LIVING ON NOTHING ATOLL

Aloha Cove

Theresa Kelly

CPH.
SAINT LOUIS

To God Be The Glory!

For David, who kept the faith.

Thank you for believing when I didn't.

Cover Illustration by Sandy Rabinowitz.

Scripture quotation on p. 213 taken from the Holy Bible, New King James Version, copyright © 1979, 1980, 1982 Thomas Nelson, Inc. Used by permission.

All other scripture quotations are taken from the HOLY BIBLE, NEW INTERNATIONAL VERSION®. NIV®. Copyright © 1973, 1978, 1984 by International Bible Society. Used by permission of Zondervan Publishing House. All rights reserved.

Copyright © 1999 Concordia Publishing House
3558 S. Jefferson Avenue, St. Louis, MO 63118-3968
Manufactured in the United States of America

Library of Congress Cataloging-in-Publication Data

Kelly, Theresa, 1952–
    Living on Nothing Atoll / Theresa Kelly.
      p. cm. — (Aloha Cove)
      Summary: Cass Devane's life is turned upside down when her mother
remarries and they go to live with her new stepfather and stepsister on
Kwajalein, one of the Marshall Islands in the Pacific Ocean.
      ISBN 0-570-05483-4
      [1. Stepfamilies Fiction. 2. Remarriage Fiction. 3. Islands Fiction. 4.
Kwajalein Island (Marshall Islands) Fiction. 5. Christian Life Fiction.] I.
Title. II. Series
  PZ7.K2985L i 1999   99–21167
  [Fic]–DC21   CIP

1 2 3 4 5 6 7 8 9 10   08 07 06 05 04 03 02 01 00 99

"My life is a living, breathing nightmare!" Cass Devane wailed to her best friend, Janette Foster, as they sat in Janette's bedroom. "And do you know what the worst part of it is?" She didn't wait for Janette's response. "The fact that I'm awake. If all this stuff with the Spencers were just a bad dream, I could count on my mother coming in to hug me and tell me everything's okay."

"Except, in this case, your mother's part of the problem," Janette said sympathetically.

"Part of the problem?" Cass laughed. "Get real. My mother is the problem." She raked her fingers through her long, red hair and confusion clouded her hazel eyes. "I don't know what's going on with her. She's never acted like this before. It's like in the past couple of weeks she's changed from a normal person—the mom I've known all my life—into a crazy woman. She's gone completely insane. I mean, how else can you explain her falling head over heels in love with a guy she dated twenty years ago? All I can say is the whole situation is nuts. And my mom's nutty as a fruitcake to be going along with it. It's one thing for Steve Spencer to be acting the way he is. But my mother should definitely have more sense."

"I know the whole thing bugs you, but I think it's kind of sweet," Janette said. "You have to admit that having Steve show up out of the blue the way he did, and sweep your Mom off her feet, is like the plot of some movie. How often does something like that happen in real life?"

"My point exactly," Cass retorted. "In movies the main characters don't have kids, and they don't live on opposite sides of the world. That makes a huge difference, don't you think? It's not so romantic when there are real people involved, especially when one of those people—namely me—hates everything about the situation."

Janette shrugged. "So you're not thrilled about your mother and Steve. So what? Everyone knows true love has its challenges. That's what makes it so exciting."

"Don't say that!" Cass ordered sharply. "I don't know what it is, but it absolutely is not love. My mother's just"— she fumbled for the right words—"going through some kind of weird phase. I mean, she just turned 37 a couple of weeks ago and all she talked about was turning 40 soon. Maybe she's just having one last fling or something. Whatever it is, though, I'm sure things will return to normal as soon as this Steve guy packs up his daughter, and the two of them head home to Kwa … Kwa … whatever the island's called that they live on," she finished with an irritated toss of her head.

"Kwa-ja-lein," Janette pronounced. "After you told me about your mother and Steve, I looked it up. It's part of the Marshall Islands and it looks like a really cool place to live. It's about halfway between—"

Cass shot her a drop-dead look and drawled, "Like it matters. *Kwa-ja-lein*"—she mimicked Janette's pronunciation—"could be an island on the moon for all I care. I just have to put up with my mother walking around all starry-eyed for four more weeks. Then Steve will be gone and this whole sorry mess will be ancient history and I'll be able to

4

get back to my normal life."

"How can you be so sure he's just going to disappear like that?" Janette asked. "From what you've said, they sound pretty serious. I mean, except for when your Mom's at work, they spend every waking minute together. Do you honestly think they're going to give that up at the end of the month? What's to stop them from getting married?"

For a moment Cass was speechless. Then she burst into hysterical laughter. "For pity's sake, Jan," she gasped when she finally caught her breath, "we're talking about my mother—Donna Maureen Devane. You remember her. Have you ever known her to do anything wild and crazy?"

"Not until Steve Spencer came to town."

Cass abruptly stopped laughing and stared wide-eyed at Jan. The blood drained from her face. "Oh my gosh, you're right. She's been acting so strange since Steve showed up. I can't count on her making rational decisions. What if she gets it into her head to do something stupid like marry him?" Moaning, she bent forward and clutched her stomach.

Janette jumped up from the floor where she was sprawled and hurried to sit beside Cass on the bed. Slipping an arm around Cass' shoulders, she asked anxiously, "You're not going to throw up, are you?"

Without looking up, Cass shook her head. "I'm okay," she mumbled, although her stomach continued to do slow, heavy rolls. "I just hadn't thought about the possibility of marriage." Cass raised scared eyes to Janette. "You don't really think she'd actually marry Steve if he was insane enough to propose, do you?"

"Of course not," replied Janette. "Your mother has too much sense to do something so dumb. Look—I shouldn't have even mentioned it. I'm sorry."

Cass gave Janette a weak smile. "It's okay. It's just a silly idea … right?" Glancing behind her at the clock on the night stand, she sighed. "I should get going. As if it weren't bad enough that Steve's coming for supper for the fourth night in a row, he's bringing the lovely Tabitha with him." She rolled her eyes. "My mother asked me to be home in time to help her get things ready."

Crossing the room, Cass picked up her sweatshirt from Janette's desk, then paused at the door. "I'll call you after supper and tell you how it went—if my mother doesn't rope me into keeping Tabitha company while she and Steve take a walk in the moonlight, that is."

As Cass let herself out of the Foster house and began the short walk home, she thought about how content she'd be if things could remain the way they'd always been. It wasn't that she didn't have problems or that she went around deliriously happy all the time. But other than Steve and Tabitha Spencer's visit, life was good. Cass loved her hometown in the mountains of eastern Tennessee. A lot of the kids at school talked about how they couldn't wait to graduate and move away, but it wouldn't bother her to spend the rest of her life in Jonesborough. She had a great group of friends, the best one being Janette. She and Janette met the first day of kindergarten at Covenant Christian School and had just finished their sophomore year. Now that they had their licenses, they were looking forward to taking some road trips when they weren't busy with summer jobs. And of course there were the activities the youth group at Cass' church had planned for the summer.

All in all, Cass thought, plucking a handful of leaves from the hedges bordering a neighbor's property, *I'd have to say things are pretty good. They'll be even better as soon as the Spencers go back to the island where they belong. They have their world, and we have ours, and the two just don't match up.*

CHAPTER 2

The front door opened as Cass started up the front steps to her house.

"Where in the world have you been?" demanded Mom. A frown marred her usually pleasant expression. "I asked you to be home early."

"I was at Janette's, where I told you I'd be. We never left the house. You could have called if you were worried about me being late," Cass said defensively. "In case you haven't noticed, though, I'm not late. You said the Spencers were coming at six. It's not even five o'clock yet."

"But I have a lot to do between now and then and I need your help."

Cass made a face as she squeezed by Mom into the house. "Oh, please. You're making a tuna casserole. We're not talking about a gourmet meal."

"You're right." Mom's mood suddenly lightened. She linked arms with Cass and accompanied her down the hall to the kitchen, a huge smile on her face. "You'll have to forgive me. I just want everything to be perfect, even though Steve's told me over and over again that he wouldn't care if I served him a peanut butter and jelly sandwich on a napkin. He says the most important thing is being together."

Cass couldn't believe her ears. The girls in her class said stuff like that when they talked about their boyfriends. Her mother was 37—she had no business acting like a lovesick teenager.

"Sweetie?" Mom nudged Cass as they passed from the hall into the kitchen. "Is something bothering you? You seem awfully quiet."

Ignoring the butterflies fluttering in her stomach, Cass decided to be honest. "Yes, I do need to talk about something," she admitted before blurting in a rush, "It's you and Steve. If you ask me, this thing with him has gone far enough. You spend every moment you're not at work either with him or talking about him. You're driving me up the wall. Janette thinks it's romantic he's come back into your life after all these years. I think it's stupid. I mean, what's the point? It's not like there's any future in it. Steve will be going home in a month, and that'll be that. You can't have a relationship with someone who lives thousands of miles away. So why don't you break it off with him now and spare yourself the heartache you'd go through four weeks from now? Don't you agree that's the logical thing to do?"

Without saying a word, Mom moved to the sink where she busied herself washing carrots and cauliflower for the vegetable plate. Cass shifted from foot to foot and waited for a response until she noticed the red flush on the back of her mother's neck below her short, blonde hair. Cass was instantly suspicious.

"Mom?" she said loudly in order to be heard over the running water. "You're blushing. Is there something going on that I should know about?"

Mom slowly turned around, wiping her hands down the front of her jeans. An uncertain smile trembled on her lips.

"Honey, Steve and I were planning to talk to you girls at supper tonight. But, since you've brought it up, perhaps I should tell you now what's happened." Mom smiled and

Cass felt her stomach sink. "Okay, here goes. Last night Steve asked me to marry him—and well, I said yes. We went to see Pastor Harrison on my lunch hour today. He agreed to do the wedding on July 5th, which is ten days before Steve's due back in Kwajalein. After I returned to the office, Steve spent the day making arrangements for the four of us to fly out of here on July 8th and spend five days in Hawaii on a family vacation before heading down to Kwajalein on the 15th." She paused a moment. "I know this comes as a surprise, but what do you think?"

"What do I think?" Cass echoed through wooden lips. She stumbled back a few steps until she located a chair and collapsed onto it, breathing hard. She couldn't take her eyes off her mother. She kept waiting for Mom to break out laughing and shout, "Gotcha!" The problem was, Mom was completely serious. "I think it, and you, are insane. How can you marry someone you've known for only two weeks? And don't even say anything about dating Steve in high school. That was twenty years ago—it doesn't count."

Before Mom could argue, Cass went on. "And what about me? He asks you to marry him and less than 24 hours later you're planning for me to leave my home and all the people I care about and move halfway around the world to an island in the middle of the Pacific Ocean? It's not fair."

Mom sat down in the chair next to her. She reached out to take Cass' hand where it lay clenched in a fist on the table, but Cass headed her off by sliding it into her lap.

"All right," Mom said calmly, "first things first. It does matter that our relationship goes back as long as it does. Even though it's been only two weeks since we met up again, we have a history together. He's been friends with Uncle Larry since Steve's family moved to town the summer before eighth grade. So I've known him that long— even though he never really paid much attention to me until my sophomore year in high school." Mom smiled at the memory. "Larry bugged Steve to death the first time he asked me out. I was thrilled. I'd had a crush on him for years so our first date was a dream come true for me."

When Mom paused, seemingly lost in thought, Cass impatiently cleared her throat. Mom gave her a guilty smile. "Anyway, as you know, we dated for two years until Steve graduated and went off to college. Before he left, we agreed to date other people, although I hoped things would still work out for us. Steve met his ex-wife at school and they got married while they were still in college. Tabitha was born a few years later."

"A month after me," Cass muttered. "How convenient that you two have daughters the same age."

"Honestly, you make it sound like we planned it that way," Mom said gently. "By the time your father and I got married just before my nineteenth birthday, I'd completely lost touch with Steve. He'd gone off to Ohio State University and didn't even keep up with Larry anymore. The only time I heard anything about him was when I ran into his parents around town. To be honest, I really didn't care what he was up to. I was very much in love with your father. After you were born, all that mattered to me was taking care of my family. Your father and I planned on having five or six kids, growing old together, and living happily ever after." She hesitated. "Unfortunately, plans don't always work out the way we want them to."

Cass could see pain filling her eyes. "Being widowed at 23 isn't something I'd recommend. If it weren't for God, you, and my family, I don't know how I would have survived. Somewhere along the line, I remember hearing that Steve's wife had left him and had run off to live in a commune out west. A few years later, someone told me he and his daughter had moved to Kwajalein. None of it registered because it had nothing to do with me. I was too busy raising you and working to think about anything else. I saw

Steve a couple of times over the years when he and Tabitha were back visiting his parents, and it was always nice to talk. But nothing clicked until he came back this time for his 20th high school reunion. We told Pastor Harrison today it's as if God waited until we'd both healed from the pain of our first marriages to bring us together again."

"Uh-uh. No way." Cass raised her hands. "I'm not going to let you get away with blaming God for this mess. You'll never convince me He had anything to do with it."

"Really?" Mom asked coolly. Her eyes narrowed as she looked at Cass. "You'll be interested to know Pastor Harrison would disagree with you. He told Steve and me he couldn't, in good conscience, marry us if he didn't believe God is the reason we're together. Since he's delighted to do the wedding"—she shrugged—"I'll let you draw your own conclusions."

Cass' heart sank. She'd counted on enlisting Pastor Harrison's support in preventing the wedding. She'd figured her mother would listen to what their pastor would have to say. Obviously, though, Mom and Steve had gotten to him first. That still left Mamaw and Papaw, and Uncle Larry and Aunt Linda. Surely they could talk some sense into her mother.

As if reading her thoughts, Mom said, "Steve and I had a little time after we talked with Pastor Harrison so we stopped by to see your grandparents and told them about our plans. In light of how you feel, you'll probably find it hard to believe that they were very excited by the news. Naturally, they were concerned about your reaction. But Papaw and Mamaw have always liked Steve, and they're very pleased we've found each other again."

Cass mentally scratched her grandparents' names off her list, hesitated, then erased Aunt Linda and Uncle Larry too. If Mom had won over Mamaw and Papaw so easily, Cass figured she didn't stand a chance with her aunt and uncle, especially since Steve and Larry had been friends. Apparently she was on her own when it came to trying to persuade her mother to change her mind.

"It sounds like everything's working out great for you and Steve," Cass said stiffly. "Everybody's thrilled you're getting married. I guess you couldn't be happier, huh?"

"Actually, I could be." Mom reached into Cass' lap and gently pried apart her entwined fingers to tightly clasp one of her hands. "I can't be totally happy if you're upset. Knowing you're glad for me would make my happiness complete."

Cass sighed in frustration. "Mom, it's not that I don't want you to get married, and the thought of having a stepfather doesn't bother me too much since Steve seems nice enough and I don't remember enough of Dad to feel disloyal or anything. It's just"—she could feel tears coming—"your marrying Steve means we have to move. If you have to get married, why can't you find somebody from around here?"

Mom smiled gently, and Cass could see the tears in her eyes as well. "For your sake, I wish I had met someone who lived here. But I've fallen in love with Steve, and I have to trust that God knows exactly what He's doing in bringing us together again, and that He has wonderful things planned for us on Kwajalein."

"That makes one of us then." Pulling her hand free from Mom's grasp, Cass brushed the tears from her cheeks, smoothed her hair, and straightened her shoulders. She lifted her chin and hoped she looked calmer than she felt. "Since I can't talk you out of getting married, I guess I'd better get used to the idea, huh? Tell me what the plans are. Are you going to have a big wedding? Will I have to get dressed up? Please don't make me wear something fancy. You know, with bows and lace and junk. What's going to happen to the house? Where will—"

Laughing, Mom held up her hands. "Whoa! I can't keep

up with you. One question at a time." She suddenly grabbed Cass in a bone-crushing bear hug. "I'm so proud of you, sweetie. I know you're still in shock, and I really appreciate the effort you're making to get used to the news and to act like you're happy for me. I tell you what." Standing, she pulled Cass to her feet. "Go upstairs and take a few minutes to let this all sink in. You look fine on the outside, but you must be falling apart on the inside. When you come back down, I'll answer all your questions while we finish getting supper ready. Deal?"

Fighting the urge to start up the argument again, Cass stared into Mom's eyes for several seconds before nodding. As she turned to leave, Cass felt a playful tug on her hair.

"I love you, Cassandra Aileen," Mom said quietly.

Cass glanced over her shoulder and the tears she thought she'd banished sprang once again to her eyes. Mom's face blurred and, for a moment, Cass thought she was looking at a stranger.

"I love you too, Donna Maureen," she replied in a husky voice, completing the ritual she and her mother had shared for as long as she could remember.

Trudging up the stairs to her room, Cass whispered, "And I love you, hallway and steps and railing and—"

She muffled the sob that caught in her throat and ran the rest of the way to her room. She slammed the door as hard as she could before flinging herself across the bed. She might not know all the details about the wedding and move yet, but Cass knew one thing for sure. As she lay crying into her pillow, she realized she might as well kiss her nice, ordinary life good-bye. Thanks to Steve and Tabitha Spencer—it would soon be gone forever.

CHAPTER 3

Cass cried so long that she didn't leave herself any time to help Mom with supper. By the time she staggered, red-eyed, down the stairs, Mom was putting the finishing touches on the table. Even though she wasn't serving anything special, she had used the good china and silver, linen napkins, and candles. Despite her unhappiness, Cass couldn't help laughing.

"Aren't you going a little overboard for tuna casserole?" she teased. "Maybe you should trash what you have and order something in from the nearest steak place. After all," she added in a strained voice, "this is a celebration, right?"

Mom set the last water goblet in place, then turned to Cass. "It's not the food that makes the celebration," she said gently. "It's the people. As long as I have the people I love around me, I'm happy."

Cass tucked a stray strand of hair behind her ear and dug the toe of her sneaker into the carpet. "Does that include Tabitha?"

Mom looked up from rearranging a napkin. "Does what include Tabitha?" Understanding dawned on her face. "Oh, you mean the people I love?"

Looking everywhere but at her mother, Cass nodded.

Mom paused, then shook her head. "I can't say that I love Tabitha yet. It's too soon. But I am quite fond of her. She's a lovely girl." She peered closely at Cass. "Does that bother you?"

Yes! Cass screamed inside her head. *It's bad enough you love Steve. I don't want you loving his daughter too.*

Aloud, she replied with a careless shrug, "It doesn't matter one way or the other to me. I was just curious how you felt about her."

Instead of responding to Cass' question, Mom asked, "How about you? What do you think of Tabitha?"

Cass gave a short laugh. "Not much," she drawled. "Tab and I are complete opposites. If we went to the same school, there's no way we'd have anything to do with each other. We come from different worlds."

Mom frowned. "Do you mean because she's lived on an island most of her life?"

Cass rolled her eyes. "Hello? Haven't you been listening to me? I said we're total opposites. Tab likes rock music. I like country. Everything she wears matches, right down to her pierced earrings. My only requirements are that my clothes are clean and comfortable. Tabitha probably considers shopping an aerobic exercise, and I'm into basketball and track. Like I said, we have absolutely nothing in common. Zero, zip, nada."

"I'm sure, in time, you and Tabitha will learn to appreciate one another's differences," Mom said, but Cass thought she sounded rather doubtful.

The doorbell rang as Cass trailed Mom into the kitchen to check on the casserole. Cass felt her stomach drop at the sound. "Go ahead, Mom," she said quickly. "I'll make sure everything's okay in here then I'll join you in the living room."

Trying to ignore the sick feeling that was threatening to overwhelm her, Cass checked the casserole and turned down the temperature so it wouldn't burn. She lifted the lid on the pot of green beans and gave them a stir. After opening the refrigerator to eye the vegetable plate and fruit salad, Cass ran out of reasons for stalling. With a sigh of self-pity, she pasted a phony smile on her face and pushed open the door leading to the living room.

"There you are!" Mom greeted her in the too-cheerful voice she used whenever she was nervous and trying to hide it. Cass figured she'd been worried she'd have to drag her out of the kitchen and make her talk to the Spencers. "Now that you're here, Steve and I can share our good news with Tabitha."

"And what news is that?" Tabitha asked with a coy look at her father and Mom.

Watching her made Cass clench her jaw. She really couldn't stand the girl. Tonight Tabitha wore perfect white shorts and a blue baby-doll T-shirt. Her blonde curls were held back by a blue hair clip, and she sported white sandals. It was almost enough to make Cass gag. Compared to Tabitha, she looked shapeless and grungy in her jeans, over-sized T-shirt, and bare feet.

Mom patted the sofa cushion beside her and Tabitha scooted closer. Steve had his arm draped along the back of the couch behind his daughter, his fingers brushing Mom's shoulder. Cass stood across the room, feeling like an outcast. She tried to signal her discomfort to her mother, but Mom had eyes only for Tabitha. Muttering under her breath, Cass collapsed into the nearest chair.

"Cass and I already talked so she knows what this is about," Mom began with a quick smile in Cass' direction.

Cass looked away. She wasn't about to let her mother get support from her for this marriage idea.

Mom turned back to Tabitha. "Anyway, unless your Dad wants to be the one to tell you, I'll go ahead." Steve nodded at her, so Mom took a deep breath and said in a rush,

"Your Dad proposed to me last night, and I accepted. We've set the wedding for July 5th. After the four of us take a"— she hesitated, searching for the right description—"well, I guess you could call it a family honeymoon, in Hawaii, we'll all head down to Kwajalein on the 15th."

Tabitha's mouth dropped open and she shot a quick look at Cass. "Even her?"

Bristling, Cass sat up straight and glared at her. "What do you mean, even me? Of course I'm going. Mom and I are a package deal."

Tabitha looked sheepish. "I didn't mean it the way it sounded," she tried to explain, sending Cass her most winsome smile. Cass sniffed and pretended to study her nails. "I just thought … you know—having to move and all …" Her words trailed off and Cass smiled inwardly. She frowned again as Tabitha turned to her father and said brightly, "Never mind that. The important thing is, you and Donna are getting married." She flung her arms around Steve's neck. "I'm so happy for you. It's about time you had someone other than me to love." Transferring the hug to Mom, Tabitha continued, "And I couldn't have chosen a better wife for Dad myself." She ducked her head and finished softly, "Or a more terrific mother for me."

I think I'm going to throw up, Cass thought sourly.

She was amazed at the scene being played out in front of her. She didn't believe for one second that Tabitha was as thrilled about the upcoming wedding as she pretended to be. She might detest the girl, but Cass had to hand it to her— Tabitha was a heck of an actress. Cass was sure Mom was comparing Tabitha's excitement at the news to her own lack of enthusiasm, and that she, Cass, was coming up the loser.

"So, Cass, are you as happy about our parents getting married as I am?" Tabitha asked from her snug position between Mom and Steve.

Cass looked into her soon-to-be stepsister's eyes, glittering with unshed tears, and at her clenched jaw and nodded. "Yeah, I'd say we're equally happy about it."

Tabitha appeared startled for a moment, then she forced herself to smile. "Just think. We're going to be sisters. Who'd have thought, when we met a few weeks ago, that we'd wind up related?"

"Only someone with a really warped sense of humor," muttered Cass.

"Oh, you," Tabitha said and giggled, waving a hand at Cass. "Are you always such a comedian?"

"Yeah, I'm a laugh a minute." Cass stood up and headed for the kitchen. "Look, why don't I get supper on the table while the three of you enjoy congratulating each other? I think I smell the casserole starting to burn."

Steve jumped up to follow Cass. "I'll give you a hand. They're"—he jerked a thumb over his shoulder at Mom and Tabitha, who continued to cling to one another—"not done crying yet and it's getting a little too damp for my liking."

There was nothing Cass could say so she nodded curtly and slammed through the door into the kitchen. Steve was right on her heels. It wasn't that she had anything against him personally. She'd meant it when she told Mom he seemed nice enough. As far as Cass could tell, there were only two things wrong with Steve. He wanted to marry her mother and he was Tabitha's father. Other than that, she liked him fine.

Maintaining a stony silence, Cass stalked across the floor and yanked open the oven door. She saw that the edges of the bubbling casserole were beginning to brown and reached for the pot holder on the counter.

"Would you like me to do that?" offered Steve.

Cass glared at him over her shoulder. "No, I think I can manage it," she drawled, her voice dripping with sarcasm.

Steve didn't take offense. "I'm sure you can. You seem to be quite self-sufficient."

Carrying the casserole to the table, Cass examined his words for hidden meanings. When she couldn't find any, she replied grudgingly, "Thanks. I try to be. I take a lot of pride in being able to take care of myself."

Steve crossed his arms and propped a hip against the counter as Cass moved back and forth between the kitchen and dining nook, getting things ready for dinner. "Which, translated, means you don't need or want me in your life so you don't understand why your Mom does."

Cass stopped in the middle of transporting the green beans to the table and gaped at him. "I … I … never said that," she stammered, wondering if he planned to report their conversation to Mom. Her mother would throw a royal fit if she thought Cass had insulted Steve.

Steve laughed at her stricken expression. "I know you didn't. I'm sorry if I put words in your mouth." As Cass continued on her way with the beans, he added, "And, just in case you're worried about it, I didn't come in here to try to trap you and get you in trouble with your mom. I have no intention of coming between you and her. You were right about you two being a package deal. I wouldn't have asked your Mom to marry me if I weren't looking forward to being your stepfather in the bargain."

Not sure how to respond, Cass mumbled, "That's very nice of you. I appreciate it."

Steve stepped to the refrigerator, opened the door to the freezer portion, and took out a couple of ice cube trays. As he dropped the ice into the water glasses, he said, "Look, Cass, I want you to know where I stand. The way I see it, when your Mom and I get married, I'm taking you on as another daughter, and I'll be just as responsible for you as I am for Tabitha. You won't owe me anything for doing it. Not gratitude, not appreciation, not affection, nothing. I'll consider it a privilege to treat you as one of my own. Okay?"

Across the table, Cass stared at Steve in astonishment.

"Then what's in it for you?"

Steve's grin made his hazel eyes twinkle. "I get another daughter. I always wanted more kids, and here I'm getting one without having to go through the hassle of teaching you how to walk and potty-training you and stuff. You come ready-made. What a deal."

Cass tried reminding herself she was mad at this man who was turning her life upside down, but it didn't work. She burst out laughing. She and Steve were still grinning when Mom and Tabitha entered the room. Tabitha's eyes narrowed to slits. Going to her father, she slid her arm through his and leaned against his side.

"Hey, what's so funny? Is it a private joke or can the rest of us get in on it?"

Steve glanced at Cass who shrugged and fussed with the vegetable plate. Tabitha's appearance had cast a chill over the warm moment she'd just shared with Steve.

Kissing the top of Tabitha's head, Steve directed her to one of the chairs. "I don't think I can explain it, honey. It was one of the times you had to be there. I'm sure you understand."

Cass hadn't realized she was holding her breath until she expelled it in a rush. For some reason, it pleased her that Steve had kept the episode just between them.

CHAPTER 4

Sitting down to eat, Cass found herself next to Tabitha and across the table from Mom and Steve. It wasn't a major problem, but it meant she had to hold hands with Tabitha while they said the blessing. Extending the tip of her index finger, Cass barely connected with Tabitha, who appeared just as unwilling to touch her. If their parents noticed, they decided not to comment. As soon as the prayer was over, Cass and Tabitha hastily withdrew their hands and dropped them into their laps.

"So, Donna," Tabitha began once the meal had been served, "tell me the plans for the wedding. Is it going to be small and simple? Or are you thinking of going all out?" Winking, she added, "I vote for going all out. I mean, it's a big day for our family. Don't you agree, Cass?"

Cass, who most certainly did not agree, thought it best not to say so. "I don't know. I figure it's up to my mom and your dad to decide what kind of wedding they want. Why should we have any say in the matter?" *Especially when we didn't have any say about whether or not they should get married in the first place,* she added silently.

"Of course you have a say," Mom said. "Steve and I welcome any suggestions either of you might have." She smiled at Steve. "Don't we, sweetie?"

Steve nodded. "You're free to be as involved, or uninvolved, as you like," he told the girls.

"In that case," bubbled Tabitha, "I intend to be very involved. When can we start looking for your wedding dress, Donna?"

Cass kept quiet. She shoveled forkful after forkful of food into her mouth in order to get finished with supper as soon as possible.

Tabitha and Mom were in the middle of discussing dress colors and styles when Cass announced, "I'm done. May I be excused?"

Mom looked from her half-eaten meal to Cass' empty plate. "Goodness, you must have been famished. Would you like seconds?"

Cass impatiently shook her head. "No thanks. I'm full. May I be excused?" she repeated.

"What about dessert?" Mom gestured behind her at the counter. "I made peach cobbler."

Anxious to make her escape, Cass thought fast. "I ... uh ... I thought I'd go by and get Janette, and we could ... um ... go to the mall for awhile or something."

"I don't think that's such a good idea." Mom reached over and squeezed Steve's hand where it lay on the table. "We're going to that new romantic comedy that just opened today. It's not Steve's kind of movie, but he was nice and said he'd take me."

"What time does the movie start? I can be back before then if you need the car."

"Transportation isn't the issue. Steve's been borrowing a friend's car while he's here." Mom hesitated. "We were counting on you and Tabitha spending time together while we went out. Outside of her grandparents, she doesn't know anyone in town, and they're busy tonight. We don't like the idea of leaving her alone."

Cass knew Mom expected her to offer to take Tabitha

along. She knew it was the polite thing to do, probably even the right thing. Unfortunately, she couldn't make herself say the words that would doom her to spending the next several hours with Tabitha.

As the silence lengthened to embarrassing proportions, Tabitha's chin came up in a show of defiance. "Don't worry about me," she informed her father and Mom. "I don't mind being on my own. I can watch TV or read a book. You have any good books lying around, Donna?"

Mom didn't respond. Instead, she gave Cass a stern look. "I think it would be a nice gesture if you invited Tabitha to go to the mall with you and Janette. Besides, you girls need to start getting acquainted."

"Really, Donna," Tabitha protested weakly, "that's not necessary. I'll be fine here by myself."

Glancing at her out of the corner of her eye, Cass thought Tabitha looked as miserable as she felt. From across the table, Mom's glare pretty much guarenteed life-time grounding if she didn't ask Tabitha along, and fast.

"Mom's right," she grudgingly conceded. "We should spend some time together, seeing as how we're going to be related and all. Would you like to go to the mall with Jan and me?"

"I'd love to. If you're sure you don't mind," Tabitha purred, putting Cass on the spot.

Cass would have liked nothing better than to wipe the smirk off the other girl's face, but with Mom and Steve looking on, that was out of the question. Mustering what was left of her dignity, she said sweetly, "Why, of course I don't mind. I apologize if I gave you that impression. As a matter of fact, I'm looking forward to introducing you to my friends. I know they're going to think you're as won-derful as I do."

Mom and Steve beamed, but Cass and Tabitha just glared at each other. Although the adults had missed it,

Cass knew Tabitha had caught the sarcasm in her voice.

"I'll go upstairs and get ready while you finish eating supper," Cass told Tabitha. She darted a hasty glance at her mother. "If that's all right with you, I mean." When Mom nodded, Cass stood and picked up her dishes to carry them to the sink. "I'll also call Jan and make sure she can go with us."

Unfortunately, Cass' phone call was five minutes too late. The Fosters' next-door neighbors had just called and asked Janette to baby-sit. She was heading over there in ten minutes.

"Sorry," Jan said and meant it. "Both about your mom getting married and about not getting to meet Tabitha. I can't wait to see if she's as awful as you say she is. Why don't you call Carly or Lauren and see if they're available?"

"No." Cass sighed. "I haven't told them about any of this stuff yet, and I'm not in the mood to act like nothing's going on. That's why I wanted you and me to go out. Even with Tab tagging along, I figured we could ditch her for a little while and talk about this whole disaster. But I guess it's going to be her and me tonight."

"I'm really sorry. If only you'd called a few minutes earlier," Janette said. "Speaking of which, I'd better go. The Olsons are meeting friends for dinner and they won't be very happy if I make them late. Call me when you get back in from your big evening with Tabitha. I want to hear all the gory details."

After hanging up with Jan, Cass moped around her room for several minutes before pulling herself together and heading downstairs. Mom, Steve, and Tabitha were just finishing dessert. Tabitha's gaze swept over Cass, her expression puzzled.

"I thought you said you were going upstairs to get ready."

Cass looked down at herself then up again at Tabitha. "I did. I put socks and sneakers on."

Tabitha's laugh was faintly mocking. "My, you're low-maintenance, aren't you?"

Cass refused to let Tabitha see how irritated she was. "I guess some of us don't require as much work as others." She smiled at Tabitha's glare. Cass went to her mother and hugged her. "Have fun at the movie."

Mom reached up to pat Cass' cheek. "We will. We're going to the 7:30 show, then we'll probably go out for coffee afterwards. We should be back no later than 11:00. You girls need to be in at 10:00."

Great—if I last that long with her, Cass thought.

CHAPTER 5

Cass and Tabitha drove the first couple of miles without speaking. The music blaring from the radio masked the silence for a time, but Cass grew increasingly uncomfortable. They couldn't spend the rest of the evening ignoring each other.

Turning the radio down a notch, Cass shot Tabitha a curious glance. "So, what do you really think about our parents getting married?"

"Uh … why do you ask?" Tabitha's tone was cautious.

"Oh, come on. You know why. It was pure acting when you came across as all happy and excited about the wedding. You know it, and I know it, even if our folks were too dense to catch on."

"I am too happy," Tabitha protested. "I'm glad my father's found somebody to share his life with."

"Uh-huh, okay," Cass said sarcastically. "I believe you."

"No, really," Tabitha insisted. She shifted in the seat. "I'll be leaving home in two years to go to college, and I'll feel better knowing he won't be alone."

"Yeah, well, if that's what I was talking about then I'm happy for my mom too." Cass paused. "Except we both know that's not what I was talking about. Don't tell me you're thrilled my mother and I are going to be invading your house and your life down on Kwa—that island you live on."

Her face set in a stubborn expression, Tabitha crossed her arms and stared out the window. "It doesn't bother me in the slightest. I'm looking forward to having a mother and sister."

Cass took her hand off the wheel to raise it in surrender. "All right, I give up. I'll just go on being the bad guy because I'm not on cloud nine about the wedding. At least I'll be able to live with myself."

"How long have you had your license?" Tabitha asked abruptly.

Cass shot her a sidelong glance. "Since I turned sixteen in April. Why?"

To Cass' surprise, Tabitha looked wistful. "I turned sixteen on May 28th, but I don't even have my driver's permit. There's no reason to since there aren't any P.O.V.'s— privately owned vehicles," she explained, "on Kwaj. People either walk, ride bikes, or call a taxi."

Cass' jaw dropped. "No way! You mean, along with everything else, I'm going to have to give up driving for the next two years?" She slammed the steering wheel. "That's great. This thing just keeps getting better and better."

"There's no place to drive," Tabitha pointed out. "I guess you haven't been listening when Dad and I have talked about Kwaj. It's three miles long by a half-mile wide. I'm not kidding. There's nowhere to go."

Cass felt like crying, but she ordered herself not to, at least not in front of Tabitha. "Man, and I thought there was nothing to do around here."

"There's a lot to do on Kwaj," Tabitha said, defending her home. "There's swimming, of course, and movies, and bowling, and I have a ton of friends."

"Yeah, I feel so much better now," Cass drawled. "I can hardly wait to get there. Movies and bowling, wow."

"You don't have to be sarcastic," sniffed Tabitha. "It's not like Jonesborough has a lot going for it. Talk about hick town. This is the longest Dad and I have ever stayed here, and I'm ready to die of boredom."

Wouldn't that be nice, Cass thought as she turned into the mall parking lot. She bit her lip to keep from saying anything out loud.

Once she parked the car, Cass slid out and started for the mall entrance without waiting for Tabitha. After a few moments, she heard Tabitha running to catch up.

"Hey, wait for me. I don't know my way around." Tabitha drew alongside Cass and matched her stride for stride. Cass just glared at her. "What? Are you mad about the hick town remark? I was just kidding."

Cass abruptly halted and swung around to face Tabitha. "Tell me how I'm supposed to know when you're kidding. I hardly know you. Or your father, for that matter. Despite that, I'm expected to walk away from my life here and spend the next two years on an overgrown rock in the middle of the Pacific Ocean with the two of you and Mom, pretending we're one, big, happy family. It's insane." Raising her face to the darkening sky, she hissed, "You hear that, God? The whole idea's insane, and I hate it."

"Talk about insane," Tabitha muttered, and started to walk away.

Aware that Tabitha was mocking her, Cass quickly composed herself. She wasn't about to give Tabitha any more ammunition with which to attack her. She forced a laugh.

"Oops, temporary nervous breakdown. Stress can do that to a person." She resumed walking toward the sprawling building.

The moment they stepped through the main entrance, she was greeted by several boys from her class standing in a group off to the left. Cass reluctantly acknowledged their hellos. The last thing she wanted was to introduce her future stepsister to her friends, but they were eyeing Tabitha with undisguised curiosity.

"Hey, Cass, who's the new girl?" B.J. asked, smiling at Tabitha.

"I'm Tabitha Spencer," Tabitha said, tossing her curls and boldly returning B.J.'s flirtatious look. "And who are you?"

B.J. appeared dazzled. "Uh ... Billy Joe Tipton," he gulped. "Everyone calls me B.J."

"Since I'm not everyone," purred Tabitha, "I'm going to call you Billy." She ducked her head and peered up at him from under lowered lashes. "Is that okay with you?"

Rendered temporarily speechless, B.J. merely nodded. The three other boys instantly clamored to make Tabitha's acquaintance.

The four of them attached themselves to Cass and Tabitha, following them from store to store as they jockeyed for the position closest to Tabitha. If it weren't so pathetic, Cass would have thought it was funny to see her friends vying for Tabitha's attention. As it was, it annoyed her to see them reduced to puppy dogs, grateful for a single word or glance from Tabitha. *But I would die to know how to do that myself*, she thought ruefully.

The boys stayed with Cass and Tabitha the entire time they were at the mall. B.J., or Billy as he'd been renamed for the evening, succeeded in being the one to buy an ice cream cone for Tabitha when they finally made their way to the food court. Chad immediately went off in search of a soda for her. After he bought one, he returned to the table and discovered the chair next to Tabitha had been taken over by Jason. He sank into the seat beside Mike and proceeded to sulk. Cass decided she'd had enough.

"I see some people I know over there." She waved in the general direction of the pizza stand. "I'm going to go say hey. I'll be back in a little bit."

The others barely noticed when Cass slipped away. Making her escape, she found a couple of friends to talk with until it was time to head home.

"Sorry to break things up," Cass announced as she came back to the table, "but Tab and I need to get going."

The boys groaned, and Tabitha smiled at them. "Oh, come on, guys," she said sweetly. "I'll still be around for a couple of weeks."

"At least I have your phone number," Chad said. "I can call you, right?"

Tabitha giggled. It was clear she was having the time of her life. "I'd love it if you did."

The boys escorted Cass and Tabitha to the car, then stood in the parking lot, waving, as they drove away. The moment the boys were out of sight, Tabitha quit grinning and whirled around to glare at Cass.

"Don't ever call me Tab," she ordered heatedly. "My name is Tabitha. Call me Tab again and I won't answer you."

"Whoa there," Cass said, laughing. "I didn't mean anything by it."

Cass could feel Tabitha studying her. "You really don't like me, do you?"

Cass didn't see any reason to lie. "Nope."

"I don't like you either." Resting her head on the seat back, Tabitha closed her eyes and sighed. "At least we have that in common. This living together isn't going to work out very well, is it?"

"Nope," Cass repeated, adding hopefully, "unless one of us changes."

"Don't look at me," advised Tabitha.

"Me either." Cass responded in the same tone.

"Finally," Tabitha said mockingly. "Something we agree on."

CHAPTER 6

"Mom, you said I wouldn't have to wear anything fancy," Cass protested. It was two weeks before the wedding and she was at the mall with her mother, Steve, and Tabitha. The first thing Mom had done was steer Cass into the shop where she'd bought her own wedding dress a week earlier. "I distinctly remember your agreeing that my purple and white dress would do just fine. I even tried it on for you so you could be sure. How come you've changed your mind all of a sudden?"

"It's not all of a sudden. I've been thinking about getting you a new dress ever since Tabitha and I bought ours." Mom smiled. "Since my dress is yellow and Tabitha's is green, I thought it would look nicer in the pictures if you were wearing green too. Come on, what do you say? Will you at least look around? For me? I promise I won't make you get something you absolutely hate, okay?"

"Oh, all right." Cass allowed herself to be pulled toward the rack of dresses at the back of the store. Passing Steve, she muttered under her breath to him, "You're lucky. You can stand up to her. I'll bet she's not making you wear green."

Steve fell into step with Cass and confided, "Sorry, you lose. Your mother bought me a yellow shirt, and a green-and-yellow tie to go with it. I didn't have a say in the matter. She handed me her purchases and told me to wear them." He pretended to shudder. "I'm just glad she didn't decide on a hot pink dress. Or a chartreuse one. I'd never live it down, especially with your Uncle Larry coming to the wedding. What self-respecting guy wears colors like that?"

Cass stifled a giggle. She still wasn't entirely comfortable around Steve, although she'd gotten over some of her anger toward him. It wasn't his fault he lived where he did, and he certainly couldn't be held responsible for Tabitha being such a snob. She had decided to save her energy for more important things—like dealing with Mom's insistence that she find a new outfit for the wedding.

When the foursome reached the dress racks, Mom and Tabitha immediately began sorting through the choices. It didn't take them long to eliminate most of the dresses, pulling out only a few for Cass to try on. Cass stood off to one side, trying to feign complete boredom.

"So, you're not exactly keen on shopping, huh?" Steve said, moving over to stand next to her. "That's refreshing in a woman."

Cass smiled slightly. "Quite honestly—I couldn't care less about clothes." She glanced down at her faded denim shorts, shapeless red T-shirt, and beat-up sneakers, then grinned up at Steve. "But I guess that's kind of obvious. I'll take comfort over style any day."

Amusement flickered in Steve's hazel eyes. "For what it's worth, you look fine to me. Then again, no one would ever mistake me for a fashion model, so maybe I'm not the best one to judge."

"Unlike them." Cass indicated the perfectly dressed and made-up Mom and Tabitha who were still busy trying to find the right dress for her. "It doesn't matter where they're going or what they're doing, they always look great. I don't get it."

Steve emitted a low whistle of admiration. "They are a fine-looking pair, aren't they?"

Before Cass could utter the snotty comment poised on the tip of her tongue, a perfectly made-up, not-a-hair-out-of-place saleswoman bustled over to Mom and Tabitha. "How may I help you, ladies?"

Mom smiled. "I'm getting married in two weeks, and I'm looking for a dress for my daughter. We don't want anything too fussy, and we're hoping to find something in green. Do you have any suggestions?"

Stepping back, the woman placed her hands on her hips, tilted her head, and studied Tabitha from head to toe. "I believe she'd look charming in something soft, perhaps a sea green," she decided. "Let me see what I—"

"Oh, no," Mom broke in with a nervous laugh. "I'm sorry, this isn't my daughter. I mean, she will be in a couple of weeks." She pointed to Cass who was listening with a stony expression. "That's my daughter over there. She needs the dress. This one"—she touched Tabitha's shoulder—"is my stepdaughter-to-be. She already has her dress."

Shaking her head, the saleswoman looked from Mom and Tabitha to Steve and Cass, then back again. "Well, I'll be." She laughed. "I would have sworn that you two were mother and daughter and that they"—she gestured over her shoulder—"were related. The similarities are remarkable."

"Gee, you poor thing," Steve murmured to Cass. "She thinks you look like me. Have you ever heard the phrase, 'a fate worse than death'?"

Actually Cass didn't think it was so bad to be mistaken for Steve's daughter. She liked his trim, athletic build and his sandy-haired, hazel-eyed looks. What bothered her was that Tabitha looked so much like Mom.

The saleswoman turned her attention to Cass and peered at her through calculating eyes. "Your coloring needs something darker than a pale green," she finally declared. "And I agree with your mother about not putting you in anything fussy." She tapped her finger against her chin and thought a moment. "I have just the dress for you. Emerald green with clean, simple lines. Let's hope we have it in your size. What are you? A five? A seven? I think I have both."

"I usually wear a seven," Cass replied grudgingly, sure the dress the woman had in mind would be hideous.

The saleswoman hurried to a rack along the side wall. Rattling through the hangers, she crowed triumphantly and pulled out a shimmering green silk. She held it up for Cass' inspection, sweeping her hand down the length of the dress to show it off like a model on a television game show.

"So, what do you think?" the woman asked after giving Cass a few moments to study the dress. "Is this gorgeous or what?"

"It's beautiful," Cass breathed, forgetting for the time being that she didn't care about clothes. She couldn't wait to try on the dress and see if it looked as good on her as it did on the hanger.

"Very nice," Mom approved.

"Did you say you have another one in a size five?" asked Tabitha. She nudged Mom. "Maybe Cass and I could wear matching dresses."

"No!" Cass yelped. At Mom's warning frown, she added more quietly, "Mom told me the dress you got is perfect for you. She said it's just the right color and style. You really don't want to change, do you?" *Please say you don't*, Cass silently begged Tabitha. *I don't think I can keep on being polite much longer, and I'm already skating on thin ice with Mom.*

"I guess not," Tabitha conceded. She cast another

glance at the dress the saleswoman held aloft and there was longing in her eyes. "That color's so much brighter, though," she pointed out with a hint of a whine in her tone. "My dress will look washed out next to it."

"No, it won't, sweetie." Mom slipped an arm around Tabitha's shoulders and gently smoothed her hair. "You're able to wear pastels and still stand out because your coloring is so vibrant. Cass needs the brighter colors to highlight her features."

Cass had stiffened at hearing Mom call Tabitha "sweetie." Now she openly glared at her. "Gee, thanks a lot," she drawled. "Let me see if I have this right. What you're saying is Tabitha's pretty all on her own, but I need the right clothes to look good?"

"That's not what I meant and you know it," Mom snapped. She combed her fingers through her hair before continuing, "Look, let's start over. Somewhere along the line we got our wires crossed. In spite of the way it sounded, I was agreeing with you. Tabitha should stay with the dress she has because it suits her. And you should try on this dress because it looks like it'll be wonderful on you." She turned to the saleswoman. "Would you show us to the nearest fitting room, please?"

When Tabitha started to follow them, Cass shot her mother a pleading look. It would be bad enough to have her mother come in with her. To her relief, Mom asked Tabitha to wait outside while the two of them went into the cubicle.

"Oh, Cassandra, I was right," Mom said in a hushed voice after Cass had slipped into the dress. "You do look wonderful. I believe this is the dress for you. Turn around and look at yourself and tell me what you think."

Cass' face lit up with delight when she saw her reflection. The emerald dress brought out the green in her eyes and made her hair and skin glow. The sweetheart neckline and V-waist showed off her petite figure to perfection. She laughed, though, when her gaze dropped to the ragged sneakers she'd forgotten to take off.

"These will definitely have to go." She lifted a foot and laughed.

Mom pretended to disagree. "Oh, I don't know. They lend a certain flair to the outfit, don't you think? Not every woman is as capable of successfully blending formal and informal as you are. It's a real gift." She laughed. "As soon as we're finished here, we'll go find some shoes." Taking Cass by the shoulders, she pointed her toward the door and gave her a little push. "Go out and show Steve and Tabitha how pretty you look."

Cass hung back. "Do I have to? Couldn't I just surprise them at the wedding?"

"Yes, you have to," Mom said firmly.

Cass sighed, yanked open the door, and stalked out into the store.

As he'd done earlier with Mom and Tabitha, Steve whistled his appreciation. He twirled his finger for Cass to turn for his inspection. She did, feeling a little silly, but also enjoying the attention. When she faced Steve again, he gave her a thumbs-up.

"You'll be the belle of the ball," he declared, and Cass' cheeks burned with embarrassed pleasure at the compliment. "Or should I say the wonder of the wedding?"

Cass shrugged, then looked at Tabitha for her reaction. The girl took her time as she studied the dress from neckline to hem.

Tabitha finally completed her inspection. "It's a nice dress," she observed flatly. "How are you planning to wear your hair?"

"My hair?" echoed Cass, her hand automatically reaching up to pat her ponytail. She hadn't given the matter a single thought.

Tossing her own cloud of curls, Tabitha drawled, "Yes,

your hair. Surely you're not going to wear it the way it is. That ponytail does nothing for you or the dress. In fact, it looks downright childish."

"I'll wear my hair any way I feel—" Cass began hotly.

"Girls," Mom interrupted, "that's enough." She grabbed Cass' wrist in an iron grip. "We don't need to discuss hairstyles right now. The important thing is Cass has found a dress that we all like. We'll take care of the other details later. Meanwhile we need to pay for the dress and see about getting her some shoes." With a sharp tug, Mom practically dragged Cass back into the fitting room.

"Who does she think she is, making snide remarks about my hair?" Cass said hotly in the dressing room. "Just because hers is so wonderful."

"Now, now." Mom carefully lifted the dress over Cass' head and reached for the hanger. "Don't make such a big deal out of what was just an innocent comment. I'm sure Tabitha meant well. I think it's sweet that she wants you to look nice for the wedding."

"I don't believe this!" Cass glared at her. "You're taking her side!"

"I'm not taking anyone's side," Mom said calmly as she re-hung the dress and smoothed out nonexistent wrinkles.

"Well, you should." Cass jerked on her T-shirt. "In case you've forgotten, I'm your daughter. You should take my side."

"Cassandra, you're not making any sense."

"Neither are you with this hurry-up wedding," retorted Cass. "If I didn't know better, I'd say you had to get married."

Silence filled the dressing room. Feeling miserable, Cass stepped into her shorts and zipped them. To avoid looking at her mother, she fussed with her shirt, tucking it in, then pulling it out again.

"I'm waiting for an apology."

"I know." Cass kept her gaze trained on the floor and mumbled, "Sorry."

"Try saying it like you mean it."

Cass whirled to face her mother. "What do you want from me? I'm doing the best I can, okay? I said I was sorry about the remark and I am. But I'm not sorry about being unhappy about the wedding. I hate that you're getting married. I hate moving and leaving my friends. I hate Ste—" Realizing that wasn't true, Cass quickly changed it to, "Tabitha. I hate my life."

"Oh, sweetie—" Mom said softly.

"Don't bother." Cass shrugged off the hand Mom laid on her arm. "Nothing you say will make me feel better. The only thing that would help would be for you to call off the wedding, and you're not going to do that. Let's just get this shopping trip over with so I can go home and spend the little time I have left here with Jan and my other friends. Besides," she added over her shoulder as she turned the doorknob, "what are you worried about me for? You have another 'sweetie' in your life now. Save the concerned-mom routine for her. Oops, silly me." Her laugh was brittle. "You don't need me to tell you that. You do it anyway."

CHAPTER 7

The next two weeks flew by in a blur of activities. When Cass wasn't sorting through her things, deciding what to take and what to leave behind, she was helping her mother make those same decisions about household items. In the middle of the second week, the movers came and dismantled Cass' bedroom furniture to ship it, along with cartons of her and Mom's treasured possessions, to Kwajalein. Cass cried as she watched their belongings loaded onto the moving van. Steve had told her it would take close to four months for their things to reach the island. The thought of living in a strange place without anything around to remind her of home filled Cass with despair. As the truck disappeared down the street, Cass realized there was no getting around it. She was witnessing the end of her life as she'd known it and her silent tears turned into harsh, wracking sobs.

The only bright spot in the remaining two weeks was the time Cass spent with her friends. After one teary afternoon, Cass and her friends agreed not to waste the time they had left crying. Instead they tried to cram a summer's worth of fun into fourteen days. Whenever the others were off from work, the group got together to go to the movies, hold slumber parties, swim, picnic, and shop until they almost dropped from exhaustion.

One night, however, it all became too much for Cass. She, Janette, and Carly were staying at Lauren's house. They'd just finished watching a tear-jerker movie and were about to experiment with hairstyles when Cass suddenly threw her pillow across the room.

"I'm so sick of the deal with my mother and the Spencers I could scream," she announced to her friends. "I'm seriously thinking about trying to find a way to stay here while my mom moves to Kwaj with Steve and his obnoxious daughter."

"Wow, could you do that?" Carly asked as she devoured a bag of potato chips. "I mean, who would you stay with? Your grandparents?"

Cass exchanged a look with Janette. They'd already talked about the possibility. "My first choice would be to stay with Jan's family. If that didn't work out, though, I think my grandparents would be okay with having me live with them."

"It'd be so great if you didn't have to leave," Lauren said. "But, honestly, what do you think the odds are that your mother would let you stay behind when she moves?"

"Not good," admitted Cass. "But I've come up with a plan about how to approach her. I'm going to run it by you guys, and you can tell me what you think." She took a deep breath. "Here goes. I've thought about saying something like, 'Mom, this marriage thing is fine for you if that's what you want. But you can't expect me to throw away my life here because you've fallen in love with Steve. Everyone and everything I know is here. I'm doing really well at school. The coach said he'll be starting me as a shooting guard when basketball season starts. I love our church and the youth group. I'll miss being with you, but I don't want to leave all this behind.'" She sat back and looked expectantly around the group. "Well, how does that sound?"

The girls shifted uneasily and avoided Cass' eyes. Carly finally spoke up. "I don't know about anybody else, but everything you said sounded perfectly reasonable to me." There were murmurs of agreement from Janette and Lauren then Carly continued, "The problem is, you know how parents are. I doubt your mother's going to buy it."

"I'm afraid you're right," Janette said while Lauren chimed in, "Yeah, me too."

Cass slumped in defeat. "So you're saying I shouldn't even try? I should just pack my bags and sail away to Kwajalein to live unhappily ever after?"

"No way!" Janette said. "What do you have to lose by trying to get your mother to see things your way? And— who knows—you might even get her to change her mind about making you move. I say go for it."

"I will." Cass brightened. "Even if I don't convince her to let me finish high school here, I'm hoping I can talk her into letting me stay the rest of the summer. That's not too much to ask, do you think?"

"Absolutely not," Janette declared loyally. "I mean, it's the least she can do since she's ruining your life." Her expression was full of sympathy as she gazed at Cass. "I know I was all for your mom and Steve's romance in the beginning, but I didn't think it would lead to this. The worst part is your having to move, but the second worst is you're getting Tabitha as a stepsister."

"Tell me about it," Cass muttered. "Y'all have to meet her," she told Carly and Lauren. "It'll explain everything about why I dread the thought of being cooped up on a teeny-weeny island with her for the next two years. One of us isn't going to make it out alive."

Drifting off to sleep a short while later, Cass felt more hopeful than she had in days.

Her optimism lasted until lunch the following day with

her grandfather. He picked Cass up from Lauren's house and drove her to the Main Street Cafe in downtown Jonesborough, one of their favorite places to eat. On the way she outlined her plan to talk to her mother. Papaw listened without comment until after they'd placed their orders at the cafe counter and settled into a booth.

"Sassafras," he began, using the nickname only he was allowed to use, "it's not going to work. Don't rob your mom of the happiness she's found with Steve by suggesting you stay behind while she moves. It would break her heart to have to choose between you and Steve. If you put your foot down about moving, I reckon there's a good chance she'd postpone getting married until after you graduated from high school."

"Really?" The possibility that she possessed such power hadn't occurred to Cass. Wow, could she ever use what Papaw had just told her to her advantage.

As if reading her thoughts, Papaw shook his head. "Don't even think about it. I would be very disappointed if you played on your mom's love and devotion to get what you wanted."

"I wasn't—" Cass began, then broke off when she saw his look.

"There's not much you can put past me, Sassafras," he advised, "so don't even try."

Cass didn't respond. Instead she proceeded to shred the paper napkin that had been sitting under her glass of iced tea.

Papaw reached across the table to lay a hand over Cass'. "Before I say anything else, I want you to know one thing. It's going to be all right, I promise. You're very sad right now. You're also angry. But you're going to get through this. Do you want to know how I know that?"

With her free hand, Cass wiped away the tears that had started sliding down her cheeks. "How?" she whispered.

"Well, you believe the Lord's in charge of your life, right?"

Cass recognized where the discussion was headed and she wasn't happy about it. Still, she had to be honest. "Yes."

"And that He can bring good out of any situation?" persisted Papaw.

Again, Cass was forced to admit, "Yes." Sighing loudly, she added, "I don't see how anything good can come out of Mom getting married and moving us so far away, though. When I think about what it's going to be like, all I can imagine is how different life is going to be down on Kwajalein."

"Different doesn't have to mean bad," Papaw reminded her.

Cass gave him a disgusted look. "Please," she sniffed, "whatever else you do, don't treat me like a baby. You know as well as I do that *different* definitely does mean *bad* in this case. In fact, it means horrible, rotten, no-good—"

"I get your point," Papaw drawled, taking a sip of tea. "But that still doesn't mean good things can't come out of it."

"Like what?" challenged Cass.

"Well, let's see." Papaw frowned and pretended to think it over. "For starters, I'd say it's good that your mom is marrying a fine Christian man like Steve who will love her and take care of her after all these years of being on her own. Not only that, you're getting a father who—"

"Stepfather," Cass broke in to correct him. "And what do I need one for anyway?" she demanded crossly. "I have you and Uncle Larry. Y'all have been like fathers to me. I don't need Steve coming in and taking your place."

"He's not." Papaw released Cass' hand as the waitress arrived with their orders. "He's freeing us up to be what we were supposed to be all along. We'll go back to being your uncle and grandfather, and Steve will take over as your dad."

More tears, this time of hurt, welled in Cass' eyes. "You mean you're tired of being my stand-in father?"

Papaw sighed. "Of course not. I reckon I'm not doing a very good job of explaining myself."

"Yes, you are," Cass said resignedly. "I'm just in a bad mood." She arranged her face into an interested expression and declared, "There, I'm better. Tell me why else I should be glad Mom's getting married."

Papaw gave her a knowing look, but continued. "Well, you can't deny the fact that your moving is certainly beneficial for your Uncle Larry and Aunt Linda. Since they'll be renting your house, it'll get them out of the tiny, cramped apartment they're in. Think how much nicer it will be for your three little cousins not to have to share a bedroom."

The bite of sandwich Cass had taken turned to sawdust in her mouth and she almost gagged. She was tired of crying and feeling miserable, but she couldn't help it. "Okay, I give up." She raised her hands in surrender. "As far as everyone but me is concerned, it's a good thing we're leaving. Except for me, it makes everybody's lives so much better, so why should how I feel count for anything?" Her lips started to tremble. "Just tell me one thing. Aren't you going to miss me at all?"

Papaw stared across the table at Cass with a face full of love. "Every minute of every day."

Once again Cass fought to bring her emotions under control. "I'm going to miss you too," she replied briskly. "But we'll write and call, and I'm sure we'll come back to visit." The words rang hollow in her own ears and she gave up the act. "If I survive, that is," she muttered. "I don't know if Mom's told you, but Tabitha and I don't like each other much. Unfortunately, Mom has this whole Brady Bunch fantasy going on in her head. She's determined to turn us into an instant family, so she keeps throwing Tabitha and me together every chance she gets. I really

44

don't mind her going out with Steve, but she usually insists on Tab and me tagging along. We go shopping together, eat practically all our meals together, go to church together. I guess I should be grateful I get to go to the bathroom by myself."

Papaw laughed. Cass took a bite of her sandwich and continued. "Anyway, it's gotten so I'm kind of glad I didn't have a family all these years. I used to feel sorry for myself because I was the only only-child I knew. But I've decided that if this is what family togetherness is all about, forget it. It's way too suffocating for my taste. I need my personal space."

"Things will settle down after a bit," Papaw predicted. "I reckon your mom's anxious about making sure everyone gets along. She'll ease up once y'all get situated in your new home."

"I hope so." Cass didn't sound optimistic. "I can't take two years of pretending to be Tabitha's best buddy. The girl makes me want to hurl."

Papaw laughed and, after a moment, Cass managed a smile. But she felt her heart break a little bit more. She knew she wouldn't die from missing her grandfather, but she figured she'd come close.

After her lunch with Papaw, Cass couldn't get his answer to her question about whether he'd miss her to stop echoing in her head. Everywhere she went for the rest of the week, and each time she saw a friend, she found herself thinking, *I'm going to miss this every minute of every day.*

CHAPTER 8

Saturday, the day of the wedding, dawned sunny and hot. Nothing stirred in the still, sultry air, but even the heat couldn't melt the ice Cass felt around her heart. Although she obediently got up when Mom called and began getting ready when she was asked, Cass' limbs were stiff and her face felt frozen. Even the beautiful green dress failed to bring her any delight. Cass stood in front of the full-length mirror on her closet door and stared at herself. With her bleak eyes, bloodless lips, and ashen complexion, it was like looking at a stranger.

Mamaw chose that moment to rap sharply at Cass' door before bustling into the room. In the mirror, Cass saw Mamaw's mouth thin into an impatient line.

"Why are you just standing there?" she asked briskly. "You're not even halfway ready yet. You know your mom wants you downstairs in fifteen minutes for pictures. Tabitha and Steve are ready."

Great, Cass thought sourly. *Of course they're here. I'm surprised they didn't camp out on the doorstep last night. Steve can't wait to make Mom, Mrs. Steve, and Tabitha's life revolves around being the center of attention.*

Cass turned from the mirror to frown at Mamaw. "Did Mom send you up here to hurry me along?"

"No, to give you these." Mamaw held out a spray of baby's breath which Cass accepted with reluctance. "The hurrying along was my idea," she added. "But don't worry, there's no extra charge for it."

Cass smiled. No one would ever mistake her grandmother for a sweet, little, old granny. She was a brisk, no-nonsense woman who always said what she thought and took charge as often as she could.

"I told Mom I won't wear flowers in my hair. I'll look stupid." Cass crossed her arms and silently dared Mamaw to contradict her.

Mamaw just raised an eyebrow. "Don't be ridiculous. You'll look fine. Tabitha's wearing her flowers and she looks utterly charming."

"That's because Tabitha has the kind of hair flowers look good in," Cass retorted. "My hair's so straight I'll look like I have clumps of weeds sticking out everywhere."

"Not if you French braid your hair the way your mom asked you to," Mamaw shot back. She took the flowers from Cass' unresisting hand and placed them on the floor beside the sleeping bag Cass had been using in place of a bed. Walking up behind Cass, Mamaw combed her fingers through Cass' long, thick hair. "I'm not an expert at this, but I reckon I can manage a decent-looking braid."

"Don't." Cass shrugged off Mamaw's touch before whirling around to scowl at her. "What part of no don't you and Mom understand? I'm not braiding my hair and I'm not wearing flowers and that's that."

"No, it most certainly isn't." Hands on hips, Mamaw returned Cass' glare without flinching. "This is your mom's day and you'll do whatever—I repeat, whatever—she wants. You owe it to her."

Cass ground her teeth in frustration. "I can't tell you how sick and tired I am of hearing about how much I owe Mom. Papaw, Uncle Larry, Aunt Linda, you. Y'all tell me I owe her.

Don't you think I already know that? I mean, she's always been there for me and I know I can always count on her, no matter what. But—" she hesitated, not sure how to say what she wanted to say. "I think I've been a pretty good daughter too, and I'm giving up a lot because of her. Can't we call it even and forget about braiding my hair and sticking flowers in it?"

"It's not up to me," Mamaw replied calmly. "Your mom told me to give the baby's breath to you and to remind you to French braid your hair. If you have a problem with following through on her instructions, I suggest you take it up with her. It's not my place to question your mom's orders."

Cass was torn. Mamaw had a valid point, but Cass preferred not to deal with Mom right now. From what little she'd seen of her so far today, she probably wouldn't appreciate a confrontation.

Cass hesitated for another moment, then turned her back to Mamaw so she could begin to braid. "Fine," she said, "but this doesn't necessarily mean I'm happy about it."

There was silence for the next several minutes while Mamaw braided, weaving strands of baby's breath into the plait. When she was finished Cass craned her neck, inspecting herself from all angles. She was relieved to see the result wasn't nearly as awful as she'd thought it would be.

Admiring her handiwork, Mamaw met Cass' eyes in the mirror. "There. That's not so bad, is it?"

Cass made a face, unwilling to let Mamaw see how pleased she was with the way she looked. "It's okay, I guess."

"Oh, you," Mamaw said. "You're as stubborn as they come. You know you look gorgeous. Would it kill you to admit it?"

"No, but it kills you that I won't," Cass replied tartly. "And that makes it worth it to keep my mouth shut." When her grandmother laughed, Cass was suddenly overwhelmed. Misty-eyed, she turned to ask softly, "Are you going to miss me, Mamaw?"

"Laws, of course I am." Mamaw avoided looking at Cass by adjusting a spray of baby's breath that didn't need adjusting. "But there's no use in getting sentimental about it. What's done is done and you still have to finish getting ready." Spinning on her heel, she marched to the door. "I'll see you downstairs in five minutes."

Cass grinned as the door swung shut behind her grandmother. She was sure she'd seen tears in Mamaw's eyes before she hastily exited the room.

Papaw is right about her, Cass thought, tugging on her pantyhose. *Underneath it all, she really is an old softy.*

The next fifteen minutes were sheer torture for Cass. When she came downstairs the photographer was finishing up his session with Mom, Steve, and Tabitha. Standing between the adults, Tabitha looked like a delicate, pale green flower. Her hair was a riot of curls with the baby's breath peeking out here and there. Compared to her, Cass felt like an old maid school teacher with her tight braid and carefully woven flowers. She groaned inwardly. It seemed no matter what she did, she wound up running a distant second to Tabitha.

"Come on, your turn." Mom gestured to Cass to join her and Steve. "We want some pictures of the three of us, then just us two, and finally all four of us." Mom smiled up at Steve. "Our first family portrait."

Cass stifled a groan. Mom was definitely losing it. How could she call it a family portrait when they were anything but a family? At best they were four people who barely knew each other. Sighing, Cass reluctantly took her place between her mother and Steve.

"Think happy thoughts and smile," coaxed the photographer.

Cass did her best, but guessed all she was producing was a sickly grin. Her suspicion was confirmed when Tabitha snickered and rolled her eyes. Cass stifled the urge to punch her.

"Pretend you're someplace else," Steve murmured to Cass. "That's what I'm doing. In my mind, I'm soaking up the rays on Waikiki. Having my picture taken isn't high on the list of things I like to do."

Cass laughed. "You, too, huh? I thought I was the only one who was camera-shy."

"Nope. Join the club." Steve's hand settled lightly on Cass' waist, providing her with much-needed support. "Let's see if we can get through this without too much trauma. Care to join me at Waikiki?"

Grateful for his understanding, Cass beamed up at Steve before turning her smile to the camera. Over the photographer's shoulder, she noticed Tabitha glowering at her. She wasn't sure what she'd done, but if it made Tabitha mad, Cass was glad she'd done it.

Being photographed with Tabitha proved to be the hardest experience of all. The photographer wanted the two of them to stand between their parents, but neither seemed about to touch each other. No matter how many times they were told to move closer, they steadfastly maintained their positions. The photographer eventually gave up and allowed them to keep the six-inch space between them. Cass heaved a sigh of relief when the photographer dismissed them and called for another grouping. She figured after this ordeal, the wedding should be a breeze.

As soon as the picture-taking was done, there was a mad scramble to pile into cars and head for the church. Cass almost screamed when she learned Mom, Steve, and Tabitha had taken off, apparently forgetting all about her. She was just about to go upstairs and get out of her dress when Papaw found her in the kitchen.

"You coming?" he asked mildly. "The last train's leaving the station. If you don't hitch a ride with me, you're going to have to walk."

"Or I could stay here"—Cass examined a fingernail—

"since my own mother obviously doesn't care if I'm at her wedding."

"Sassafras, you saw how confused it was for a few minutes there," Papaw said. "She didn't leave you behind on purpose."

"She made certain Tab was in the car," Cass replied sourly. "I can tell who Mom's favorite is going to be."

"Sugar, you know your Mom loves you and wouldn't deliberately hurt you. Now please get in the car so we can get to church. The wedding can't start without you and, in my opinion, your mom's waited a powerful long time for this day to come. It's not right to make her wait any longer."

Cass smiled weakly and allowed Papaw to take her arm to escort her to his car. As they drove to church, the butterflies in Cass' stomach kicked into overtime. Cass stared out the window, the scenery flashing by not registering with her. "So you honestly think Mom's doing the right thing marrying Steve?" she asked after a few minutes. "You don't think they'll come to their senses a couple of months down the line and realize they've made a humongous mistake?"

"If I didn't think your mom were doing the right thing, I wouldn't be on my way to the church," Papaw assured Cass. "I'd be back home in my garden, promising the Lord anything He wanted in exchange for Him stopping the ceremony."

"I'm glad you decided not to waste your time. I already tried it." Cass managed a crooked smile. "It didn't work."

"That's one of the problems when it comes to dealing with God," Papaw agreed solemnly. "He knows better than to give us what we think we want. He insists on giving us what's best for us."

"Don't I know it. If I were in charge of the universe, I'd sure run things differently." Cass laughed. "Of course, it's probably a good thing I'm not in charge, especially where

Tabitha's concerned. I'd zap her with zits and flabby thighs so fast it'd leave your head spinning."

"Hmm"—Papaw arched an eyebrow at her—"imagine what she'd do to you."

The parking lot was nearly full when Papaw reached the church. Cass knew most of the people streaming into the building and appreciated their show of support for her mother, even if she wasn't in favor of the marriage. Privately, though, she wondered what Mom's friends and co-workers really thought of her whirlwind courtship and hurry-up wedding.

Papaw led Cass to the pastor's office where Mom, Steve, Tabitha, and Mamaw waited. He retrieved Mamaw, kissed Mom's cheek, shook hands with Steve, and left. Cass waited until the door closed behind her grandparents before confronting Mom.

"Thanks a lot for forgetting me," she drawled. "You really know how to make a person feel wanted."

A blush appeared above the collar of Mom's dress. "I'm sorry, sweetie. We got in such a rush, but I knew someone would make sure you got here."

"Besides," Tabitha piped up with just a hint of a smirk, "there wasn't any room in the car for you anyway. We wound up taking two of Uncle Larry's kids with us. They were crammed into the back seat with me." She smoothed an imaginary wrinkle in her dress. "It was fun, but I was afraid I'd be a mess by the time we arrived. Thankfully, our little cousins behaved."

Cass steamed at hearing Tabitha refer to her relatives as hers. The girl had some nerve, moving in on her family the way she was. What was next? Calling her mother Mom?

Before Cass could respond, Steve said, "I apologize for leaving you stranded. Believe me, it wasn't intentional. Chalk it up to pre-wedding jitters. But I'd still like to make it up to you. How does going out for a macadamia nut ice cream cone one afternoon in Hawaii—just the two of us—sound?"

Cass had never tasted macadamia nut ice cream, but it sounded glorious to her, especially since she'd skipped breakfast. "It's a date," she replied, and added with a mock finger-wagging, "And don't even think about forgetting because I'm going to hold you to it."

"But, Dad," protested Tabitha, "you know macadamia nut is my favorite. Why can't we all go?"

"Because I want to personally thank Cass for being a good sport and forgiving us for abandoning her," explained Steve.

It was Cass' turn to smirk, and she didn't hold back. Tabitha responded by glaring at her and then turning her head.

Pastor Harrison arrived to let them know it was time to assemble at the back of the church. While he strode down the aisle to the altar, Mom smoothed an errant strand of hair behind Cass' ear, then leaned forward to kiss her. "I love you, sweetie. Thank you for being here."

Like I had a choice, Cass thought silently. Aloud she replied, "I love you too. I hope this makes you as happy as you think it will."

Briefly caressing Cass' cheek, Mom murmured, "The one thing I'm sure of is that this is God's will for all of us."

As Mom turned to Tabitha to hug her, Cass found herself facing Steve and feeling awkward. Shaking hands would be silly, but she didn't feel comfortable enough with him for an embrace. Steve solved her problem by draping an arm around her shoulders for a quick squeeze. Cass allowed herself to lean into him for just a moment before stepping away. The organ music swelled and her breath caught in her throat.

"Here we go," Mom whispered, positioning herself next to Steve. "It's showtime."

Cass and Tabitha preceded their parents down the aisle. Cass walked with her eyes straight forward, barely smiling, even though she knew Tabitha was smiling and waving at everyone they passed. While Tabitha seemed to enjoy being on show, Cass just wanted to reach the front row as quickly as possible so she could slide in next to her grandparents and disappear from view.

The wedding itself passed in a daze. Later, all Cass could recall was Steve's ringing declaration of his vows, followed by Mom's soft recitation in the hushed sanctuary. Everything else was a blur until Pastor Harrison's joyful announcement that they were husband and wife, and Uncle Larry's laughter-producing, "Amen and hallelujah!" Cass averted her eyes when Mom and Steve engaged in a lingering kiss, then looked back in time to see Mom holding out her hand to her to join them in walking out of the church.

Cass could barely endure the small reception that followed in the fellowship hall. She lost count of how many times she smilingly assured people that yes, she was quite happy her mother had gotten married, and yes, she was looking forward to living in a tropical paradise.

I wonder if I'm in even more trouble with God for lying in church, Cass thought as she helped herself to punch and cookies.

Looking up, she realized Tabitha was across the table from her. To her surprise, the other girl looked as glum as she felt.

"Having fun?" Cass murmured.

"About as much as you are," Tabitha shot back.

"Hmm." Cass wasn't sure how to respond, so she

changed the subject. "You're spending the next two nights with your grandparents while Mom and your dad go on their honeymoon, right?"

"Uh-huh." Tabitha nibbled on a cookie and studied Cass. "What would you say to coming over and picking me up tomorrow so we could go to the mall or something? Now that our parents' marriage is a done deal, I guess it's time to bury the hatchet."

"I'd say, why would I want to waste my time with you when I could be with my friends, enjoying myself?" Cass smiled sweetly. "I hope you know I mean that only in the nicest way."

Tabitha's face hardened into a furious mask. "You are the most despicable person I've ever met."

"Really?" Cass assumed an innocent expression. "You must not get around much." Lowering her voice, she continued, "And don't ever try to use me again. You just wanted to bury the hatchet because you thought you could con me into rescuing you from your grandparents. How stupid do you think I am?"

"The jury's still out on that." Sashaying away from the table, Tabitha added over her shoulder, "Ask me again in a few weeks. I should know you well enough by then to be able to answer you."

It took all Cass' self-control not to hurl her cup of punch at Tabitha's retreating back.

A short while later, after cutting the cake and bidding their daughters farewell, Mom and Steve left for their honeymoon. As Cass stood on the church steps, waving forlornly, she glanced to her right. Tabitha stood three people away with tears glistening on her cheeks. If Cass didn't dislike her so much, she might have felt sorry for her. She turned her head and watched the car holding Mom and Steve disappear down the street.

The wedding guests lingered for another half-hour, then

gradually took their leave. Steve's parents, with Tabitha in tow, stopped to say good-bye to Cass as she helped her aunt and uncle clean up after the reception. She smiled politely when they invited her to drop in whenever she wanted to over the next two days, but said nothing. There was no way she was going to spend any more time in Tabitha's company than she had to.

Mamaw and Papaw treated Cass to a late lunch on the way home. Although they kept up a steady stream of conversation, Cass didn't join in. A throbbing headache threatened to reduce her to tears at any moment. She ate her burger and fries without tasting them, then followed her grandparents out to their car where she collapsed in the back seat with one arm flung over her eyes to shut out the blinding sunlight.

A visit that afternoon from Janette, Lauren, and Carly did little to cheer Cass up. The aspirin she took managed to dull the headache pain, but didn't erase it entirely. When her friends offered to treat her to a movie, Cass begged off.

"I think I just need to be by myself for a while," she said apologetically. "Besides, I don't think I'd be very good company right now."

Janette waved her dismissal of such a silly notion. "You know we don't care how grouchy you are. We love you no matter what." The others chimed in their agreement. "If you really don't feel like it, though, that's fine. I'll call you first thing in the morning and we'll decide what we're going to do tomorrow."

Heavy silence settled over the group. Tomorrow would be Cass' last day with her friends. Janette finally pushed herself to her feet from where the four of them had been sitting in a circle on Cass' bedroom floor.

"We'll leave now so you can take a nap or whatever," she announced, motioning to Carly and Lauren to stand. "If you feel better, call me. We could still do the movie thing or just"—she shrugged—"I don't know, hang out. okay?"

Cass nodded. "Okay, but don't expect to hear from me. I think it's going to be a long time before I feel better, and I'm not just talking about my head. I mean my whole life."

"Yeah, that's what I figured." Janette flashed Cass a small smile. "Hang in there, okay? Remember, if you need anything, all you have to do is call."

Cass spent the remainder of the afternoon in her room. Every time Mamaw checked on her, she pretended she was asleep. As much as she loved her grandparents and appreciated their concern, Cass couldn't face another lecture from them on how everything was going to be fine. She knew the truth. She was leaving her home the day after tomorrow and heaven only knew when she was going to be back.

After picking at the fried chicken and mashed potatoes Mamaw fixed for supper—usually a favorite of hers—Cass declined her grandparents' invitation to watch television with them and returned to her room. She got ready for bed at eight and was stretched out on top of her sleeping bag by eight-thirty.

The moment Cass closed her eyes, images from the wedding started racing through her head. To chase them away, she opened her eyes and stared up at the ceiling, willing herself to relax. As soon as the tension began to seep from her muscles, she shut her eyes, only to have the wedding video start up again. This process repeated itself over and over for the next two-and-a-half hours. Although Cass was exhausted, it was impossible to sleep.

She folded her arms under her head and gazed up at the shifting patterns the moonlight created on the ceiling as it shone through the branches of the tree outside her window. Cass once again recalled the questions Papaw had asked when they'd gone out to lunch a few days ago.

"Lord," she finally whispered, "I do know You're in

charge of my life and that everything You have planned for me is good. So please"—hot tears slid down her temples to pool in her ears—"please help me get through the next couple of days. I don't know why You're making me leave the people and places I love. But You are, so You've got to help me. I can't do this on my own. I don't have any strength or hope left. Please see me through saying good-bye."

Finished, Cass rolled onto her stomach and settled her head on the pillow with a deep sigh. It took another hour, but the last thing she heard before she fell asleep was the clock downstairs in the living room chiming midnight.

CHAPTER 9

"I'm in Hawaii. Somebody pinch me because I can't believe it. I am actually in Hawaii," Cass gushed for the fifth time in the five minutes since they had gotten off the plane in Honolulu. Her eyes and nose worked overtime, trying to take in the dizzying sights and smells that came at her from every direction.

"We know. We know. In fact, half the airport knows by now." Tabitha wearily brushed a stray curl off her forehead. "So you're in Hawaii. Give it a rest, will you?"

As Cass prepared a nasty retort, Mom touched her arm. "Let it go," she advised quietly. "It's been a long trip and we're all tired. Don't say something you'll regret later."

"Like there's anything I'd regret saying to Miss High and Mighty," Cass muttered. "Unless I said something nice by mistake. That's the only thing I'd be sorry for."

Cass glared at her stepsister who stood a few feet away, looking bored as she fanned herself with a magazine. Ever since they'd left Tennessee almost twelve hours ago, Tabitha had been acting insufferably superior. She had gone on and on about all the places on Oahu she couldn't wait to see again, asking Cass each time she mentioned a new location if she'd ever heard of it. Over and over, she'd shaken her head in amazement when Cass admitted she hadn't. Then Tabitha started a conversation with Steve about the fun they'd had during their previous stays in Hawaii. Unable to stand it any longer, Cass had scrunched down in her seat, closed her eyes, and feigned sleep. It wasn't very original, but it worked.

I will not let her ruin this for me, Cass told herself as she shot resentful looks at Tabitha, who pretended not to notice. *It's my first time here. I'm allowed to be excited. If Tabitha "I'm Too Cool For Words" Spencer doesn't like it, that's just tough.*

Feeling somewhat better, Cass turned to her mother with a grin. "It's incredible. We haven't even left the airport and I already love this place. I can't wait to get out of here and see the rest of it."

Mom's answering smile erased the lines of fatigue from her face. "I know what you mean." She inhaled deeply. "The air even smells different here, like exotic flowers and coconuts."

Laughing, Cass glanced around the terminal. "What do you think is keeping Steve? I wish he'd hurry so we can get going while it's still light. I want to be able to see things on the drive to the hotel and it'll be dark soon."

Mom frowned. "He said he was going to pop into the restroom for a minute. I can't imagine what's taking him so long. Unless maybe he's gotten sick," she added in a worried voice.

Cass suddenly spotted Steve walking toward them, a broad grin on his face. She nudged Mom and pointed. "Here he comes. And I don't think he found those in the bathroom. At least I hope not."

Dangling from Steve's hand were three leis. He held them up for Mom's and Cass' admiration as he made his way through the crowd, a beaming smile on his face.

Mom looked enchanted. "Is he a sweetheart or what? Honestly, I'm the luckiest woman in the world."

Cass gagged. "Yuck! Don't tell me this is what it's going to be like living with newlyweds."

Mom gave her a sweet smile. "This is exactly what it's going to be like living with *these* newlyweds so you might as well get used to it." She smacked her lips with great relish. "The mushier, the better."

Cass was still groaning when Steve reached them. He went first to Mom and tenderly placed the garland of plumerias around her neck. Not yet accustomed to their displays of affection, Cass blushed when the couple kissed. Steve turned next to her.

Slipping an identical lei over Cass' head, Steve kissed her cheek and whispered, "Aloha. Welcome to Hawaii, daughter."

Touched by both the gesture and what he'd said, Cass watched through misty eyes as Steve walked over to Tabitha and repeated the ritual. Fingering the fragrant purple flowers of her lei, she thought, *Mom's right. He is a pretty special guy. I can see why she fell in love with him. But,* she reminded herself, *that doesn't mean I forgive him for turning my life upside down.*

The next thirty minutes were hectic as they collected their luggage, tracked down the rental car, and arranged and rearranged the suitcases so they would all fit in the trunk. The sun was a dazzling ball of orange sinking into the Pacific when Steve fianlly pulled out of the airport parking lot and headed east toward downtown Honolulu.

In the backseat, Cass nearly gave herself whiplash trying to look in every direction at once. She gaped at the towering palm trees and craned her neck to catch a glimpse of the beach between the oceanfront buildings. Ignoring Tabitha's derisive snorts, Cass exclaimed at each new sight—the vibrant colors of the clothes, the tiki torches blazing on the sidewalks, the horse-drawn carriages taking people on tours of the city.

Steve had managed to wrangle reservations at the Royal Hawaiian, a world-famous hotel. Wanting to be the first one to spot it, Cass eagerly scanned each high-rise they passed, searching for a name. When Steve turned right onto a driveway that led up to a pink stucco building, Cass' heart sank.

This is a famous hotel? she thought in confusion. *It doesn't look half as nice as most of the places we passed on the way in.* Disappointed, she climbed out of the backseat when Steve parked the car near a tree covered with flaming red flowers.

"Here we are," Steve announced, gesturing grandly toward the hotel. "The Royal Hawaiian. What do you think?"

"It's beautiful," Mom murmured. She came around the car to snuggle against Steve's side. "I can't imgagine a more romantic place to spend our honey ... "—she glanced at the girls and chuckled—"oops ... make that family-moon."

Steve smiled and kissed the top of Mom's head before turning to Cass. "How about you? Do you like it?"

"It ... uh ... looks fine," Cass hedged, adding truthfully, "It's not quite what I expected, though."

Tabitha laughed. "What she means is, it's not good enough for her. She'd rather stay in one of the newer, bigger places." Smirking, she shook her head. "Some people just don't have any class. What does she care that the Royal's the most prestigious hotel in Hawaii?"

Steve gave her a fierce scowl. "That's enough, Tabitha Joi. Being tired is no excuse for rudeness. Apologize to Cass, pronto."

Cass tried not to look smug when Tabitha, her face flushed with embarrassment, muttered, "Sorry." Cass saw Mom and Steve exchange exasperated glances and wondered if they were asking themselves what they'd gotten into. There was no denying that their daughters weren't nearly as crazy about each other as they were.

They're in for some honeymoon, Cass thought, almost feeling sorry for Mom and Steve. *How much fun can they have with the two of us at each other's throats the entire time? Oh, well.* She mentally shrugged. *They knew what they were getting into. It's not like Tabitha and I ever hid the fact that we hate each other's guts.*

Cass carefully maintained her distance from Tabitha as they trailed their parents into the hotel. Entering the lobby, Cass stopped dead in her tracks, her mouth and eyes wide with astonishment.

"Sort of takes your breath away, doesn't it?" Steve asked, backtracking to Cass' side once he realized she was no longer with them. "That's how I felt the first time I saw it."

Cass nodded. "It's ... it's the most beautiful place I've ever seen. I can't wait to tell my friends I got to stay in a place like this."

"I knew you'd like it," Steve said, his pleasure at Cass' reaction evident in his voice. He draped an arm across her shoulders and grinned down at her. "Nothing but the best for my girls."

"This is better than the best," Cass assured him.

Taking her time as she looked around, Cass felt as though she'd walked into a fairyland. Arches and columns soared up to ceilings that featured gleaming crystal chandeliers. The glow from the chandeliers glittered in the mirrors lining the walls and in the black stone floor beneath Cass' feet. As if that weren't spectacular enough, one end of the lobby opened to the ocean lawn and the beach beyond. Flames from tiki torches fluttered in the breeze and the sound of the surf breaking on the shore could be heard between snatches of conversation.

"Honestly! Will you come on already?" Tabitha's voice broke Cass' spell. "You may be having the time of your life gawking at everything, but some of us are tired and would like to get to our rooms."

Cass allowed Steve to nudge her along to where Mom and Tabitha waited. Reaching them, she said sweetly to her glaring stepsister, "You know, I actually feel sorry for you. It's really sad that you've gotten so used to all this that you can't appreciate how wonderful it is. I plan to enjoy every minute of our time here."

"Oh, goody. Five days of being stuck with a *haole*." Tabitha said. "That means mainlander, in case you're interested."

"Wow! You speak Hawaiian?" Cass exclaimed, forgetting she should be insulted. "What else can you say? If I'm a ha—whatever you called me, what are you?"

Smirking, Tabitha replied, "Dad and I are what's known around here as *kamaainas*—oldtimers."

Steve laughed. "Don't let any of the genuine kamaainas hear you say that," he advised Tabitha, who made a face. "I'm sure they still consider us *malihinis*—newcomers."

Fascinated with the new words, Cass repeated them to herself while Steve checked in at the front desk. Following the bellhop down the corridor, she told herself to remember to ask Tabitha to teach her more Hawaiian when they reached their room. The sooner she learned the language, the sooner she could stop being a haole and pass herself off as a malihini.

They spent the next fifteen minutes getting settled in their rooms. While Cass flitted from window to patio—or lanai, as Tabitha curtly informed her it was called—Tabitha unpacked and claimed the top two drawers in the dresser for herself. Cass was enjoying herself too much to mind being stuck with the one bottom drawer. As soon as her suitcase was empty, Cass brushed off her hands and announced she was ready to go. Tabitha, who was busy hanging up her shirts and dresses, turned from the closet with a scowl.

"Where are you planning on going? You're not going to be allowed out by yourself."

"I assumed we'd all head out. I'm so excited—I don't want to hole up here." She swept her arm toward the lanai. "There's a great big world of exciting things to see and do out there, and I'm anxious to get started."

"Tomorrow will be soon enough." Tabitha shut the closet door and sat down on the bed closer to the bathroom. Yawning, she eased off her sandals and rubbed the soles of her feet on the carpet. "All I want to do is go to bed. I'm exhausted."

"From what? Sitting on a plane?" Cass moved restlessly about the room. "Come on, don't you want to go out and have fun?"

"Nope." Tabitha began to unbutton her blouse. "I already told you. I want to sleep."

A knock at the door halted Tabitha's unbuttoning. Cass looked through the peephole then opened the door to admit Mom and Steve. To her delight, Mom was carrying her purse which meant they were going out. She emitted a silent cheer.

"Who's up for some supper?" Steve glanced from Cass to Tabitha. "I called the Palace and got reservations for eight-thirty. We need to leave in five minutes, though, if we're going to make it on time."

"All I have to do is comb my hair and I'll be good to go." Cass headed for the bathroom, adding over her shoulder, "What kind of restaurant is the Palace? Do they serve Hawaiian food? What is Hawaiian food anyway? Probably lots of different fish and fruit, right?"

"I believe she has a bit of an adrenaline rush going," Cass heard Mom say to Steve and Tabitha. "It hasn't sunk in yet that she's actually running on empty. She'll probably crash in another hour or so. But, in the meantime, I'm afraid she's going to be annoyingly chatty and hyperactive. I've been through this before with her."

"No problem. I can handle it," Steve said. "It's a nice

change of pace from the jet lag queen over there."

Cass smiled, but through the door she could see Tabitha glaring at her father. "I heard that. Excuse me for not being like Cass and driving everyone crazy. Besides," she added, "you never used to mind me being tired after a plane trip. How come you're mad this time? Because you have someone to compare me with?"

Cass caught Steve rolling his eyes as she stepped back into the room and she smiled inwardly.

After dinner, Cass was still ready for sightseeing. To her dismay, she was voted down by everyone else.

"What a bunch of party-poopers," she grumbled. "We're in Hawaii, and all you want to do is go back to the hotel."

"I'll tell you what," Steve offered when the foursome was settled in the car, "I'm game for a walk on the beach if you're still up to doing something when we get to the Royal Hawaiian. How's that for a compromise?"

"I suppose it's better than nothing," Cass replied without enthusiasm. Realizing how ungrateful she sounded, she added hastily, "I mean, that would be nice. Thanks."

"But I don't feel like going for a walk," whined Tabitha.

"Who said you're invited?" Cass retorted.

A loud, exasperated sigh was heard from Mom in the front seat. "For pity's sake, Cassandra, it's a free beach. Anyone is free to walk on it. Nobody needs a special invitation. The same holds true for going back to your room. You're free to do that if you choose. Will you two please stop arguing about every little thing?"

Stung, Cass subsided into silence. She was really beginning to hate being put in her place in front of Tabitha.

Back at the hotel Tabitha seemed to waver between accompanying the others and heading to the room. She finally decided to turn in, but not without a backward glance at her father, Mom, and Cass as they headed through the lobby for the beach.

"I'll say it again. I've died and gone to heaven!" Cass kicked off her sandals, and her feet sank into the cool sand. "I forgot how good sand feels," she marveled. "We've only been to the beach—what, Mom?—once, twice?"

"Twice," Mom answered. "But you were too small to remember the first time. You were a beach baby even then, though." She laughed. "You threw a tantrum when it was time to go back to the motel."

"A tantrum? Me?" Cass pressed a hand to her chest and assumed an innocent expression. "Surely you jest. I can't believe little ol' me ever threw anything even faintly resembling a tantrum."

"Uh-huh," drawled Steve. "Especially when you consider how laid-back and easygoing you are now."

Cass raised an eyebrow at him. "Don't think I don't recognize sarcasm when I hear it."

Steve caught Cass to him in a quick hug that surprised her, but also gave her a warm feeling. "Don't worry," he assured her. "I still like you, no matter how un-mellow you are. You're the kind of person who gives life zing. Everyone should have somebody like you around to keep things interesting."

The pleasure Steve's words gave her tingled all the way through her. She was thankful it was dark because she was sure she was beet-red from blushing.

"If you'd like to walk on ahead, sweetie, it's okay. I'm sure you'd rather not be seen on the beach at night with a couple of old fogeys. Just stay where we can see you. Hawaii may seem like paradise, but bad things still happen."

Cass turned to her mother with a wicked grin. "Oh, please, you don't fool me," she teased. "You know you want me out of your hair so you and Steve can be alone and act all lovey-dovey." She made exaggerated kissing sounds.

Mom chuckled and entwined her hand with Steve's. "Do you blame us?" she shot back. "After all, how many couples take their children on their honeymoon with them?"

"Duh, Mom." Cass hit her forehead with the heel of her hand. "Most newlyweds don't have kids. At least that's the order you've always told me it's supposed to be done in."

Spinning on her heels, Cass sashayed off down the beach. She smiled to herself when she heard Mom and Steve's appreciative laughter behind her. It occurred to Cass that if Tabitha could somehow be erased from the picture, she wouldn't mind her mother and Steve's marriage so much. She liked having a new audience to play to. The problem was, as it had been from the start, Tabitha.

Cass' energy level finally began to bottom out after thirty minutes of strolling the beach. As much as she hated to admit it, she confessed she was ready to call it a day. She was practically crawling by the time they reached the hotel and didn't resist when Steve put a supportive arm around her waist to guide her to the room she shared with Tabitha. The other girl looked up from the bed when the door opened, and Steve helped Cass into the room.

"There you go." Steve ruffled Cass' hair. "Home, safe and sound. Why don't you get into bed before you fall asleep on your feet?"

Cass' smile was slightly woozy. "I guess I kind of overdid it, huh?"

"Yes, but I admire your zest for life." Steve turned Cass by the shoulders and, pointing her in the direction of the empty bed, gave her a push. "Sweet dreams, honey."

He waved at Tabitha. "You too. Don't forget, Donna and I are right next door if you need us."

Tabitha, her eyes narrowed to angry slits, didn't respond to her father. When Mom came into the room to kiss the girls good-night, Tabitha did, however, lift her face to receive her peck on the cheek. When it was her turn, Cass threw her arms around her mother's neck.

"Thank you for the walk. It was exactly what I needed."

She blew a kiss to Steve. "Thank-you even more since it was your idea."

"You're welcome." Grinning, Steve bowed. "The nice thing about you is you're so easy to please. A cheeseburger and a walk on the beach, and you're a happy girl. Boys must love you."

Cass, who'd collapsed backwards onto the bed, raised her head to reply fervently, "Well, we'd hope so anyway."

Mom and Steve left the room laughing. Cass laughed too—until she glanced over at Tabitha and caught her stepsister glaring at her.

"You're really angling for the parents' pet award, aren't you?" Tabitha asked.

"I have no idea what you're talking about." With her last spurt of energy, Cass bounced off the bed and stalked to the dresser to retrieve her pajamas. "Don't take it out on me because you decided to stay here and miss out on all the fun."

"Ooh, some fun." Tabitha rolled her eyes. "Spending the evening with your mother."

"Your father was there too," Cass reminded her. She started for the bathroom, hesitated, then added sweetly, "And you know what? The more time he and I spend together, the more we realize how much we like each other. Isn't that great?"

Without giving Tabitha a chance to reply, Cass ducked into the bathroom and closed the door. When she emerged about twenty minutes later, Tabitha was asleep, or pretending to be, so Cass turned off the light and climbed into bed.

CHAPTER 10

To no one's suprise, Cass was the first one up in the morning. Making as much noise as possible, so as to wake Tabitha without deliberately appearing to do it, she took a shower and got dressed. Coming out of the bathroom, though, Cass discovered Tabitha was still curled in a ball on her bed.

You're either an incredibly heavy sleeper, Cass thought as she watched her sleeping stepsister and wondered what to do, *or you should win an Academy Award for acting. I guess there's only one way to find out.*

"Aloha, Tab!" she called loudly. "Come on, rise and shine."

Tabitha responded with a grunt and rolled over, facing away from Cass.

Cass smiled, then launched one of her pillows and hit Tabitha in the back of the head.

"Ow!" Tabitha sat up. "What's going on?" She rubbed her eyes in confusion then peered blearily at Cass. "Did you throw something at me?"

Sidestepping the question, Cass said, "It's eight o'clock. Time to get up." She snapped her fingers. "Let's go, Tab. Time's a'wasting. Wikiwiki."

Tabitha groaned and flopped back down. "Oh, man, I knew it was a mistake to teach you Hawaiian. And don't call me Tab," she added in a gravelly voice.

"Whatever." Cass waved aside the order, more concerned with getting the Hawaiian language right. "Did I use the wrong word? Doesn't *wikiwiki* mean quickly?"

"It does." Yawning, Tabitha covered her eyes with her arm. "Only I don't feel like doing anything wikiwiki this morning. I just want to be left alone so I can sleep. I don't know how you can be up and going this early."

"Come on—you'll feel a hundred percent better once you've had a shower. I do. In fact, I'm starved. Where can I get something to eat around here?"

"Go get on Mom and Dad's case and make them take you to the dining room. If I remember right, the hotel has a terrific breakfast buffet." Tabitha sounded like she was on the verge of falling back to sleep.

Cass suddenly forgot about being hungry. "Excuse me. Since when did you start calling my mother *Mom?*"

Tabitha turned her head, opened a sleepy eye, and swept the tousled hair off her forehead. "Since last night. While the three of you were out walking, I decided I felt comfortable enough to begin calling her Mom. She told me I could start whenever I felt I was ready, so I don't know what you're getting all worked up about. It's not like it was my idea. Mom's the one who asked me to, not the other way around."

"It's too soon." Cass folded her arms and glowered at Tabitha. "Your father said I could call him Dad, but I wouldn't dream of taking him up on the offer until they've been married—I don't know—six months, at least. You don't just jump into these things. You ease into them."

Propping herself up on her elbows, Tabitha laughed at Cass' earnest expression. "Is that a rule out of some step-family handbook? Look, you can call my father Superman

71

for all I care. But don't get on my case because I'm comfortable calling your mother Mom." A sly look appeared in Tabitha's eyes. "You know, I'm starting to think you're jealous because Mom and I get along so well."

"Your father and I get along too," asserted Cass.

"Oh, really?" Tabitha's arched brows disappeared beneath her bangs. "If that's true, why aren't you ready to call him Dad?"

"I—because it's—" Cass sputtered, furious at herself for not coming up with an answer.

"Oh that's right. I forgot. It's too soon." Tabitha snuggled back against the pillows with a tinkly laugh that set Cass' teeth on edge. "Silly me."

"You can laugh at me all you want. I don't care." Cass flounced off the bed and stomped across the floor. "I'm going next door to wake up my mother and—what did you say to call him?—Superman. Should I tell them you won't be getting up to eat with us?"

"Nah, I might as well join you. You've already ruined my plans to sleep in." Tabitha flicked her hand at Cass as if dismissing a servant. "Tell them I'll be ready in thirty minutes."

"OK, Miss I-Have-To-Be-Perfect," Cass jeered and prepared to slam the door on her way out of the room.

"Oh, and be sure to say hi to Mom for me," Tabitha responded sweetly.

All Cass could do was kick the door when it banged shut behind her. Belatedly, as she limped down the hall to Mom and Steve's room, she realized it wasn't the smartest thing to do since she was wearing sandals.

For a day that began so badly, it turned out to be wonderful. After breakfasting on croissants, fresh pineapple, and kiwi, they spent the morning touring downtown Honolulu. Cass couldn't decide which she liked better—the International Market Place with its waterfalls, tropical birds and vegetation, and Swiss Family Robinson-style tree house, or King's Village, where the streets were made of cobblestone and the salespeople in the stores dressed in costumes from the turn of the century.

The family spent the afternoon on the stretch of Waikiki Beach that fronted their hotel. Cass couldn't believe the beauty of the Pacific Ocean. Growing up in Tennessee, she remembered seeing the Atlantic just once in her life when she and Mom vacationed in South Carolina four summers ago. She'd been fascinated, but frightened, by so much water. Today, however, she ran fearlessly into the waves and swam out to the raft anchored about a hundred feet off-shore without thinking about drowning or sharks or any of the other dangers that had kept her hugging the sand back at Myrtle Beach.

If Kwajalein is anything like this, Cass thought several times throughout the afternoon, *then maybe it won't be so bad after all. I could get used to this life without too much difficulty.*

Her feelings about Hawaii were summed up in the postcard she sent to Janette after a dinner cruise on their third night. She wrote, "You wouldn't believe this place! It's as close to heaven as you can find on earth. I'm having the best time! I wish you were here (instead of Tabitha the grouch). Don't forget me. Love, C."

In fact, during the five days in Hawaii, the only cloud on Cass' horizon was Tabitha. Her stepsister frequently whined about being bored to anyone within earshot, which was why Cass usually placed herself as far away from Tabitha as possible. She'd lost count of how many times Tabitha grumbled, "Being here is so lame. I wish we were back in Kwaj already. I feel like I've been gone a lifetime."

Cass finally got up the courage to complain to her mother about Tabitha when she and Mom were resting under a banyon tree at the Polynesian Cultural Center. Steve and a sulky Tabitha had gone in search of cold drinks and Cass turned to Mom with a frown as they watched the pair stroll away down the path.

"All right, it's just the two of us so tell me the truth. Is it me or is Tabitha driving you crazy too?"

Mom shrugged and fanned herself with one of the center's brochures. "She does seem a little out-of-sorts," she replied. "She's not the same happy-go-lucky girl I got to know back in Tennessee. My guess is she's tired of traveling since she's obviously anxious to get home."

"And leave all this?" With a sweep of her arm, Cass indicated the stunning beauty surrounding them. "I know Kwajalein's a tropical island too, but I can't believe it even begins to compare to this place. I wish we could stay another month."

Smiling, Mom lifted the hair off her neck to expose it to a passing breeze. "It is pretty spectacular, isn't it? It's a dream come true to be honeymooning in Hawaii."

"Except for being stuck with Tabitha and me along to ruin things," Cass pointed out. "That has to be the nightmare part of your dream."

"Uh-uh," Mom protested. She let go of her hair and shook it back into place. "Steve and I love having you girls with us. We look at it as killing two birds with one stone. We're learning how to be a married couple and a family at the same time. When you think about it, it's actually a very efficient way of doing things."

Cass laughed. "Leave it to you to plan an efficient honeymoon. You're one weird woman, Mom."

"I love you too." Mom affectionately butted her shoulder against Cass'.

"I know." A wry expression twisted Cass' features as she stared at the path Steve and Tabitha had taken. "You mentioned learning how to be a family. I'm starting to wonder if I'll ever learn to love Tabitha. She's such a pain."

"I've said it before and I'm going to keep saying it until it sinks in. Give it time," advised Mom. "We're still getting to know one another. I think things will settle down once we get to Kwajalein."

The name made Cass' stomach sink. Other than hoping her new home resembled a miniature Hawaii, she tried not to think about Kwajalein. Now that Mom had brought the subject up, however, the place suddenly loomed large in her imagination.

"Are you … nervous … about finally seeing what it's like down there?" she asked haltingly.

"A little bit," Mom admitted. "Mostly I'm excited. I've been so busy that I haven't had the opportunity to do many adventurous things in my life." She laughed. "Moving halfway around the world is definitely an adventure."

"What if Kwajalein turns out to be an absolutely dreadful place?" Cass peered at her mother, curious to hear her answer. "Have you thought about what you'll do?"

"Honey, you know I don't like to talk in terms of 'what if.' It's a waste of time. Nine times out of ten the things we worry about never come to pass." Picking up the brochure she'd laid in her lap, Mom began fanning herself again. "Besides, Kwajalein is going to be a terrific place to live. I feel it in my bones." She winked at Cass. "And you know my bones are hardly ever wrong."

Cass refused to give up so easily. "But what if it's not?" she persisted. "What will we do if it's so awful there that we just can't stand it?"

Mom hesitated before responding. "I made a promise to Steve, and I will honor it, no matter what. Even if Kwajalein turns out to be the nastiest place on earth—which, by the way, I'm sure it's not—I'll stay because Steve is my husband, and I want to be wherever he is."

"I didn't make any promises," Cass muttered.

"Ah," Mom nodded. "Now we come to the heart of the

matter. You want to know whether or not you have an out if you decide you don't like Kwajalein."

Cass lifted her chin in a show of defiance. "Is that so wrong?" she challenged. "Moving down there wasn't my idea. I'd like to know if I have any options if I wind up hating the place."

Instead of answering right away, Mom gave Cass a speculative look. "What brought this on all of a sudden? I didn't realize you were worried about Kwajalein. I thought you were having a great time here."

"I am." Cass avoided Mom's eyes by toying with the hem of her shorts, folding it up, then smoothing it down, over and over again. "But Hawaii isn't Kwajalein, not by a long shot. The closer we get to heading down there, the worse the feeling gets in the pit of my stomach." She shrugged. "I don't know. Maybe it has something to do with the fact that Tabitha likes Kwajalein so much. I figure, anything she likes, I'm bound to hate on sight."

Mom laughed softly. "Oh, sweetie, you're one of the most honest people I've ever known." She pulled Cass close, and Cass briefly leaned her head on Mom's shoulder before straightening and glancing around to make sure no one had seen her. "As far as your options are concerned," Mom continued, "I'm fully aware that it's the last thing you want to hear, but you don't have any."

Cass stiffened and drew away from her mother to glare accusingly at her. "Meaning?" she asked in a frosty tone.

"Meaning Kwajalein is your home for the next two years. You need to know I will not consider for one second the possibility of sending you back to Tennessee to live. You're my daughter, which means I'm responsible for raising you. I still have two years left on my commitment and I'm not about to turn you over to someone else's care."

"But—" Cass began.

"No buts," Mom cut her off. "The discussion is closed. You're living in Kwajalein for the next two years and that's that."

Cass realized any further attempts at arguing would be futile. Mom didn't use that tone of voice often. "Okay," Cass relented with what she hoped was passable cheerfulness. "No harm in asking, right?"

She unfolded the hem of her shorts and squared her shoulders. "It just gets me sometimes that starting my junior year back in Jonesborough was all the excitement I planned on this year." She flung out her arms. "Now look at where I am, and where I'm going."

"I know," Mom said sympathetically. "But, sweetie, I promise you—"

"Everything will be fine," Cass finished the rest of the sentence for her. "You know, Mom, if I had a dollar for every time you've told me that, I'd be able to buy my own ticket back home by now." *And maybe I'd actually be able to convince myself that you're right,* she added glumly to herself.

CHAPTER 11

The family's final day on Oahu was spent relaxing on the beach. Cass was amazed to realize how quickly she'd adapted to the sun, surf, and sand. Back home she'd always avoided the sun as much as possible since she would usually just burn. Janette used to laughingly tell her someone needed to invent a sunblock with an SPF of 100 for people like her. Now underneath the freckles blanketing her skin was the beginning of a tan, and she couldn't be more thrilled.

After lunch Cass was floating blissfully on an inflatable raft, half-asleep, when a splash hit her in the back. Glaring, she leaned up on her elbows, expecting to find that Tabitha had decided to amuse herself by bugging her. She was surprised to discover Steve grinning at her as he treaded water a couple of feet from the raft. Cass bit back the nasty comment on the tip of her tongue and smiled in return.

"Are you up for that ice cream date I promised you right before the wedding?"

It was all she could do to keep from breaking into an ear-to-ear grin. As the days had passed, she'd concluded that Steve had forgotten about his invitation.

"I can't keep treading water forever," Steve teased when several seconds passed without a response from Cass. "I'm pushing forty, you know. Do you want to go for ice cream or not?"

Cass laughed. "I'd love to. I can be ready in fifteen minutes."

Steve flipped onto his back and gave her a thumbs-up. "That's one of the many things I like about you. All you need is a moment's notice and you're set."

Unlike Tabitha, you mean? Cass almost asked, then thought better of it. After all, Tabitha was Steve's daughter, and she was foolish to think he might prefer her in any way over his own flesh and blood.

Steve was already sitting on the blanket with Mom and Tabitha when Cass paddled ashore. Dragging the raft behind her, she walked carefully across the hot sand, aware that Tabitha's eyes were like laser beams tracking her every step of the way.

"I hear you and Steve are heading out for ice cream." Mom smiled up at Cass. "You're in for a treat. I tried the macadamia nut when Steve and I went out last night, and it's so good it's almost sinful."

Now that Cass had reached the blanket, Tabitha refused to look at her. Instead, she dug in the sand beside her with a sulky expression. "Macadamia nut's my favorite and I haven't had any since we got here."

"We can all go out together after supper," Steve suggested. "I don't believe there's a law against having macadamia nut ice cream twice in one day."

"You and I haven't done one single thing by ourselves, though," Tabitha continued in a whiny voice that made Cass want to hit her. "Why does she"—this was said with a definite sneer—"get to go out with you and I don't?"

"Come on, Tabitha, you know why." A hint of irritation had crept into Steve's voice. "Donna and I explained to you girls that we wanted to use the time here to get to know each other. What better way to get acquainted than going one-on-one?"

Tabitha lifted her head to glare at him. "Fine," she spat out. "Go ahead, take all the time you need to get acquainted with your new daughter. I just hope that in the process you don't forget you already have a child."

"Tabitha—" Steve began.

Tabitha jumped up and stalked toward the water before he could finish. Cass refrained from sticking out a foot to trip her as she swept past.

Cass left the raft with Mom, located her towel among the several strewn across the blanket, and knotted it around her waist. As she and Steve headed for the hotel she shot him a troubled look.

"Uh ... I'm sorry I made Tabitha mad at you," she haltingly apologized. "If you'd rather cancel on the ice cream, I'll understand."

Steve dismissed her concern with an airy wave. "You're not getting rid of me that easily," he assured Cass. "First of all, nobody can make someone else feel anything. We choose how we react to situations. Tabitha chose to be angry. She could have just as easily chosen to be gracious. Okay?" At Cass' nod, he continued, "Secondly, I've been looking forward to treating you to macadamia nut ice cream ever since I suggested it. If you'd prefer to skip it, that's up to you. Speak now or forever hold your peace. Otherwise, there's nothing that could make me back out of introducing you to one of my all-time favorite taste sensations."

"I don't want to back out." Cass hesitated, took a deep breath, and forged ahead, "I've ... uh ... been looking forward to it too."

Steve gently tugged a strand of her dripping hair. "I'm glad. Now let's get a move on. My stomach's starting to growl."

Ten minutes later Cass was knocking on Mom and Steve's door. After rinsing off the salt in the shower, she'd braided her wet hair, dug her nicest shorts and a shirt from her drawer, and topped off her appearance by exchanging her ragged flipflops for the new pair of sandals Mom had bought her the day before. She blushed when Steve whistled at her, but she also couldn't stop grinning.

"You know, I learned something from you." Emerging from the hotel, Cass paused to put on her sunglasses.

"Really? What's that?" Steve directed Cass to the International Market Place across the street.

"Well, I thought about what you said while I was getting ready. You know, about people not being able to make other people feel something." At a break in traffic they hurried across the road. "At first, I decided you were wrong. I thought about all the times I'd said to people they'd made me happy or mad or whatever. Then I thought about the times other people were affected by something and I wasn't. For example, I remember one time when my friend, Janette, and I watched a movie. She wound up crying her eyes out, and I sat there thinking, 'What's the big deal?' because I couldn't summon up a single sniffle." She interrupted herself to gaze up at Steve. "Is this making any sense or am I babbling?"

"You're making perfect sense." Steve steered Cass toward an ice cream shop. "In fact, you've caught on to something a lot of the adults I know haven't learned yet. People and situations may provoke us, but it's up to us how we respond. Just as people can't force us to love them, neither can they force us to get angry at them. We're responsible for how we act, not the other person."

"So what you're saying is, it's a cop-out when people say someone or something made them fly off the handle or whatever, right?" Cass looked to Steve for his confirmation.

"You got it," said Steve. "All kinds of circumstances exist in the world—fun, exciting, scary. We choose how to react to them, and we can't lay the blame at anyone else's doorstep." He opened the door to the ice cream shop and stepped aside to allow Cass to go in first. "But enough lecturing. I declare all serious discussion off-limits for the next thirty minutes. Let's talk about pleasant subjects." He winked. "Like your mom and how crazy I am about her."

The man behind the counter handed Cass her macadamia nut ice cream cone and she took a tentative nibble. All fears of disappointing Steve by not liking it fled instantly.

"You were right. This is delicious. Let's come back here after supper for dessert." Steve laughed and she joined in. "Better yet, let's see what time they open. We can stop in tomorrow morning for breakfast on our way out to the airport. Do they have macadamia nut down on Kwajalein?"

"Sometimes." Steve took another bite before continuing. "It depends on what gets shipped in on the barges each month. Sometimes a special treat is flown in on one of the flights when the crew finds a little extra cargo space left over. They'll announce on the radio that there's a shipment of fresh something or other in, and there's a run on the grocery store that beats anything you've ever seen during the worst Christmas rush."

"Really?" Cass asked faintly. She couldn't imagine people going wild over food.

Steve smiled at her dubious expression. "I know it sounds strange, but you'll see for yourself when you get to Kwaj. You'll soon find out that living there isn't anything like living in Jonesborough."

"I've pretty much figured that out already," Cass muttered.

"Don't look so worried." Steve reached across the table to lightly tap Cass' nose. "Once you get used to it, you'll think it's the greatest place on earth."

Cass didn't want to argue with him, but she didn't think that would ever happen. "How long did it take you to get used to living there?"

"I don't know." Steve shrugged, trying to recall. "Two, three months tops. In my case, moving to Kwaj was a godsend since it meant I could provide for Tabitha without spending all my time at work like I had been. I suppose that's one of the reasons why I have such positive feelings about the place."

"I suppose." Not wanting to dwell on the topic of Kwajalein, Cass turned back to devouring the ice cream cone. "I guess I'll just have to wait and see for myself what it's like."

"You'll know by this time tomorrow," Steve said cheerfully before biting into his cone.

Thanks a lot, Cass thought sourly, the ice cream turning to sawdust in her mouth at Steve's comment. *You sure know how to ruin a good time.*

Try as she might, she could no longer push aside thoughts of Kwajalein as she had done for the past five days. Ready or not, Cass was heading to her new home and new life tomorrow.

And I am not the least bit ready, she reflected, wishing there were some way to delay their departure. At this point, not even the world's best ice cream could make her feel better.

CHAPTER 12

The next morning the family was at Hickam Air Force Base airfield by seven. Cass was slumped in a chair, still blinking sleep from her eyes, when their flight was announced. She obediently shuffled into line behind Mom, Steve, and Tabitha, and followed them out the door.

As she neared the plane, Cass happened to glance up and was so startled she came to an abrupt halt.

"Mom?" she called.

Her mother looked back. "Cass, what's the matter?"

"What's the problem?" Steve asked, and they both came back to join her, pulling Tabitha along. "Are you sick?"

Shaking her head, Cass gestured toward the plane. "What is that?"

Tabitha rolled her eyes. "Let's see. Wings, cockpit—could it be a plane?"

Steve silenced her with a look. "Only military aircraft fly in and out of Kwaj, Cass. Their primary mission is to bring in supplies, so what you're looking at is a cargo plane. That's why it doesn't have any passenger windows and is painted olive drab."

"Does it have seats?" Cass asked, and Tabitha laughed.

Once again, Steve frowned at her. "They outfit it with

the required number of seats. The rest of the area is taken up with cargo, although the various crates and boxes are usually concealed behind a canvas curtain. Once you're inside you'll notice cargo netting lining the walls." He chuckled. "I'll admit it's a different way to fly, but it's completely safe. Plus, you'll be served the best food you've ever eaten on an airplane since MAC flight meals are provided by the Air Force."

"Okay." Some of the wariness drained from Cass' face and she started moving toward the aircraft's stairs. "I was looking forward to looking out the window, though, like I did on the way here."

"Don't worry," Tabitha breezily assured her, "all you'll miss seeing are two thousand miles of ocean. Big deal. That hardly qualifies as a tragic loss in my book."

Neither is you accidentally falling out of the plane at a couple of thousand feet, Cass silently retorted.

Once Cass was settled inside the plane, which was as dreary as the outside, she realized how exhausted she was. With a five-hour flight ahead of her, and Tabitha in the neighboring seat, Cass decided her best option would be to sleep away as much of the time as she could. Within fifteen minutes of take-off she was curled under a blanket, sound asleep.

It took Mom vigorously shaking her shoulder as the plane made its descent into Kwajalein's airport to finally rouse her. Her stomach lurched when she realized what was happening, and she again longed for a window so she could get her first glimpse of what Mom's hasty marriage had gotten her into. Forced to wait, Cass sat rigidly in her seat while the plane touched down and taxied to a stop. Her breath came in short puffs when the passenger door swung open and sunlight and fresh air flowed into the craft.

Suddenly it was if someone had taken a soggy, steaming towel and wrapped her in it. The air was hot—stiflingly, almost sickeningly, hot and she hadn't left the plane yet.

She couldn't imagine what it was going to be like once she stepped out of the dim interior of the aircraft into the blinding white light that streamed through the door. She could feel the perspiration prickling at her scalp and gathering between her shoulder blades and she figured she'd be dripping wet before she even set one foot out of the plane.

Turning to ask Tabitha if it was always this sweltering on Kwajalein, Cass was startled to see that her stepsister's face was bright with anticipation. Tabitha stared intently at the open door as though she couldn't wait to get out.

"I'm so glad to be home," Tabitha said. "I hope Kira got my letter and told everybody about the change in dates. I can't wait to see all my friends."

"But particularly Kira's brother, Micah, right?" Steve asked from behind Cass and Tabitha. "Has Tabitha told you about the huge crush she has on Micah Alexander?" he asked Cass.

Tabitha blushed a deep red. "Don't start, Dad," she warned. "For the umpteenth time, I do not have a crush on Micah. He's Kira's brother. What am I supposed to do? Ignore him? We're just friends. Nothing more."

"Oh, yeah, right. I forgot."

Steve winked at Cass between the seats, and she quickly turned away to hide her grin from Tabitha. All of a sudden, she couldn't wait to get off the plane, if only to see the boy who could make her stepsister so flustered.

With Tabitha practically pushing her over, Cass stood up and took her place in line with the other disembarking passengers. The moment she stepped onto the platform beyond the door, she paused for a few seconds to take a quick look around.

Well, it's definitely not Hawaii, not by a long shot.

Kwajalein was completely flat. Although there were scores of palm trees clacking their fronds in the ever-present tradewinds, there was none of the lush greenery that made Hawaii the tropical paradise it was. And the smell! Cass wrinkled her nose. Instead of the fresh, flowery air of Hawaii, Kwajalein smelled like a bathroom after a long, hot shower—moist and slightly mildewy.

"Come on, move!" Tabitha jabbed Cass in the back with her tote bag. "The last thing I want to do is stand up here in the sun all day. I have places to go and people to see."

"Like Micah?" Cass tossed over her shoulder as she started down the steps.

"Oh, shut up," Tabitha retorted. "You don't know anything about my life here on Kwaj, so quit acting like you do." As soon as she reached the tarmac, Tabitha pushed past Cass and hurried toward the terminal.

"So what do you think of your new home?" Steve came up behind Cass. "Or isn't that a fair question, seeing as how you haven't had a chance to look around yet? I suppose I should give you a few minutes to get your bearings before I start peppering you with questions, huh?"

"I already know one thing—it sure is hot here." Cass tugged at the neckline of her T-shirt to permit the air to circulate against her sweaty skin. "It must be a hundred degrees, at least. I thought Hawaii was warm, but this place is like an oven."

"Actually, the temperature rarely goes above ninety, even though we're practically sitting on the equator. You can thank the tradewinds for that. And, believe it or not, you will get used to the heat."

Cass raised an eyebrow and Steve laughed. "I'm not kidding. Within a couple of months, I guarantee you that you'll be reaching for a sweater when the temperature drops below eighty."

Cass groaned and mopped her forehead. "Just the thought of a sweater could be enough to put me over the edge. The terminal had better be air-conditioned."

"Steve!" The exuberant greeting interrupted Steve's

response. "Great to have you back, buddy. And this must be your lovely bride."

Cass turned in the direction of the hearty voice booming across the tarmac. A tall man with Oriental features was headed toward Steve with an outstretched hand. He grabbed Steve's hand in what appeared to be a bone-crushing grip. Cass winced, hoping the handshake wasn't as painful for Steve as it looked.

"Ed! It's good to see you." Steve drew Mom to his side. "I'd like you to meet my wife, Donna. Honey, this is Ed Nishihara from the radio station."

Mom extended her hand and, unlike with Steve, Ed gently enfolded her hand with his. "It's nice to meet you, Ed. Steve's told me a lot about you." Mom laughed. "And, in case you're wondering, all of it was good."

"He must have lied his fool head off then," Ed said, grinning. "I'm pleased to meet you too, Donna. When Steve called to say he was bringing back a wife, I thought he was joking. But I can see you've already worked miracles for the guy. I believe I've seen him smile more in the past couple of minutes than in the five years I've known him. Any woman who can make a friend of mine this happy is all right in my book."

Mom smiled at Steve. "I promise I'll do my best to keep him smiling."

Cass, growing hotter by the second, began to edge away from the adults. Even though Steve hadn't answered her, she assumed the terminal was air-conditioned and decided to get inside before she collapsed on the tarmac.

Cass' movements caught Ed's attention and he turned to her with the same wide, welcoming grin he'd given Mom. Not wanting to seem rude, Cass immediately abandoned her attempt to escape.

"You must be Cass." Ed's eyes narrowed as he searched her face. "You're not feeling too well, are you? I don't blame ou. Our heat and humidity take some getting used to." Lifting the carry-on bag from Cass' shoulder, he grasped her elbow. "Come on. Let's get you inside where it's cooler. We don't want you passing out on us."

Cass gratefully allowed herself to be steered into the white cinder block building. She gasped at the cold air that instantly raised goosebumps on her arms.

Ed grinned as she shivered. "We believe in going from one extreme to the other around here," he cheerfully explained. "We like to keep people guessing. We've fixed it so you're either freezing or baking. There's no in between."

"He's kidding," Steve added hastily, seeming to sense her dismay. "I agree the terminal's chilly, but you'll be quite comfortable in our house. And, honest, you'll hardly notice the heat after a little bit."

"If you say so."

Although Cass wasn't convinced, she was too weary to put up an argument. She was tempted to find an out-of-the-way corner of the terminal to crawl into and hide. The problem was the Kwajalein Airport was too small to have any out-of-the-way corners—it was just one large room. Sighing to herself, Cass squared her shoulders and waited for whatever came next in this nightmare she was living.

"By the way," Ed said, turning to Steve and Mom, "I borrowed one of the government cars so you wouldn't have to take a taxi home with all your things. Donna, after Steve and I collect the luggage, how would you like a tour of the island before you head on to the house? It won't take long. There's not much to see, but I thought you might enjoy a quick look around."

Mom looked at Cass, who shrugged and looked away. *Like you care what I want anymore,* she thought bitterly.

Mom shifted her attention back to Ed. "I'd love a tour. Thank you. I have to admit I'm curious to see what the rest of the island looks like."

As Steve and Ed started toward "baggage claim"—a haphazard pile of the passengers' luggage—Tabitha suddenly appeared with a small crowd in tow. Cass blinked. She almost didn't recognize this happy, bubbly person.

Boy, can she switch gears fast, Cass marveled. *No one would ever know what a crab she's been the past six weeks.*

"Dad, is it okay if I go to Kira's for a little while instead of going straight home with you guys? We haven't seen each other in a month and a half, and we have a bunch of catching up to do." Tabitha produced her most winsome smile for her father. "You know how it is."

"Well—" Steve hesitated, glancing at Mom. "I'd prefer we all go home together first. Then you could head over to Kira's after a while. Hi, Kira," he added, waving at the dark-haired girl standing behind Tabitha. "It's good to see you again. I hope the summer's been treating you well."

Kira returned his greeting with a smile and a wave. "Not bad, but I sure haven't had as much excitement as you and Tabitha."

At her father's words, Tabitha's expression had instantly clouded over. "Can't I please go to Kira's?" she whined. "Why do I have to go back to the house anyway? Mom and Cass don't need me around to get settled. You can show them where everything is. I promise I'll come home any time you tell me to, no complaints, no arguments."

Mom answered her after a moment's hesitation. "I think spending time with your friends is a fine idea. I'm sure y'all have a lot to talk about." She and Tabitha shared a knowing smile that twisted a knot in Cass' stomach. "Just be sure to be home by five so we can have our first supper together as a family in our own home. How does that sound?"

"Sounds great!" Tabitha's brilliant smile was back in place. "Thanks, Mom," she added, shooting Cass a spiteful smirk. "You're the best."

"Thanks, Mom," Cass mimicked her under her breath.

She had no clue why Tabitha had given her that look. If anyone had bothered to ask her, she'd have told them she couldn't care less if her stepsister spent the next two years at Kira's house.

Cass watched Tabitha leave surrounded by her friends, a great wave of jealousy washing over her. She missed Janette and the rest of her crowd from home so much it hurt. She tried to picture what they might be doing right now and then remembered that Kwajalein and Tennessee were on opposite sides of the International Dateline. She'd gained a day when the plane flew over the Dateline so it was still yesterday back home.

How am I supposed to keep up with what's going on in my friends' lives when we don't even share the same day of the week? she thought. She bit her lip to keep from crying.

Breaking in on Cass' thoughts, Mom murmured, "I believe the tall, dark-haired boy walking next to Tabitha is Kira's brother, Micah." They watched Tabitha's crowd exit the terminal. "I wasn't watching them every second, of course, but I don't think he's left Tabitha's side since she got off the plane."

Cass studied him with interest. "I think you're right," she agreed. "Look at how he can't keep his eyes off her." *I guess there's no accounting for taste*, she added silently.

"They certainly make a striking couple, with Tabitha so fair and Micah so dark." Mom turned to Cass when the door closed behind the last girl in the group. "Steve says they haven't officially dated yet, although they spend a great deal of time together since they hang out in the same crowd. From what I saw, it's just a matter of time before he asks her out."

Cass tuned her out. She had absolutely no interest in Tabitha's love life.

CHAPTER 13

Steve and Ed came back with their luggage and Ed led the group out of the building to a nearby olive green car with official-looking letters and numbers stenciled in white on the door. Cass climbed into the back seat of the car and slid over to make room for Mom. They left the doors open while Ed and Steve stowed the suitcases in the trunk. The two men sat up front when they were done, although Steve angled himself in the seat so he could talk to Mom and Cass.

Ed pulled the car into the road with barely a glance over his shoulder, since there wasn't any other traffic to be concerned about. "As you can see," he began, acting the tour guide, "the airport takes up almost half the island. The number of people who work here on Kwaj is about evenly split with the number who commute to Roi-Namur, another island in the Kwajalein atoll chain. I'm sure Steve told you that the U.S. Government rents the two islands from the Marshallese government and operates missile-tracking stations on both. Missiles are shot from bases in California and tracked across the Pacific before they splash down in our lagoon."

"In the lagoon?" Cass echoed, her voice squeaky and her eyes wide. "Isn't that dangerous? What if they miss?"

"You don't have anything to worry about," Ed said lightly. "We haven't had one hit us yet, and they've been shooting at us for almost thirty years. In fact, it's considered a big deal around here when a missile's headed our way. A lot of people congregate on the beach to watch the splashdown. It's a pretty impressive sight, particularly at night."

"I wonder what else they do for excitement—watch the palm trees grow? Or maybe throw rocks in the ocean?" Cass muttered, earning herself a stern look from Mom.

"As I'm sure you already know," Ed continued, turning the car down a stretch of road that paralleled the runway, "Kwajalein is cresent-shaped, measuring roughly three miles long by a half-mile wide. It's not very big, but I think you'll find it has most everything you need for a good life. Anyway, it's a coral island which means it wasn't formed by volcanoes like the Hawaiian islands were, but from coral and algae piled by the ocean over the span of thousands of years. That explains why the highest point on the island is only seven feet above sea level and why we don't have any freshwater streams or ponds. The water we drink comes from the rainwater we collect during the rainy season. Sometimes our supplies get a little low by the end of the dry season and we have to ration water usage until it starts raining again."

A pounding headache was starting to form just behind Cass' eyes. She tuned out Ed's geography lesson and turned her attention to the scenery flashing by the window.

Her first impression that Kwajalein wasn't as lush as Hawaii was unfortunately proving to be correct. Although coconut palms, banyan trees, and, surprisingly, pine trees abounded, the rest of the plant life was scawny. Where there was grass, it grew low to the ground and in patchy clumps. Even the flowers were scraggly instead of luxurious. Everything looked as though it fought a daily battle to cling to life in the island's sandy soil.

"This is our golf course." Ed's voice intruded on her dreary thoughts. "All nine holes of it." He chuckled and gestured toward the ocean. "There's only one water hazard, but it's a doozy, especially if you're unlucky enough to hit your golf ball into the shark pit."

Cass gulped. "The what?"

Since she was sitting directly behind Steve, he had to turn in order to give her a reassuring smile. "The place where the island's garbage is dumped into the ocean is called the shark pit because sharks regularly show up to feed on what's put out. There's no cause for concern, though. They've never been known to go anywhere near the lagoon where we swim. They keep to their side of the island and we keep to ours."

"There's always a first time for everything," Cass pointed out, vowing to never venture any farther into the lagoon than ankle-deep water. "What if they don't like the trash one day and decide to browse in the lagoon for something tastier?"

"Don't be ridiculous, Cassandra," Mom said before Steve could respond. "Fish don't think like that."

Cass shot her mother an exasperated look. "Sharks aren't exactly your ordinary, run-of-the-mill fish. I've watched enough nature shows to know it's a good idea to keep my distance from them. They've been known to kill people."

"Not here, they don't," Steve informed her. "If I thought there was any danger, believe me, I'd never let Tabitha within a hundred yards of the lagoon. But there hasn't been a single shark attack in the eight years we've lived here."

"That's a relief." Feeling slightly better, Cass decided she might risk going up to her knees in the lagoon. After a few months, if nothing had taken a chunk out of her calves, she'd seriously consider venturing into waist-deep water.

At that rate, it'll be a year before I finally get my hair wet, Cass mocked herself. *But at least I won't give a shark the chance to make a snack out of me.*

When the tour ended fifteen minutes later, Cass realized for the first time just how limited her new world was. She'd seen everything Kwajalein had to offer in less than a half-hour. Ed had driven them by the one restaurant; the combination post office and department store; the combination library, radio station and bowling alley; the supermarket; and the elementary and high schools.

I thought Jonesborough was small, Cass thought, *but this place is miniscule. No wonder it's just a dot on the map.*

Ed pulled up in front of a one-story cinder block house painted a faded green. Cass stared at it in shock for several seconds. Even the fragrant hibiscus and bougainvillea that grew in profusion on either side of the walk leading to the front door and bloomed along the foundation couldn't lift her spirits. She hadn't been expecting much, but the house looked like a dump.

"Here we are," Steve announced, opening the car door. He sounded anxious, but Cass wasn't about to muster any concern for him. "Home, sweet home."

Cass forced herself to move while Mom clambered out of the car and hurried to Steve's side. Slipping an arm around his waist, she leaned her head on his shoulder.

"Why, honey, it's lovely!" she exclaimed. "It's even nicer than you told me it was. I can't wait to see the inside."

Cass blinked in confusion. She'd never known her mother to lie, so how could she stand there and call the house lovely? Couldn't she see how tiny and rundown it was?

Mom and Steve walked up the flower-bordered path, followed by Ed who carried a couple of suitcases. As they neared the front patio (*It's called a lanai here,* Cass reminded herself), the door to the other half of the duplex flew open. A woman with very blonde hair and very tanned skin appeared, grinning and waving.

"Why, Steve Spencer!" the woman called in a drawl that Cass' Tennessee ears recognized as being from Georgia. "So the grapevine was right for once. You did go and get yourself married. Tom said he heard it from some of the men at work, but I told him I'd believe it when I saw it with my own two eyes." She propped her hands on her hips and beamed her approval. "Well, all I can say is, praise the Lord! It's about time."

Laughing, Steve detoured across the meager lawn. "Donna, this is Charlie—short for Charlene—Simpson. She and Tom and their three boys have been our neighbors for four years. Charlie, this is my wife, Donna, and my stepdaughter"—he pointed to Cass who remained by the car and lifted a limp hand in greeting—"Cassandra, otherwise known as Cass."

Charlie extended her hand to Mom. "Welcome to the neighborhood, Donna. You'll find we're a friendly, informal bunch. I sure am glad somebody finally took pity on this boy and married him. I really was afraid he was well on his way to turning into the male version of an old maid, and everyone knows a man needs a good woman to keep him on the straight and narrow."

Cass could tell by Mom's burst of laughter that she liked Charlie, and it was yet another thing, in a growing list of things, she didn't understand. She thought the woman entirely too loud and pushy.

With a promise to come over once Tom got home from work, Steve and Mom made their way back across the pathetic scrap of lawn. After unlocking the front door, Steve scooped Mom up in his arms and triumphantly carrying her across the threshold. Mortified, Cass glanced up and down the street, hoping no one, other than Ed, was around to witness this ridiculous display. She shook her head at Steve's retreating back.

Just when I was starting to like you, you had to mess it up by going and doing something really dumb.

"Hey, Cass, what are you waiting for? Come on in," Mom called from somewhere inside the house.

Sighing, Cass trudged up the flagstone path, dread building in the pit of her stomach with each step. She paused at the door to take a deep breath then walked inside. Immediately a relieved whoosh of air escaped Cass' lips.

The living room was bright and cheery, despite the fact that the house had stood empty for six weeks. The walls were white, as was the vinyl floor. Steve had chosen vivid yellows, greens, and blues for the furniture, curtains, and rugs. The effect was very dramatic compared to the pastels Mom had decorated their old house with and Cass decided she preferred the bolder colors.

The living room led directly into the dining room which had a window that spanned the entire wall and overlooked the ocean. The curtains were open, and Cass lingered a moment to marvel at the realization that the Pacific Ocean was now her backyard.

The dining room was separated from the kitchen by a short counter and, off the kitchen, Cass spied a porch. Although everything looked decent enough, and not nearly as dilapidated as Cass had feared, it was cramped compared to their house back home. She couldn't imagine what it would be like living in such close quarters day after day. It occurred to her that, even if the island were big enough for both her and Tabitha, the house definitely was not. They'd be tripping all over each other.

"Let me show you your room." Steve sounded proud as he beckoned to Cass to follow him down the short hall to the first bedroom on the left. "I know it will feel strange to you until your own things arrive. I'm sorry it's going to take so long for them to get here, but I think you'll like it once you're settled in. It's important to me that you feel at home as soon as possible."

Cass peered around Steve into the room and she crumpled inside with despair. It looked to be half the size of her bedroom at home. She'd never suffered from claustrophobia, but she could see herself developing a raging case of it in a place this small.

"It's nice, don't you think?" Mom asked from behind Cass. "When your furniture gets here, it'll be very cozy. Your own, private hideaway, just like your bedroom back in Tennessee was."

Cass wanted to be polite, she really did. She knew it wasn't Steve's fault he lived in such a tiny house. She knew he hadn't married her mother just so he could haul her halfway around the world and make her life a living nightmare. Cass knew all that, and she meant to say something pleasant in response to her mother's question. But what came out of her mouth was a long, anguished wail.

"No, it isn't a nice room or a cozy room. It's a dump. The whole house is a dump." Tears streamed down Cass' cheeks. Out of the corner of her eye she saw Ed quickly retreat down the hall. "I can't believe I actually have to live here. You know what I kept thinking as we drove around the island? This place is nothing. You took me away from my home, my family, and my friends, and brought me down here to live on ... on ... nothing atoll."

"Sweetie, don't," Mom said softly, reaching out to touch her. "It's going to be—"

"Don't say it," Cass ordered. Putting her hands over her ears, she backed away from Mom. "I don't care what you think, it's not going to be okay. I don't want to hear it. I hate it here, and nothing in my life is ever going to be okay again."

"All right," Steve said gently but firmly, "you've had a long day and you're tired and upset. Your mom and I understand. Perhaps you'd feel better if you lay down for a little while. Things won't look so bad after you've had some time alone to think about them."

"Are you sending me to my room?" Cass demanded angrily.

Smiling, Steve shook his head. "Don't worry. I'm not sending you anywhere. I'm merely suggesting you might like to be by yourself for a bit. If you don't want to, that's fine with me. Your Mom and I will be glad to have your company."

Some of the tension drained from Cass. "Maybe you're right," she conceded. "Let me get my stuff out of the car and—"

Steve caught her by the arm as she turned to leave. "I don't want you moving a muscle. I'll get whatever you need. That's what dads are for. You go in there and start working on relaxing." He gave Cass a gentle push.

Cass obediently headed into the room, grateful to Steve for taking charge. She was almost back to liking him again. When she turned to close the door behind her, she was surprised to see Mom still there and grinning at her.

"What?" Cass asked suspiciously.

"I just want you to know I think you're really something. Who else but you would come up with a catchy phrase like 'nothing atoll' to describe Kwajalein?"

While she wasn't ready to see any humor in the situation yet, Cass felt some of the ice around her heart melt at Mom's compliment. She quietly shut the door instead of slamming it as she'd planned to do only moments earlier.

After Steve brought in her luggage Cass stretched out on the bed, her arms folded beneath her head. There was a window opposite the bed and sunlight streamed into the room. Its brilliance made Cass' eyes water—or at least that's what she told herself was the reason for her tears.

Papaw always says whenever I'm feeling blue, I should cheer myself up by counting my blessings, she thought bitterly. *Even though I don't feel particularly blessed at the moment—in fact, I feel downright abandoned by God—I'll give it a try.*

She stared out at the cloudless blue sky and hibiscus bush framed by the window. *Well, I guess I'm thankful Tabitha wasn't here to see me lose it. I know she'd have gone straight to her friends to tell them how I threw a fit because I didn't like my room. Thank You, Lord, for sparing me that humiliation.*

And thank You for keeping the plane in the air during the flight from Hawaii and for landing it safely on the island. And thank You that I don't have to share a room with Tabitha. Cass shuddered at the image of her and her stepsister locked up together in the same space and decided not to think about it any more. Her mind drifted off to nothing and before long she fell asleep.

CHAPTER 14

When Cass woke up she could smell the tantalizing aroma of frying chicken coming from the kitchen. As she slowly came awake, her glance flickered around the room, and for a few minutes she was unsure where she was. Remembering, she groaned and flung her arm over her eyes.

"So it wasn't all just a bad dream," she muttered.

She got up and went to the bathroom across the hall to wash her face and brush her hair. She'd already discovered one advantage to living in a sunny climate—her red hair was developing golden streaks, and Cass loved the way they looked. She couldn't wait to send some pictures back to Janette. Her friend would be green with envy.

Emerging from the bathroom, Cass followed the supper smells and sounds of conversation down the hall to the kitchen. Steve sat at the dining room table, reading aloud from what looked to be a miniature newspaper while Mom and Tabitha worked at getting dinner ready and made comments on the various news stories. Suddenly uncertain as to what her role was, Cass hesitated at the edge of the living room rug.

"There you are, sleepyhead," Steve teased when he glanced up from the paper and noticed her standing there.

"We were wondering if you were going to put in an appearance."

"I'd have been here sooner if somebody had come and gotten me," Cass replied stiffly. She didn't like feeling like an outsider.

"Ooh, someone woke up on the wrong side of the bed," teased Tabitha.

Torn between ignoring her stepsister and responding in kind, Cass decided on the latter. "Wow, are you just naturally funny?" she drawled. "Or did you have to go to comedy school to learn to be such a riot?"

Tabitha just glared at her and turned her back on Cass. Suddenly feeling much better, Cass crossed the floor to the kitchen.

"What can I do to help?" she asked her mother.

"Nothing," Tabitha snapped instantly. "Mom and I have everything under control. In fact, Dad made the comment that we operate like a well-oiled machine. He said nobody would ever guess we haven't been doing this for years."

"Why don't you set the table?" Mom suggested before Cass could respond. "Steve can help you since he knows where everything is."

Steve promptly folded the paper and set it on the counter. "I'd be honored to be your kitchen detail partner," he informed Cass with a playful tug on her hair. "There's nothing I like better than sharing the workload with somebody." He glanced at Tabitha, then smiled. "In the old days, I had to prepare supper and set the table all by my lonesome."

Tabitha's cheeks flushed an angry red. "That's not true and you know it. We used to split the chores fifty-fifty."

Steve just laughed. "I'd say it was more like sixty-forty, maybe even seventy-thirty."

Cass smiled at the glare Tabitha gave him. It was about time somebody put the girl in her place.

She and Steve worked well together and got the table set in no time. While Mom and Tabitha finished preparing dinner, Cass and Steve sat in the living room and laughed at the condensed stories in the Kwajalein Gazette.

"Not having a real newspaper gets to me sometimes," Steve admitted. "I'm a news junkie—especially fresh news. The papers we get in from Hono—our nickname around here for Honolulu," he explained, "are anywhere from three days to a week old. I suppose this"—he held up the four-page Gazette—"is better than nothing, but just barely. I'm grateful I work at the radio station where the ticker-tape machine keeps me up-to-date on the latest breaking stories."

"I'm into the news too," Cass informed him, pleased to discover they had something else in common beside a love of macadamia nut ice cream. "Maybe I could come down to the station sometime and see the ticker-tape machine and all the other ... you know ... radio stuff."

Steve looked pleased. "I'd be honored to have you visit. I was planning to ask you after giving you a couple of days to settle in. You just tell me when you're ready and we'll set it up."

"Set what up?" Mom asked as she carried the platter of chicken to the table.

"A time for Cass to visit the station." Steve said.

Following Mom with biscuits and a bowl of mashed potatoes, Tabitha piped up, "I can take her by. I haven't been to the station in ages."

Steve laughed. "That's because the last time I mentioned it, you said, and I quote, 'I'd rather be tied up and dropped into the shark pit than have to go to the station and suffer through another boring tour.' "

Tabitha blushed and muttered, "That was a couple of years ago. I was going through my snotty stage. I don't feel that way anymore."

Steve draped an arm across her shoulders. "Does that mean you're just about through your snotty stage, then?"

Tabitha shrugged off his arm. "Why do you keep picking on me?" she complained. "You never have anything nice to say to me anymore. Not since she—" Tabitha stopped abruptly, then finished sullenly, "anyway, it's been a long time."

Inwardly, Cass grinned, even though Steve gave Tabitha a hug and said, "Come on, Tab. We've always kidded around with each other. I'm sorry you're taking exception to it at the moment."

Once the food was on the table and everyone was seated, the family held hands while Steve said a blessing. Cass, whose internal time clock was going haywire because of jet lag, had been sure she wouldn't feel like eating for a couple of hours. When the chicken was passed, however, she helped herself to two pieces, then piled a mound of mashed potatoes on her plate. Since she'd been given the chair facing the window, she was treated to a panoramic view of the ocean during the meal. If not for Tabitha, Cass actually thought this domestic little scene might be quite pleasant.

"Can I go back over to Kira's after supper?" Tabitha asked, reminding Cass that unfortuantely, Tabitha *was* on the scene.

"*May* I go back to Kira's?" Steve corrected her.

"Whatever." She smiled so sweetly, Cass almost choked on her chicken. "May I?"

Steve glanced over at Mom. "As long as Donna doesn't have any objections."

"Mom?" Tabitha folded her hands into a prayerful position and turned appealing eyes in Mom's direction. "Please tell me you don't have any objections."

"None whatsoever," Mom assured her.

"Great!" Tabitha was almost bouncing in her chair.

As Steve resumed eating, he glanced at Tabitha. "What do you think about the possibility of Cass tagging along

104

with you when you head back to Kira's?" he suggested casually. "I'm sure she'd like to meet your friends."

"But, Dad," Tabitha whined at the same time that Cass protested, "Steve, no."

They glared at each other, then at Steve. Cass couldn't believe he'd practically begged Tabitha to spend time with her.

What does he think I am? she fumed. *Some kind of charity case?*

"Don't get angry," Steve said calmly. "It was only a suggestion. Nobody's ordering you to do anything."

Realizing she wouldn't be going anywhere, Cass relaxed a bit. She could tell Tabitha wasn't about to let go that easily. She glowered at her father while picking at her biscuit, rolling the pieces she tore off into tiny balls before dropping them on her plate.

"Yes, Tabitha? You'd like to say something?" Steve asked after a minute.

"It's just … I mean … I can't believe you'd try to force Cass on my friends like that," she said angrily. "She can find her own friends. There are enough people on the island for her to choose from. I don't appreciate you encouraging her to take mine."

Cass knew she should stay out of the discussion, but she couldn't help herself. Widening her eyes innocently, she asked, "What? You own your friends? They're yours to keep or give away as you see fit? Is that some kind of island custom I'm not aware of?"

"Shut up!" hissed Tabitha. "I was talking to my father so you can just stay out of it. When I want your two cents' worth, I'll ask for it."

"There's such a thing as free speech, you know," retorted Cass. "I don't have—"

"That's enough!" Mom broke in. "This is an absolutely ridiculous conversation and I refuse to listen to it for one more second. Tabitha, your father already said you didn't have to take Cass with you, so drop it. And, Cass, quit baiting your stepsister. You two are going to learn to be civil to each other if it's the last thing I do."

Cass bit back a reply and went back to eating. *There's no way you'll live to be that old, Mom.*

After the dishes were cleared, Tabitha hurried out of the house, calling out a promise to be back by ten. Cass watched her go with a mixture of relief and envy. She was glad to be rid of her stepsister for the next three hours, but she hated that Tabitha had someplace to go. She tried to picture what Janette and the others might be doing right now. She wondered if any of them were missing her.

She offered to help with the dishes, but Steve dismissed her with a wave. "If Tabitha has a pass on kitchen duty tonight, so do you. In fact"—he tugged on Mom's arm—"I propose we all play hooky. How would you ladies like to take a walk on the beach? It's low tide. Do I have any takers?"

Cass glanced at Mom, willing her to say yes. The house was beginning to close in on her and she needed to escape.

Mom glanced at her and smiled. "A walk sounds heavenly. Let me find my sandals and we're off."

The sun sat atop the palm trees on the lagoon side of the island as they set off up the oceanside beach toward the airport. With the waves breaking about fifty yards out, the roar of the surf was muted, and the threesome was able to talk without having to raise their voices. Crabs skittered for safety, dropping into the nearest hole, at the humans' approach. To her surprise, Cass found the whole scene rather peaceful. In fact, when Mom finally suggested they return home for brownies and ice cream, she was almost—almost—starting to feel better.

By the time they reached the house, the sun had dropped below the horizon and the first stars were making their appearance.

Noticing the sudden darkness, Cass frowned. "That's weird. There was hardly any twilight. It was light then—poof!—it was dark."

Steve, holding Mom's hand as he walked with her, looked over his shoulder at Cass who was bringing up the rear. "That's because we sit just a few degrees north of the equator. We're almost directly beneath the sun so it doesn't have the long slide to the horizon like it does in the northern and southern latitudes. If you're ever up for a sunrise, you'll find the same thing happens. It's dark, then the sun pops up and it's day."

"Weird," Cass said. "I guess I never thought about how different it is in other parts of the world. All I ever cared about was life in Jonesborough."

Actually, that's still all I care about, she added silently, and all the good feelings about Kwaj suddenly vanished.

Over her dessert, Cass, much to the amusement of Mom and Steve, erupted into a jaw-cracking yawn. When she finished, she glanced at them with a sheepish expression.

"I guess I'm more tired than I realized." She took another spoonful of ice cream, then pushed it away. "My body doesn't know what time zone it's in anymore." She checked the clock over the sink. "It's after eleven yesterday evening in Hawaii, which means it's"—she rapidly calculated—"around four in the morning back home." Moaning, she leaned her head on her hands. "I'm so confused. I wish we hadn't crossed the International Dateline."

Mom smiled sympathetically. "Why don't you go on and get ready for bed?"

Cass tried to stifle another yawn, but failed. "But it's only eight o'clock," she protested. "No self-respecting 16-year-old goes to bed at eight. Besides, I thought you wanted us to play Monopoly or some other game when Tabitha got back."

"We don't have to do everything our first night here." Mom smoothed the hair back from Cass' face then gave her a gentle nudge. "Go on before you fall asleep at the table and Steve has to carry you to your room."

"Now that would be the ultimate humiliation," Cass said lightly with a sassy look at Steve. She stood up. "Okay, you talked me into it. I'll see y'all in the morning."

Hesitating, Cass looked from Mom to Steve. She was accustomed to kissing her mother good-night, but she wasn't sure about including Steve yet. She decided to sidestep the issue with humor.

" 'Night, everybody." She flicked an airy wave at them both. "If I'm not up by ten"—she paused so that Steve and Mom would give her their full attention before assuming her sternest expression—"then don't bother me! If you know what's good for you, you'll leave me alone."

Cass exited the room on a gust of laughter from Mom and Steve. Sauntering down the hall to her room, she reviewed the evening and decided it hadn't gone badly at all.

The key is to keep Tabitha out of the picture, she realized. *It's actually kind of nice to have Mom and Steve to myself. Please, Lord, make Tabitha and Micah fall in love so she spends all her time with him. If I have to be here, at least that will make it more bearable. And I promise,* she added as she opened her bedroom door, *if You do work things out for Tab and Micah, I'll owe You big time. Thanks.*

CHAPTER 15

Another cloudless day. As she gradually came awake, Cass squeezed her eyes shut against the brilliant sunshine streaming into her room and groaned. *Doesn't it ever rain around here?* she wondered grumpily before remembering Steve had said they were in the middle of Kwajalein's dry season. Other than an occasional shower, they wouldn't see any significant rainfall for another three months. *What I wouldn't give for a good thunderstorm with torrential rain and the sky glowing with lightning and thunder that shakes the house.*

Cass sighed. "Fat chance of experiencing that any time soon," she whispered bitterly, forcing open her eyes.

She sat up, checked the clock, and sniffed the air. It was eight (*Four o'clock yesterday afternoon in the real world*, she reminded herself), and the mouth-watering aroma of bacon and eggs told her Mom was once again fixing breakfast for Steve before he left for work.

Although this was the third morning Cass had awakened to the smells and sounds of her mother cooking breakfast, she still wasn't used to it. Not that she minded. Back home, their mornings had been a whirlwind of showers, hair drying, and dressing for work and school with barely enough time for a bowl of cereal or a piece of toast. But while she liked the leisurely pace here, it was just another reminder of how different her life was now from what it once was.

There was a light knock on her door and then Steve peeked into the room. He smiled when he saw Cass was awake. "Good, you're up. Your Mom sent me to tell you breakfast is ready if you feel like joining us. Otherwise, you're on your own. Personally, I wouldn't pass up your Mom's eggs."

Just to be ornery, Cass thought about telling Steve she wasn't interested, but the rumbling in her stomach overruled her. "Okay, I'll be there in a minute."

Still shy around Steve, Cass waited until he shut the door before she kicked off the sheet and reached for the robe hanging on the bedpost. Hearing him wake up Tabitha almost made her turn and crawl back into bed. Her stepsister was enough to ruin even a starving person's appetite. Cass was tired of listening to Tabitha go on and on every morning about her plans for the day, who she'd be seeing, and where she'd be going.

Not that there are that many places to go, Cass thought with a frustrated look out the window. *Still, anywhere Tabitha and her friends go has to be better than sitting in the house day after day.*

By the time Cass made her way to the dining room, Mom, Steve, and Tabitha were already at the table. Mom greeted her with a smile as she took her usual seat. Cass' lips barely twitched in response. Just the sight of Tabitha, sitting in her chair like a queen on a throne, soured Cass' attitude.

"Just in time," Mom said, much too cheery for that early in the morning. "We were about to say the blessing."

Sighing inwardly, Cass reached a hand to the left to hold Steve's and a fingertip to the right for Tabitha.

"So what are everyone's plans for the day?" Mom passed the bacon, followed by the dish of scrambled eggs. She smiled at Tabitha. "You first, sweetie. Anything exciting?"

Cass ignored the superior look Tabitha sent her way in

response to Mom calling her "sweetie" and heaped her plate with more eggs than she could possibly eat in one setting. She decided to show their parents she could be the better person.

"My friends and I are going swimming, then having a picnic at Eamon Beach," Tabitha answered. "You probably don't remember from your tour the first day, but there's a pavilion with tables and grills." She turned to Steve. "Which reminds me, Dad, I'm in charge of bringing the hot dogs. Can I have some money to shop at Surfway? The trip back to the mainland bankrupted me."

Steve nodded. "By the way," he added in an offhand manner, "is this picnic something Cass could go on too? I'm sure she'd appreciate a change of scenery."

Cass, about to pick up her orange juice, froze and wished the floor would open up and swallow her. After the discussion at supper the other night, she was amazed Steve would broach the subject again. Out of the corner of her eye, Cass saw Tabitha stiffen.

"Dad, I don't think—" Tabitha began.

"I don't want to hear it," Steve interrupted. "I don't believe you're making the slightest effort to do what you and I talked about after you got home from Kira's the other night. You agreed to help make Cass feel welcome. One of the ways we discussed you could do that would be to introduce her to your friends. Do you recall our conversation?"

Tight-lipped, Tabitha nodded.

Steve seemed to disregard Tabitha's sullen expression. "Then why haven't you followed through?"

"Because—" Tabitha said at the same time Cass mumbled, "It's okay, Steve. Don't worry about it. I'm perfectly happy here with Mom."

While Cass was happy to see Tabitha so uncomfortable, she was also dying of embarrassment. It was downright humiliating to hear Steve all but order Tabitha to spend time with her. It was even worse learning they'd talked about her behind her back.

Steve hesitated, looking from Tabitha to Cass. "All right," he conceded. "I won't push it this time. But I'm giving you fair warning, young lady." He pointed to Tabitha who sullenly stared at her plate. "The next get-together you and your friends plan had better include Cass or you can forget about going. Do you hear me?"

"Loud and clear," Tabitha snapped.

"If you don't have any plans," Steve said to Cass, "how would you like to come down to the station and let me show you how it operates?" He was both the radio station's manager as well as one of its announcers. He worked the day shift and Ed Nishihara split the night shift with another man. "We're not a large operation so the grand tour takes about fifteen minutes. If you come around noon, I'll throw in lunch as part of the deal."

"I don't know," Cass replied slowly, thinking fast. Although she'd expressed interest in seeing the station the day she arrived, that had quickly faded. Feeling that it was somehow a betrayal of what she'd left behind, Cass didn't want to start having anything to do with any aspect of life on the island.

"I guess it'll be okay to visit," Cass finally responsed, not able to come up with an excuse not to. "What time should I be there?"

"I take my lunch hour between twelve and one so let's say you meet me at quarter to twelve. That way you can watch me work a little while before Ed takes over."

"I know this will sound stupid"—Cass glanced warily at Tabitha who was bound to make a snide remark—"but I'm not sure where the radio station is. I don't remember much from the tour. You'll have to give me directions."

Cass thought she saw Tabitha roll her eyes, but her stepsister said nothing.

"How about I take you there myself?" volunteered Mom. "I need to do some shopping at Macy's, then I want to visit the library."

Cass frowned. "Macy's is the teeny, tiny department store connected to the post office, right?"

Mom nodded, smiling. "Naming it after the New York store is an example of island humor. Anyway, let's plan on bicycling over together."

Cass nodded. She guessed there was no way to avoid getting out on the bike Mom and Steve had bought her two days ago. Except for the government-owned cars, there were three ways to get around the island: People walked, rode their bikes, or took taxis. The taxis were actually delivery vans with benches placed along both sides of the windowless cargo areas. Several people were usually crammed into a taxi at a time. Cass rode in one with Mom her first full day on Kwajalein and vowed she'd never do it again. That left walking and biking as her only means of transportation. Since she'd given up bike riding as too juvenile the day she got her driver's permit, Cass had resisted the idea until today. She was sure Mom wouldn't take no for an answer when it came to heading out to the radio station. Her mother had said several times that she truly enjoyed pedaling all over the island. She liked the exercise and the wind whipping her hair. Cass thought she was nuts.

After Steve left for work Tabitha lingered at the table talking with Mom, so Cass hurried down the hall to claim the bathroom. If Tabitha got there first, she tended to take an hour or so. When she reappeared a short while later, Tabitha was in her room with the stereo blasting and Mom was puttering around the kitchen.

"You sound so happy. You're always singing and stuff." Cass leaned her elbow on the counter and propped her chin on her hand. "Do you actually like it here that much?"

Mom glanced over her shoulder and grinned. "I don't

just like it here. I love it." Turning from the sink, she waved a soapy hand at the window above the counter where Cass leaned. "Just look at the view we have. Palm trees and the Pacific Ocean only fifty feet from our house. How could anyone not love it here?"

"Easy," Cass grumbled. "All a person has to have is a single, functioning brain cell in order to notice how hot, tiny, and boring the place is. The ocean's okay," she conceded, "but I'd rather see mountains and fields outside the window any day."

"I know you're homesick," Mom said gently, "but don't let that keep you from seeing the positive things Kwaj has to offer. There are more of them than you're willing to admit at the moment. Try to keep an open mind. Remember, God works good in every situation. As well as in every place," she added after a meaningful pause.

Cass was about to say something sarcastic when the doorbell rang. Panicking, she looked at Mom who was up to her elbows in soap bubbles and didn't show any signs of answering the door. The music blaring from Tabitha's room told Cass there was no way her stepsister had heard the bell. As she stood rooted to the spot, the bell chimed again.

"What are you waiting for? Aren't you going to answer that?" Mom asked over her shoulder.

Not seeing any way out of it, Cass swallowed hard. "I guess so."

Up until now, she'd gone to her room whenever Tabitha's friends came around and had hidden there until they left. Now she was about to meet them, whether she wanted to or not. Opening the door, Cass took a deep breath and reminded herself to smile.

There was a slight hesitation before the girl on the front step said, sounding surprised, "Well, hi there. You're Cass, aren't you? I was starting to think you'd taken one look at Kwaj and hightailed it back to the mainland. Nobody's seen you since that first day at the airport." Her brown eyes crinkled at the corners when she grinned. Her teeth were startlingly white against her brown skin. "I'm Kira Alexander, by the way. It's nice to finally meet you."

"It's nice to meet you too," Cass echoed, overwhelmed by the girl's friendliness. She'd expected Tabitha's best friend to be as snobby as she was.

"The tall guy's my brother, Micah," Kira continued, gesturing over her shoulder at the two boys behind her. "The other one is Logan Russell. He's new to Kwaj, too, so you guys have something in common. You can compare notes on how well you're adjusting."

Cass nodded at the boys while carefully avoiding their eyes. Although she hated admitting to herself that it mattered, she suddenly wished she was wearing something other than her jean shorts and oversized T-shirt.

"Uh ... is Tabitha here?" Kira asked after several seconds of awkward silence. "We're supposed to go on a picnic and she told us to come by to get her at around nine-thirty."

"Yes, of course. I'm sorry." Cass stepped aside and opened the door to allow Tabitha's friends entrance. "Come on in. I'll tell her you're here."

Drying her hands on a towel, Mom came around the corner from the kitchen as the trio stepped into the living room.

"Hey, y'all," she greeted them. "You're becoming as familiar a sight around here as Cass' friends were back in Tennessee."

Way to make me feel even worse, Mom, Cass drawled silently. Aloud, she muttered, "I'll get Tabitha."

"No, let me." Kira laid a brown hand on Cass' arm to detain her. "I want to bug her about not being ready. As usual," she added with a laugh. "I love Tabitha dearly, but she has no concept of time."

Kira disappeared down the hall, leaving Cass to stare

after her and wonder what she should do now. She couldn't very well stand there and make small talk with two boys she'd just met. Fortunately, Mom came to her rescue.

"Why don't you boys sit down?" she suggested. "There's no telling how long Tabitha will be. She and I chatted a while after breakfast and she just took off for her room a few minutes ago. I don't think she's even showered yet."

"Oh, great." Shaking his head, Micah rolled brown eyes that were identical to his sister's.

Studying him from under lowered lashes, Cass decided he was one of the most spectacular looking guys she'd ever seen. She wondered about the exact nature of the relationship between Tabitha and Kira's brother.

Micah grinned at Mom. "It looks like we might be having our picnic in the middle of your living room, Mrs. Spencer."

"It sounds like you know Tabitha pretty well." The remark popped out before Cass even realized it was on the tip of her tongue.

Micah turned his heart-stopping smile in Cass' direction and she almost melted under the intensity of it. "Tabitha has a lot of great qualities, but punctuality definitely isn't one of them. That's one of the reasons life on Kwaj suits her. We tend to be pretty laid-back about schedules around here. Tabitha takes it to the extreme, though. As the saying goes, she'll be late to her own funeral."

"Yeah, but she'll look terrific," Cass said. "All the other corpses will be green with envy."

Laughing, Micah and Logan followed Mom into the living room. They each claimed a corner of the Hawaiian print couch while Cass perched on the edge of the rocking chair. She had a couple of attractive guys all to herself and she had no idea what to do with them.

"You don't need an old, married lady hovering over you," Mom said lightly to the group, diminishing Cass' hopes that she'd help with the conversation. "I'll leave you three to get acquainted." Mom started down the hall leading to the bedrooms. "I still have laundry to do and a bed to make."

Cass looked longingly after Mom's retreating back, but managed to stay seated. Her stomach churning, she wracked her brain for something to say. At home her friends could never get her to shut up, so why was it so difficult for her to come up with something to talk about now?

Finally she asked, "So ... uh ... Logan, how long have you been here?"

Okay, so it's lame, she silently acknowledged, *but at least it's better than nothing*.

Logan's green eyes turned toward Cass and he smiled shyly. "It'll be four months tomorrow. We got here the third week in March."

So far, so good, Cass congratulated herself.

Aloud, she continued, "Kira was right. You are a newcomer. Where did you come from?"

"Harrisburg, Pennsylvania."

Excited because it wasn't that far from her hometown, Cass leaned forward in the chair. "Really? Harrisburg? My mother has an aunt who lives there and we visited a couple of times. It's a nice place. I'll bet you miss it."

Logan's face tightened. "Nope, not at all. I haven't been homesick once since we left Pennsylvania. I like Kwaj a lot better."

"Yeah, right," Cass drawled, thinking he was kidding. She waited for Logan to laugh. When he didn't, she realized he wasn't joking and frowned. "But ... how can you not miss Pennsylvania? I mean, it's so different here. Why do you like it more than where you came from?"

"I don't know. I just do."

Cass was confused. "But it doesn't make any sense," she persisted. "How can—"

"Hey, Cass, I have an idea," Micah broke in. "Why don't you come on our picnic with us?"

Cass turned to Micah in surprise. "Me? You want me to go on your picnic?"

Micah leaned back against the sofa cushion and grinned, obviously enjoying Cass' surprise. "You're the only Cass in the room, aren't you?"

"Yes, but ... I ... well ..."

"I think it's a wonderful idea," Mom called from the bathroom. "Tell him yes, Cass."

"But what about Steve? He's expecting me and I wouldn't feel right standing him up," Cass protested. She turned to Micah and Logan. "I'm supposed to meet my stepfather at the radio station for lunch."

"Don't worry about Steve. He'll understand." Mom carried a basket of clothes into the living room. "I'll call him and tell him there's been a change of plans. He'll be delighted you're spending time with people your own age."

"Then what about"—Cass glanced over her shoulder and lowered her voice, although her stepsister was nowhere to be seen—"Tabitha? I don't think she'd be too happy about me coming along."

"I'll talk to her," Micah said. "I'm not one to brag, but she's usually pretty good about listening to me." He flashed his smile again. "I'll turn on the charm and she won't be able to resist me."

Cass laughed. "Well," she hedged, surprised at how much she suddenly wanted to go with Tabitha and her friends, "if you think it would be all right. I don't want to make her mad."

"It'll be fine," Micah assured her. He stood up and headed toward Tabitha's room. "Why don't you get your stuff ready while I let Tabitha and Kira know what's going on?" As he passed Cass, he squeezed her shoulder. "Go ahead. I promise I won't take no for an answer. You'd be amazed at how persuasive I can be."

A short while later, Cass found herself heading off on her bike with Tabitha and the others. Although it was clear from Tabitha's sullen expression and frequent sighs that she was unhappy about Cass' presence, her friends readily accepted it. They included Cass in their conversation and Logan positioned his bike next to hers as they pedaled away from the house. They stopped first at Surfway, the island's one grocery store.

"This is it?" Cass asked as she came through the door. "It's so tiny. How can it stock enough to feed everyone? I'll bet this place is one-tenth the size of the supermarkets back home."

Although Tabitha had been marching along at the front of the group, she spun around at Cass's words. "Cereal, milk, juice, bread, meat, fruits, vegetables. It may be small compared to what you're used to," she snapped, "but it has everything we need. So quit complaining. Nobody cares what your life was like back in Tennessee. All that matters is what's here and now."

"I wasn't complaining," Cass said, attempting to defend herself, but Tabitha had already stalked off in search of hot dogs. Frustrated, Cass stared at her retreating back. She could never do or say anything right as far as her stepsister was concerned.

"Don't worry about it," Kira said, coming to Cass' side. "Tabitha gets a little touchy about Kwaj sometimes. She thinks it's the greatest place in the world so she doesn't like anyone criticizing it."

"I wasn't," Cass protested. "All I did was make a simple comment about the store. It wasn't a criticism."

Kira shrugged. "You know that and I know that. But Tabitha"—she nodded toward her friend who was busy deciding what franks to buy—"thinks you were insulting her beloved Kwaj and that's one thing she absolutely won't stand for."

"So what am I supposed to do?" demanded Cass. She glared at her stepsister. "Keep my mouth shut because anything I say might upset Tabitha?"

Kira laughed. "Now you're getting the idea. Maybe that way you and Tabitha won't wind up killing each other after all."

A reluctant smile tugged at Cass' lips. "You don't know me very well if you think I can keep from putting my two cents in indefinitely. My mouth is just too big."

Kira laughed again, but since Tabitha was making her way towards them, didn't say anything else.

When the group rode into the Eamon Beach pavilion about ten minutes later, Cass was stunned by the breathtaking beauty of the place. She'd paid scant attention to the view when Ed had stopped here as part of the tour the first day, so the lagoon was a very pleasant surprise. Blinding white sand bordered the turquoise Pacific which stretched as far as Cass could see. The sunlight sparkling on the water dazzled her eyes despite her sunglasses, and she had to squint as she continued to gaze at the ocean.

"It's something, isn't it?" Logan murmured, stopping his bike alongside Cass'. "I've been coming here nearly every day for the past four months and I'm still not tired of the view. I've never seen such clear, calm water. Or so much of it," he added with a laugh.

"I thought the beaches in Hawaii were beautiful," Cass breathed, "but this ... this is incredible."

"Yup," agreed Logan. "Maybe now you'll start to see why I don't miss Pennsylvania. What does the mainland have that can compare with this?"

Before Cass could respond, Logan moved on to join the others who were unloading the contents of their bicycle baskets onto a picnic table in the pavilion. Cass took another look at the ocean. *Sure, it's nice, but it's going to take a lot more than pretty scenery to make me stop wishing I were back in Tennessee.*

As the five began talking and laughing, Cass began to enjoy herself. Tabitha was still cool towards her, but the friendliness of the others made her realize just how lonely she had been in the last few days.

They sat down to eat the hot dogs Micah grilled. Without thinking, Cass bowed her head to say a quick, silent prayer. When she looked up, three pairs of eyes stared curiously at her. Tabitha had already bitten into her hot dog and was gazing at the lagoon as she chewed. Cass' cheeks burned with embarrassment.

"Were you praying?" Kira broke the awkward silence. "It's okay if you were," she added hastily, "I was just wondering."

Belatedly wishing she'd skipped her normal routine, Cass reluctantly nodded. "I always do before I eat." Deciding she couldn't make it any worse for herself, she went on, "Most of my friends back home do too. A bunch of us went to a Christian grade school together and I guess I got into the habit. I didn't think about it bothering anybody."

"Kira didn't say it bothered us," Tabitha said quickly. "Maybe we're not as holy as your friends back in Tennessee but it doesn't bother us to see someone praying."

Before Cass could respond, Micah jumped in. "I don't know about you guys, but I'm starved so I'm going to eat." With that, half his hot dog disappeared in a single gulp.

Cass bit her lip. She really wanted to respond to Tabitha, but she figured now probably wasn't the best time. *Should I not have prayed? I don't want to get myself in this situation again, but—* she broke off the thought. She'd worry about it later.

After eating the group disappeared into separate dressing rooms to change into their swimsuits before heading for the water. When they all met again on the beach, Cass found herself comparing her freckled skin to the others' tans. She caught Logan's sympathetic glance and they exchanged rueful smiles.

"It looks like you're the burn and peel type too." He held out the tube of sunblock he was rubbing into his skin. "I don't know what kind you brought with you, but this stuff works pretty well. I haven't wound up looking like a boiled lobster yet."

Cass gratefully accepted the lotion and squeezed a generous amount into her palm. "Don't you hate being a redhead sometimes?" she complained good-naturedly. "Do you think we'll ever get as brown as they are?" She gestured toward the three friends splashing in the waist-deep water.

"I doubt it." Logan heaved a dramatic sigh. "Kira and Micah are half Jamaican, so they're miles ahead of us, and Tabitha—" he shook his head. "In this crowd, we're doomed to always stick out like a couple of sore thumbs. I think the best we can hope for is getting enough freckles so they eventually blend and look like a tan."

Cass laughed. "Sounds like a plan to me." She held out her arm for Logan's inspection. "But what I wouldn't give for a nice, even tan."

"Who would I have to gripe with then?" Logan draped a friendly arm across Cass' shoulders. "Hasn't anybody ever told you we redheads have to stick together?"

Cass was enjoying Logan's arm around her so much that she didn't notice Tabitha, Kira, and Micah sneaking up behind them. She yelped with surprise when Kira and Micah grabbed her hands and began dragging her into the water. Although she dug in her heels and yelled, it was all for show. In truth, Cass didn't mind getting wet. The water was even clearer and warmer than it had been in Hawaii. Besides, Micah had explained that the rock jetty which formed the breakwater for the lagoon also kept the sharks away. Cass had almost no qualms left about swimming.

Breaking away from the Alexanders, Cass dove under the

water and swam a couple of yards. When she resurfaced, Logan, Micah, and Kira applauded her style and Cass took several bows. She decided to ignore the look Tabitha gave her.

The group spent over an hour in the water, staging water fights and races, before heading back to the pavilion to snack on chips and sodas. That became the pattern for the rest of the afternoon. They'd swim until they were exhausted, then go back to the picnic table to take a food break. Cass couldn't believe it when Micah pulled a watch out of his shorts pocket and announced it was four-thirty.

"No way!" she exclaimed. "You mean we've been here six hours? That's impossible."

"Time flies when you're having fun." Kira rummaged through the picnic basket until she located the chocolate chip cookies Mom had sent along. Choosing one, she bit into it and grinned. "And this has definitely been fun. There's nothing I like better than doing nothing." She popped the rest of the cookie into her mouth. "Except eating, that is."

"Don't you think we ought to be getting home?" Cass turned to ask Tabitha. "Mom might be worried. We didn't say how late we would be."

Tabitha waved airily. "She knows there's nothing to worry about. I mean, we're on an island in the middle of the ocean. But I guess we should still go. I need to shower and stuff before supper."

The others decided to leave too. As everyone pitched in to clean up, they made plans for their next outing. It didn't take Cass long to realize she was automatically being included in the plans and she wasn't sure how she felt about it.

"We could come back tomorrow and I could bring my snorkeling gear," Logan suggested to Cass. "You mentioned that you've never been snorkeling. It's a great way to explore the lagoon and I'm a pretty good instructor, if I do say so myself."

"I don't know," Cass hedged and concentrated on loading picnic gear into the basket hanging from the handlebars of her bike.

As much as she'd enjoyed the day, she was suddenly anxious to return to the house. She hadn't given Janette and the rest of her friends a single thought all afternoon. It was the first time since leaving Tennessee that she'd forgotten them for more than a couple of minutes and she felt disloyal, like she needed to get home and write everybody long, newsy letters.

"Uh … can I get back to you about the snorkeling?" Cass asked Logan.

Logan shrugged agreeably. "Sure thing. I'm not going anywhere. Just let me know when you're ready to give it a try." He laughed. "My calendar's not exactly booked solid so I'll be on your doorstep the minute you call."

Cass smiled, but inside she was confused. *Do I really want to be part of Tabitha's crowd?* She asked herself. *Maybe I'll just spend the next two years by myself.*

Cass was silent on the ride home. Kira and Tabitha rode side by side, talking and laughing, and Cass burned with jealousy. She wished Janette were here or, even better, that she were back home with Janette. She'd admit the afternoon had been pleasant, but it was so diffeent from the way she and her friends spent their vacation time. There was no mall to while away the hours in, no miniature golf to play, no afternoon movies to attend.

I want to go home, Cass thought, tears stinging her eyes. She was thankful for the sunglasses that hid them from the others. *It doesn't matter how much fun I have here. It will never be as good as home.*

Steve arrived at the house at the same time the girls did and the trio walked in together. Mom turned from the stove where she was stirring something in a pot and smiled.

"Oh, good, my happy wanderers have returned." She lifted her face for Steve's kiss. "Did everyone have a nice day?"

"Except for missing you, I did." Steve peered over Mom's shoulder into the pot. "What's that?"

"I'm making chocolate pudding to have later tonight." She playfully slapped Steve's hand as he tried to take the spoon from her. "No tasting. Be a good boy and wait nicely." Mom glanced at the girls. "How about you two? Did you have fun at the lagoon?"

"I had a blast," Tabitha said. "After being gone so long, I'll never take my friends for granted again. Every time we're together, I realize how much I missed them." Her sidelong smirk told Cass Tabitha had intended her words to hurt, but she pretended concern as she continued, "Everybody was so nice to Cass. I was really proud of them for the way they just accepted her. I know how hard it's been for her to leave her friends behind and I was glad we could help her over her blues a little bit."

Why you lying little — Cass wanted to shout, particularly when she saw how Mom beamed her approval at Tabitha.

Aloud, she said testily, "You're making it sound like your friends let me tag along because they felt sorry for me. Might I remind you it was Micah's idea for me to spend the day with y'all?"

Tabitha glared at her. "Probably because you sat there in front of him with that pathetic 'somebody please pay attention to me' look you get," she sneered. "What choice did he have but to invite you along?"

"Girls, stop fighting," Steve ordered irritably. "I'm not in the mood to listen to you two taking potshots at each other." He withdrew the Kwaj newspaper from under his arm and unfolded it with a snap. "I'd like to read the paper in peace if you don't mind."

Unused to being scolded by a male voice, Cass started to turn away.

Tabitha, on the other hand, stood her ground. "But, Dad, she started it. All I said was—"

Steve fixed her with a steely look. "If you're trying to be placed under house arrest, just keep it up," he warned.

Tabitha turned with a flounce and Cass took off running. With a few seconds head start, she figured she could get into the bathroom before Tabitha did.

CHAPTER 16

After dinner Mom and Steve went next door to visit with the Simpsons while Cass and Tabitha cleaned up. Cass was content to not talk, but she knew Tabitha was uncomfortable with lengthy silences. It didn't surprise her when Tabitha began a conversation.

"I'm sorry about what I said earlier to Dad," she said, so softly Cass wasn't sure she actually said it. "I mean, about you practically begging Micah to come with us today."

Cass wasn't sure where this was leading. "Don't worry about it."

"It's just that I'm not used to the idea of sharing my friends," Tabitha added, as if Cass hadn't spoken.

Cass shrugged. "I guess I'd probably be the same way if we were in Tennessee," she admitted grudgingly. She hesitated. "Do you realize we're actually having a civil conversation? Quick. Run next door and get our parents. They'll never believe it."

"Dad would believe it of you." Tabitha's good mood abruptly soured, making Cass sorry she'd said anything. "He thinks I'm the problem."

"Aw, he's just being nice because I'm the new kid," Cass said lightly.

Tabitha shook her head. "No, it's more than that. He really likes you. Sometimes I think he likes you better than me," she added softly.

"Don't be ridiculous." Having run out of dishes to dry, Cass started putting away the ones stacked on the counter. "You're his daughter—real daughter, I mean. I doubt he'd ever love me as much as he loves you."

Tabitha brightened a bit. "Maybe you're right. He probably is just being nice to you."

Way to make me feel wanted, Cass wanted to retort, but held her tongue.

Aloud, she replied, "Exactly. He wants to make sure he stays on Mom's good side. What better way to do it than to be nice to me?"

Tabitha laughed. "They really are crazy about each other. I wasn't too sure about the marriage at first," she confided. "But Dad's so happy, I'm glad they found each other. I thought it would be kind of annoying being around newlyweds, but it's actually pretty sweet. It makes me look forward to getting married someday."

Cass shot her a quizzical look. "Really? I can't imagine myself as somebody's wife. Probably because I don't have any memory of my parents' marriage. I was so young when my father died."

"Unfortunately, I remember some stuff from when my parents were together." There was a tightness to Tabitha's voice and in the set of her mouth. "If that's all I had to go on when it came to what being married is like, I'd probably decide to die an old maid. Being around Mom and Dad has given me hope."

Cass was dying to know what Tabitha meant, but she wasn't sure how to ask her about her father's first marriage without appearing nosy. "I had a couple of friends back home whose parents got divorced," she remarked casually. "For one of them, things went pretty smoothly and her folks are still on speaking terms. For the other one, though, it got really ugly. Even though it happened two years ago, she still didn't like to talk about it."

"I know how she feels," muttered Tabitha. Lowering a pan into the soapy water, she began vigorously scrubbing. "Sometimes it's better to leave things alone. A few years ago, Dad wanted me to talk with a counselor because he thought the divorce was still bothering me. I told him I was fine and I wasn't interested in dredging up ancient history. He took me to the counselor anyway, but I got the last laugh. I sat there for an hour without saying a single word. Dad never took me back. I can be stubborn when I want to," she finished smugly.

They worked in silence for a few minutes then Tabitha asked, "Did you ever miss having a father?"

Cass shrugged. "It's tough to miss something you never had. I'd get jealous sometimes when my friends talked about stuff they'd done with their fathers, but other than that, I've never really thought about it much. Besides, my grandfather and my uncle lived in town so whenever I needed a substitute dad, they were always happy to fill in." She hesitated then took the plunge. "Do you miss your mother?"

"No," Tabitha replied tersely. "Mom's already been more of a mother to me in two weeks than my birth mother ever was."

Cass was taken aback by the coldness in Tabitha's voice. She felt a spurt of sympathy for her stepsister, but had no idea how to express it. Tabitha must have sensed something, though, because she turned to glare at Cass.

"And don't you go feeling sorry for me," she ordered through clenched teeth. "I was happy when it was just Dad and me, and I'm even happier now that I have Mom. I don't want your pity. Or anybody else's, for that matter."

"Okay, okay." Cass raised her hands and backed up a

step. "Wow—I just asked a simple question. Don't jump down my throat."

Tabitha gave an embarrassed laugh. "Sorry. I've gotten enough 'poor motherless girl' comments to last me a lifetime. I used to want to take out a full-page ad in the paper to tell everyone I was fine and that I didn't need a mother. Having Dad was good enough for me."

"That's the way I felt about Mom," Cass said, surprised that they had something in common. "I guess that explains why they fell in love. They're a couple of special people."

"Amen to that," agreed Tabitha.

Once the dishes were done, Cass wandered into the living room while Tabitha headed to the phone. Plopping down on the sofa, Cass picked up the remote control and clicked on the TV. She'd discovered that television viewing was an adventure on Kwajalein. A station on the neighboring island of Ebeye broadcast eight hours of programming a day, beginning at three o'clock. The first four hours were shows someone had taped in Honolulu and sent down, and the second four hours were re-runs of what had been shown from three until seven. Cass never knew what she would find when she turned on the TV. Sometimes it was a soap opera, other times a children's program, still other times a sitcom. She didn't know who taped the shows up in Hawaii but whoever the person was, he had strange tastes.

Squinting, Cass recognized the program as a medical drama she used to enjoy back home. She settled in to watch, even though she'd already seen the episode. It was better than nothing and besides, it was obvious that whatever truce she and Tabitha had reached was over. She could hear her stepsister on the phone, complaining about her father always taking Cass' side.

Mom and Steve returned from next door midway through the show. By that time, Tabitha was closeted in her room, listening to her stereo at an earsplitting decibel.

"Did you two have another fight?" Steve sounded more resigned than concerned.

Without looking away from the screen, Cass shook her head. "Believe it or not, no. We actually managed to have a conversation while we did the dishes. Then she went her way and I went mine."

Mom smiled at Steve. "Will wonders never cease?"

"Don't get too excited," Cass advised, muting the television as a commercial came on. "It's not like we're suddenly getting along."

"But it's a step." Mom gestured around the room. "We left you two alone for a whole hour and, look, no blood. Nothing's broken. I consider that a miracle."

Cass rolled her eyes at her. "I know you think you're funny, but you're not. Quit making such a big deal out of it."

Steve draped an arm across Mom's shoulders as she pretended to pout. "Don't worry, dear, I think you're funny. You can't see it, but inside I'm laughing hysterically."

Mom fluttered her lashes at him. "Oh, thank you, darling. You always know exactly what to say to cheer me up."

"All right, enough." Cass shifted on the sofa so her back was to the adults and turned the volume back up on the TV, even though the commercial wasn't over. "I'm going to throw up if you two don't stop it."

"We have quite an effect on people, don't we, pumpkin?" Steve said cheerfully.

Mom exchanged a broad grin with him. "Yes, we do, honeybun. I'm so proud."

From the couch, Cass emitted a loud groan and covered her head with a pillow.

Tabitha came down the hall as the program resumed. "Kira invited me to spend the night at her house," she announced. "That's okay, isn't it?"

Mom shrugged. "I suppose so. What are your plans for tomorrow?"

Tabitha frowned. "I don't know. Why?"

"You know why." Steve nodded in Cass' direction.

Cass slid down on the couch. She didn't want any part of this confrontation.

"Aw, come on, Dad, don't start that again," whined Tabitha. "I was a good girl today. I did what you wanted. Don't I deserve a reward?"

"Not when you take that attitude with me." Steve's voice was low, but menacing.

"You're not going to make me take her with me, are you?"

Even though Tabitha had whispered the question, Cass still heard it, and that was the final straw. Faking a huge yawn, she turned off the television and stood up. Avoiding the others' eyes, she muttered, "You know, I just realized I'm pooped. I guess the swimming really took it out of me. I'm going to bed."

Before anyone could say a word, she escaped to her room.

"Are you happy now?" she heard Steve as she went down the hallway.

There was a pause before Tabitha answered. "Look, can I go to Kira's or not?"

"If it's all right with your dad, it's all right with me," Mom said, much too nicely as far as Cass was concerned. She resisted the impulse to slam the door at Mom's words and shut it quietly instead.

Even after her stepsister was gone, Cass couldn't bring herself to rejoin their parents. She'd never felt so lonely in her life. Mom and Steve had each other. Tabitha had Kira. Who did she have?

Some useless pictures of friends who are eight thousand miles away, that's what, she answered herself. *For all the good that does me.*

Flopping on her bed, Cass dug those pictures out of her nightstand and began to cry. *Well, if I can't talk to them, at least I can write to them,* she thought. She knew Janette would like reading about how horrible Tabitha was.

The odd thing was, Cass discovered she wasn't entirely comfortable scribbling sentence after sentence complaining about Tabitha. She kept remembering their conversation as they did the dishes. It had been almost—well—*nice,* having a sort-of sister to talk to.

Cass shut her eyes tightly, feeling the tears about to start again. "Oh, Lord," she prayed, half out-loud, half inside, "I know I'm part of the problem with Tabitha. I really don't want to be enemies with her. Help me to see her good qualities and to quit focusing on the negatives. If I truly believe You're in control of everything, then I'm going to have to accept the fact that You put us together for a reason." She paused. "I'd really appreciate some advice. I know I can't do this on my own."

Cass kept her eyes closed for another few minutes, half hoping for a response. When none came, she got up and took her time getting ready for bed, then made a brief appearance in the living room to say good-night to Mom and Steve. She'd just turned off the light and climbed into bed when a thought came to her.

Cass turned the light back on and pulled her Bible from the bookshelf next to her bed. She thumbed through the pages until she found the passage she'd highlighted during a youth group meeting.

"Here it is," she whispered. "Romans 12:18. 'If it is possible, as far as it depends on you, live at peace with everyone.' " Cass leaned back against the wall and sighed. "I guess it doesn't get much clearer than that." She raised her eyes heavenward. "Okay, but You'd better give Tabitha the same message or this isn't going to work."

CHAPTER 17

"Do you consider Tabitha a real Christian?"

Sitting side-by-side on a boulder behind the house, Cass and Mom watched the tide come in. For some strange reason, Cass found pleasure in observing the clocklike regularity of the tides, especially the incoming surge of high tide. At the moment, the water barely tickled her and Mom's dangling feet. Once the tide was in, however, the water would cover their legs and they'd be drenched with spray from the waves slamming against the rocks.

Tabitha had left a short while ago to meet her friends at the swimming pool. Although she'd been invited to join them, Cass had begged off. She wanted to talk with Mom.

"How do you define a 'real' Christian?" Mom asked with a frown.

Wrinkling her nose, Cass stared at the horizon where the tall blossoming clouds resembled distant mountains. "I know Tabitha goes to church, but she doesn't act like my friends back home. Remember me telling you how surprised she was the other day at the picnic when I prayed before I ate?" she reminded her mother. "Not that she was the only one. They all were. Anyway, it's like Tabitha's a Christian only when she's around us. When she's with her friends, it's almost like she's a different person. I don't have any idea if her friends go to church or anything. I'm not sure how I'm supposed to act around them."

"First of all, the most important thing is to live out your faith, no matter whom you're with," Mom said. She gave a rueful laugh. "I'm not saying that's always easy. Sometimes it can be downright uncomfortable, the perfect example being when you're the only one in a group who's praying."

"Tell me about it," Cass muttered. "I wanted to crawl under the table."

Mom laughed. "I know. I've been in that position a few times myself. I'm sure Tabitha and her friends weren't being unkind, though. They were probably more curious than anything else, particularly if they're not accustomed to seeing someone their age pray in public like that."

"But that's my point about Tabitha," Cass persisted. "How come she doesn't pray unless she's with us? Isn't she being a hypocrite?"

"Well, none of us knows what's in another person's heart," Mom said carefully. "Only God knows, so He's the only one entitled to pass judgment. Plus, it might help if you kept a couple of things in mind. Tabitha wasn't brought up in the church. She and Steve became Christians just three years ago. She didn't have the advantages you did of going to a Christian school and belonging to a church youth group, so the things you're used to doing don't come as naturally to her."

Cass stared open-mouthed at her mother. "Are you telling me there aren't any youth groups on Kwaj?"

"I'm afraid not. Steve said there were a couple when he first moved here. After the former pastor left about four years ago, they died out, probably from lack of interest. Apparently the current pastor hasn't done anything to start them up again."

Cass sighed. "The one thing I was looking forward to

was joining the youth group," she said. "I figured it might make it seem a little bit like home. Now what am I supposed to do? Just go to church and that's it? How do I get to know anyone?"

"You can still meet people at church without going to a youth group," Mom said.

"Yeah, but it's not the same and you know it."

Over the pounding of the surf, Cass heard the shrieks of laughter coming from the pool located about twenty yards from the house. A concrete wall enclosed the side of the pool facing the house, but every now and then Cass caught a glimpse of someone flying through the air off the diving board. A couple of times she was sure she spied Logan's coppery hair glinting in the sunlight as he executed a soaring cannonball, and she couldn't help but wonder if he missed her company. Part of her wished she'd accepted Tabitha's invitation to swim instead of staying behind for this depressing conversation with Mom.

"I guess the fact that there isn't a youth group is another strike against Kwaj, huh?" Mom said softly.

Cass shifted her attention away from the pool to make a face at her mother. "Kwaj has so many strikes against it, one more hardly makes a difference."

"You know, there's always the chance the pastor will decide to start up a program for the youth." Mom's voice held that overly cheerful tone she used whenever she was working at being optimistic.

"After four years of doing nothing?" said Cass. "Yeah, right."

Mom seemed to ignore her sarcasm. "Maybe you could talk to him about it when we go to church Sunday."

"Oh, sure. I can picture it now," Cass drawled. Pretending to shake hands with someone, she tilted her head to one side and chirped, "Hi there, Pastor So-and-So. I'm Cass Devane. I just moved here from Tennessee and I'd

136

really appreciate it if you'd get the youth group going again. You will? Great. Thanks a lot." She dropped the pose and turned to Mom with a short derisive laugh. "Do you honestly think it'd happen like that?"

"No," admitted Mom. "But then that's not quite how I imagined the encounter. I thought perhaps the two of us could make an appointment to sit down with the pastor and talk about what it would take to get the ball rolling on a youth group. I wouldn't be surprised if Steve wanted to join us."

"I'm not the tiniest bit interested in being in on starting up a group." Sighing, Cass folded her arms and gazed at the water foaming and swirling around her feet. "I wish we never left Jonesborough."

"Cassandra—" Mom began.

A shout interrupted her. "Hey, Mrs. Spencer!"

Cass and Mom turned to look over their shoulders. Kira stood on the flagstone path that led from the front of the house to the lanai. She waved when she saw she'd gotten their attention.

"Tabitha sent me to ask you if I could bring some lemonade back to the pool," Kira yelled. "We're dying of thirst over there. Is it okay if I go inside and get it myself?"

"I'll be happy to get it for you," Mom called back. She stood up and headed for the house. "Besides, I might even throw in a treat or two if I'm feeling generous."

With a last look at the water now covering her ankles, Cass got to her feet and followed Mom across the yard.

"Hi, Cass," Kira said cheerfully as Cass came closer to where she stood.

"Hey."

Cass ducked her head, still unsure around Tabitha's friends. Mom disappeared into the house and Cass hesitated, wanting to join her but not wanting to appear rude to Kira.

"Why didn't you come swimming with us? The pool's a fun change from the lagoon. It has a diving board for you to show off all your fanciest moves."

"I wanted to talk with my mom about some things and this seemed like a good time, with everyone else in the house gone." Cass tried to sound nonchalant.

"Are you two finished talking?"

"I guess so." Cass looked at her curiously. "Why?"

Kira winked and flashed a huge smile. "Because Logan's been asking about you. He was very disappointed when Tabitha showed up at the pool alone. I think it would make his day if you decided to put in an appearance."

Cass eyed Kira with suspicion. "Is this some kind of joke?" she asked warily, "because, if it is, I don't appreciate it."

"Believe me, I never joke about matters of the heart," Kira assured her. "You can ask anyone. They'll tell you I'm a born matchmaker and I take the job very seriously. I love putting people together. I've been trying for a year to get my brother and Tabitha together, but I've put them on hold for the time being. You and Logan are my new project."

Although Cass laughed, she remained skeptical. "How do you know either of us is even interested in getting together?"

"Well, I don't really," Kira admitted, not sounding the least bit concerned. "If something doesn't work out, I usually keep trying different combinations until I hit on the right one. Except for Micah and Tabitha," she added with a laugh. "They're going to wind up as a couple if it's the last thing I do. But back to you and Logan. What do you say?" she coaxed. "Won't you change your mind and come swimming with us?"

"Oh, okay," Cass agreed with feigned reluctance, knowing full well she wasn't fooling Kira. "But I'm only going because I'm hot and bored and I'm done talking to my mother. Logan Russell has nothing to do with my decision."

"Yeah, whatever," Kira murmured as Cass turned to hurry into the house. She smiled innocently when Cass looked back to glare at her.

Five minutes later Cass pushed open the squeaky gate leading to the pool. Along with her towel, Cass carried a tote bag containing cups, napkins, and some brownies her mother had made. Behind her, Kira swung a jug of lemonade by its handle. Micah cheered when he caught sight of them.

"All right! Food!"

Micah swam to the side of the pool and hauled himself out of the water. Logan followed suit while Tabitha used the ladder. Good-naturedly jostling each other, the trio clustered around the table to which Kira had directed Cass.

After her conversation with Kira, Cass found it difficult to look Logan in the eyes. She couldn't help wondering if Kira had exaggerated Logan's interest in her, then lied by telling herself she didn't care.

Trying to look busy, Cass unpacked the cups and brownies onto the table and slipped off the T-shirt that covered her blue and green striped swimsuit.

"Boy, am I glad you changed your mind and decided to join us," Micah told Cass as he waited for his turn at the lemonade jug. He crammed a brownie into his mouth and picked up another one. "And not just because you brought food."

Cass laughed. "Well, you can thank Kira for my being here. She talked me into coming. Or maybe I should say she bullied me into it."

Micah grinned. "That's my sister." He rumpled Kira's curls, easily fending off her attempts to bat his hand away. "She could talk Eskimos into buying freezers if she set her mind to it. I just hope she's like Superman and continues to use her powers for good and not evil."

Everyone laughed except Tabitha, who stood off to one side, glaring at Cass over her cup of lemonade.

Cass quickly got over her initial akwardness with Logan. He was the same easygoing boy he'd been on the picnic and Cass soon found herself joking and laughing with him. If he was attracted to her, he hid it well. Cass couldn't decide if she was relieved or disappointed.

After everyone had eaten their fill·of brownies, Cass followed the others into the pool. Gasping, she discovered that the water was frigid compared to the lagoon. Logan explained it was chlorinated ocean water which, for some reason, rarely warmed up above the seventy-degree mark. But once she quit shivering, she had a good time. Following one exceptionally splashy dive, she was declared the cannonball queen by the others and treated to a thorough dunking to celebrate the honor.

They stayed well into the afternoon. Other friends of Tabitha arrived and the crowd swelled to a dozen. Cass volunteered to run home and raid the kitchen, and Logan immediately offered to go with her. Ignoring Kira's knowing smirk, Cass accepted his offer. They donned T-shirts and slipped on their sandals for the trip next door.

"You seem like you've settled in pretty well," Logan remarked as they crossed the gravel-covered area separating the Spencer house from the pool.

Cass shot him a wry sidelong glance. "Really? I must be a better actress than I thought."

"You still don't like it here?"

"Give me a break," Cass drawled. "It's only been six days. I've barely had time to get over jet lag and you expect me to be completely adjusted already."

Logan gave her a sheepish smile. "You're right. The least I can do is give you a week." He paused and laughed. "Remind me to ask you tomorrow how things are going."

Laughing, Cass and Logan let themselves into the

house. Curled into a corner of the couch, Mom looked up from the book she was reading. Country music played softly in the background and the aroma of simmering pot roast wafted through the air. Cass realized she'd never seen her mother look so peaceful and content.

"Don't tell me you've finished off all the brownies and lemonade already." Setting aside her book, Mom tried to look stern but Cass could see the smile twitching at the corners of her mouth.

"Some kids we weren't expecting showed up," explained Logan. "What could we do? We had to share with them." He held out the lemonade jug. "Please, Mrs. Spencer, may we have more?"

Mom laughed. "I just happened to mix up another gallon. And there may be more food around here someplace."

Mom poured ice and lemonade into the jug and packed the tote bag with cookies and chips. The song that had been playing on the radio ended and Steve's voice came on to announce the times for that night's softball games. Logan nodded toward the stereo in the living room.

"Must be pretty neat to have your dad on the radio."

"Stepdad," Cass corrected him, her tone frosty.

Logan's eyebrows lifted in surprise. "Sorry," he apologized in exaggerated fashion. "I didn't realize it was so important to make the distinction."

Cass felt her cheeks burn with embarrassment. She knew she had no reason to snap at Logan. She shook a finger at him and pretended to give him a lecture. "Apology accepted this time. But don't let it happen again."

Logan laughed. Mom, on the other hand, shot Cass a reproving look as she handed her the jug.

"Do me a favor and remind Tabitha that she and your *stepfather*," she emphasized the word, making Cass squirm, "are signed up for the bowling competition tonight. She needs to be home by four-thirty at the latest so she can eat before we have to leave for the bowling alley."

Cass avoided Mom's eyes as she accepted the jug. "I'll tell her. Uh … if you talk to Steve before I get back," she added, trying to make amends, "would you ask him if he minds if I tag along? I wasn't planning on going, but now I think it might be fun."

"I was going to call him as soon as y'all left." Mom gave Cass' arm a reassuring squeeze. "He'll be glad to hear you changed your mind. You know how much he enjoys your company."

Cass smiled. The last thing she wanted to do was be mean to Steve, even if she couldn't stand his daughter.

Cass and Logan returned to the pool and the rest of the afternoon was spent eating, splashing, and joking around. Cass realized at one point that Logan was spending a lot of time with her, but she was having too much fun to think any more about it. All in all, by the time Cass and Tabitha headed home at four-thirty, the only thing on Cass' mind was the cookout planned for tomorrow evening at Kira and Micah's house.

CHAPTER 18

Going to church on Sunday reminded Cass of her discussion with Mom about the lack of a youth program. Glancing around the A-shaped, open-sided building as she waited for the service to begin, she counted eleven teens and about fifteen younger kids. Cass wasn't surprised that Logan and the Alexanders weren't there.

Pastor Thompson, who appeared to be in his early thirties, didn't look to Cass like someone who'd be against youth groups. She decided she might take Mom's advice and talk to him about starting one. Maybe she'd do it next week after she thought about it some more.

Or, then again, maybe she'd never do it. After all, there was a part of her that secretly liked being miserable about the move. Why should she do anything to make life on Kwaj more bearable? She wanted to be able to continue to complain about how moving had ruined her life, and starting a youth group would eliminate one of her gripes.

Following the service, Cass, Tabitha, and their parents biked to the island's lone restaurant for brunch. As they slid their bikes into the rack and chained them, Cass squinted at the sign over the door that read *Yokwe Yuk*.

"Uh … how is that pronounced again and what does it mean?" she asked Steve, pointing to the strange name. She kept her voice down, trying to keep Tabitha from hearing her. "I know you've told me, but I forget."

Tabitha's sigh of exaggerated irritation meant she'd mangaged to overhear after all. "*Yuck-way yuck,*" she replied before Steve could. She slowly and distinctly enunciated each syllable, making Cass want to hit her. "Honestly, Cass, it's not that hard to remember. It sounds just like it's spelled."

Cass stiffened. "Well, excuse me," she drawled. "You seem to have forgotten you've had several years to learn the language. I've only been here a week. I apologize for not being able to speak Marshallese like a native yet."

"Hmm." Steve stepped between the two of them. "What was it Pastor Thompson preached about this morning?" He rubbed his chin as if he couldn't remember, then snapped his fingers. "Oh, yeah, I remember. 1 Corinthians 13— 'Love is patient. Love is kind.' "

Cass looked away, picking up on Steve's rebuke.

"Now," he continued as they headed into the restaurant, "to answer your question more fully, Cass, *Yokwe Yuk* is Marshallese for 'good times' or 'happiness.' It's similar to the Hawaiian word, *aloha.* It has a variety of meanings. Does that help?"

Cass nodded and, in light of Steve's non-lecture, resisted the temptation to turn and smirk at Tabitha.

Once the family was seated at a window table, Cass spent several minutes studying the menu. She had no problem deciding to pass up shark steak and mahimahi in favor of a good old American cheeseburger.

"So what did you think of the service?" Mom asked Cass after their orders had been taken by a Marshallese waiter whose dark skin and gleaming smile reminded Cass of Kira and Micah. "It was different, wasn't it?"

Cass nodded vigorously. "I'll say. I've never been to a church without walls before. It was like being in a"—she searched for the right description—"giant tent. Plus, I'm used to dressing up more to go to church." She glanced down at her plaid shirt and shorts with a bemused smile. "Mamaw would have a fit if she knew I'd gone to church in shorts. And the service was—I don't know—both strange and familiar, if that makes sense."

"That's because it's an all-purpose Protestant service," explained Steve. "Since it's the only church on the island, it blends the different worship styles of several denominations. There's a little bit of Baptist, Lutheran, and Presbyterian all mixed together. As if that's not enough, there's a Catholic mass at 11:00. The Jewish people who live here, as well as the Mormons and Jehovah's Witnesses, hold their services in homes."

"Oh." Cass suddenly felt like the island was getting smaller and smaller.

"I was impressed with what I saw of Pastor Thompson, especially considering how young he is," Mom commented. "He certainly seemed like someone you could talk to about starting up a youth program, don't you think?"

"Huh?" Tabitha suddenly quit staring out the window and joined the conversation. "What's a youth program and who's planning to start one?"

"Our church back home had a Sunday night program for kids in junior high and high school," Mom explained. "Each session opened with prayer and a short devotion. Then, depending on the kids' ages, they'd plan different events. Sometimes they stayed at the church and played games and had Bible studies; other nights they would go out for a servant event or have a bonfire."

Tabitha stared at Cass. "You and your friends liked to do this stuff? You'd actually go every Sunday?"

Annoyed by her tone, Cass had to bite her tongue to

keep from blurting out a nasty comment. She took a deep breath to calm herself and nodded. "I loved it. It was fun and I learned a lot about the Bible and other"—at Tabitha's derisive snort, Cass' voice trailed off—"you know … things."

"Wow—how exciting," Tabitha said sarcastically. "And you want to start one of those groups here?"

"Absolutely," Mom replied. "Cass and I talked about the possibility the other day and she'd love to see a group get organized. It's something she's always enjoyed and I think a group might help her adjust to Kwaj more quickly."

Cass blushed and she glared across the table at her mother. Mom made it sound like the only reason she wanted a youth group was to ease her homesickness. Although that was partly true, she didn't want Tabitha to know. She figured it would be just like her stepsister to use her newfound knowledge to her advantage.

"I'm going on record as predicting it'll never catch on." Tabitha took a sip of her Coke. "The kids here aren't as religious as Cass and her friends back in Tennessee were." She shot Cass a spiteful look. "We're used to doing normal stuff. We're not into hanging out in church all the time. I honestly don't think anyone would show up for the meetings."

"What a stupid thing to say!" snapped Cass. She glared at Tabitha. "You don't know—"

"Obviously I didn't do a good job of explaining what a youth group is," Mom cut off Cass' angry outburst. "I helped run our church's senior high program for several years so I can personally attest to the fact that the kids had a great time while they were learning about their faith. We had parties and went bowling and"—she shrugged—"went more places and did more things than I can think of right now. But trust me, they had a blast."

As Mom talked, a brilliant idea occurred to Cass. As soon

as Mom stopped speaking she leaned forward, her words tumbling over each other in her excitement. "That's it! That's the answer, Mom. I can't believe we didn't think of it before. You do it. It'll be perfect. You know how, and I'll bet there are other parents who'd help you."

Mom held up her hand. "Whoa. slow down. What is it I'm supposed to do?"

"Lead the group," Cass replied as if it were the most logical suggestion in the world. "Talk to the pastor and tell him you're willing to be in charge. I bet he'd be happy to have a youth group if he knew he didn't have to lead it."

Mom glanced at Steve. "You know, she might be on to something. I really enjoyed myself when I helped out all those years. And now that I'm not as busy as I was in Tennessee—" She paused to smile. "I think I'd get a kick out of organizing a youth program. Kwaj could certainly use one and I've always liked a challenge."

"Excuse me? Hello?" Tabitha broke in. "Didn't you listen to a word I said? I've lived here half my life. I know what the kids are like. They're not interested in spiritual stuff—they're not going to want to join a church group. It won't work."

"Well, I, for one, am in favor of your talking with Pastor Thompson and getting this thing going," declared Steve. "I've been telling Tabitha for years that there's more to life than swimming and cook-outs. It's high time she found out I'm right. It'll do her good to get involved with a group of Christian young people."

Cass smiled when Tabitha's jaw dropped. "What do you mean?" Tabitha sputtered. "Are you saying you don't like my friends?"

Steve shook his head. "I think the world of your friends and you know it. All I'm saying is you and they could find more worthwhile ways to spend your time. As far as I'm concerned, a church youth group is just the ticket."

"Why doesn't anybody believe me?" Tabitha said, sighing deeply. "My friends aren't going to like the idea any more than I do."

Steve helped himself to one of the breadsticks from the basket the waiter had left. "I hardly think you're qualified to speak for your friends. You may find yourself very surprised by their reaction to the idea."

"No way." Tabitha's expression was confident. "In fact, I'm so sure I'm right that I'd bet you a hundred dollars. If I had a hundred dollars," she added with a laugh.

"And I'm so sure I'm right," Steve shot back, "that I'll bet you a month of taking your turn doing the dishes."

"You're on!" She shot Cass a victorious smile. "Life hardly gets any better than this."

"I wouldn't count my chickens before they're hatched if I were you," said Steve.

"I'm not," Tabitha good-naturedly retorted. "I'm counting my hours of freedom. Fifteen minutes a night adds up to a nice chunk of time." She pretended to think. "Hmm. I wonder what I'll do with all my free time. Maybe—oh, I don't know—spend it with my friends?"

Steve just smiled and shook his head at her. "Don't forget, pride goeth before the fall."

"I thought summer goeth before the fall," Tabitha said, laughing. "And winter goeth after."

Cass gritted her teeth as Mom and Steve burst into laughter.

What happened? she mused grumpily. *The conversation was going so well. I was the center of attention for once. Then— boom!—Tabitha turns on the charm, and, all of a sudden, I'm the ignored, forgotten one again. How does she manage to do that time after time?*

"Penny for your thoughts," offered Steve.

Cass gave him a guilty smile. Fat chance she was going to tell Steve what she'd been thinking about his beloved daughter.

"I was thinking how nice it is we're all out together like

this," she said, earning herself pleased nods from Mom and Steve. Beside her, Tabitha snorted so softly that only Cass heard her. It made her day to know she'd succeeded in irritating her stepsister. "I'm hoping we can turn this into a celebration, though."

"What do you mean?" Mom asked.

"I really want you to be the youth group leader." Cass leaned forward to gaze earnestly across the table at her mother. "It would mean so much to me to have you be the one to get the group started."

Mom exchanged a glance with Steve, who shrugged. Mom looked back at Cass and grinned.

"That settles it. As long as Steve is in agreement, it looks like the Kwajalein Community Church has itself a youth leader. Pending the pastor's approval, of course," Mom added.

Steve covered her hand and squeezed. "He'd be crazy to turn you down."

Cass whooped with delight, then hastily covered her mouth in embarrassment as several other diners looked her way. Tabitha rolled her eyes at the ceiling.

"Mark my words, it's not going to work," she muttered with a frown.

"You're just afraid the group will be a success and you'll wind up looking like a fool," Cass replied with a small smile.

"Cassandra," Mom said warningly.

Cass didn't respond. Instead she slumped down in her chair and began tearing her straw wrapper into confetti-sized pieces.

Cass and Tabitha barely touched fingertips when the family held hands for the blessing over the food the waiter brought a few minutes later. As Cass listened to Steve's deep voice thanking God for His provision, she blinked back bitter tears. Hard as it was to accept, she'd finally come to the conclusion that it didn't matter how much Tabitha provoked her, Mom was always going to blame her for the problems between them. Cass conceded there were times she said things she shouldn't. But couldn't her mother give her a break? Why did she have to be perfect all the time when Tabitha could get away with murder?

Determining there was no answer to the dilemma, Cass sighed heavily as Steve ended his prayer and immediately removed her finger from Tabitha's.

That afternoon Cass found Mom sitting in the wicker swing on the porch, reading and sipping from a glass of iced tea. Cass plopped down in the chair opposite the swing. She pulled the floral pillow from behind her and set it in her lap.

"Where's Steve?"

Mom looked up from her book and smiled. "He's lying down in the bedroom. He decided a nap was in order. Church and lunch tuckered him out."

"Aw, poor baby," mocked Cass. Her grin took any possible sting out of her words. Cass studied the pillow in her lap, playing with the button in the middle of it.

"Do you miss working?" she asked abruptly.

Mom gave a startled laugh. "Heavens, no! What made you ask that? Do I act like I miss it?"

"No, but I've been thinking about it since lunch." Cass quit fiddling with the pillow's button and began poking at the stuffing to even it out. "I mean, you've always worked. I thought maybe one of the reasons why you want to work with the youth group is because you miss being busy."

"Actually, I'm busier than I've ever been, only in a different way." Mom gazed out the window. "I never planned on working after I had children, but after your dad died—

well, my working became a matter of survival." Mom's expression grew sad. "I hated that I couldn't always be there for you."

Sudden tears stung Cass' eyes. "But, Mom, I understood why you had to work. Honest. I never held it against you."

Mom gave her a faint smile. "Thanks, honey." She cleared her throat. "Anyway, to get back to your question about me organizing the youth group. It's a blessing to have the time now to volunteer at the church and do whatever other activities come along, as well as to make a real home for you, Steve, and Tabitha. That's what I mean by being busier than ever."

Cass frowned. "My definition of a real home doesn't include Tabitha. Having her around turns it into a house of horrors."

"Now, now," Mom said softly. "Aren't you being just a tad bit melodramatic?"

"Oh, come on," scoffed Cass. "You know what she's like. You heard how negative she was about the youth group. She's not going to do anything to help make it a success. I wouldn't put it past her to badmouth it to her friends so they don't show up."

Mom looked skeptical. "I doubt she'd go that far. Besides, once she sees how much fun the group is, I'll bet she's turns out to be one of its most enthusiastic supporters."

"Are you going to make her attend the meetings?"

"I expect her to give the group a try, yes." Mom's tone was firm. "If she really doesn't like it after going—oh, I don't know—four or five times then Steve and I will consider letting her drop out. But once she tries it, I think she'll like it."

Cass made a face. "We'll see. I'm not nearly as confident as you are. Plus, I'm afraid she'll put a damper on things if you make her come. In case you haven't noticed, Tabitha can get pretty crabby when she doesn't get her way."

Mom winked at her. "Ah, but you're forgetting how I get when I don't get my way. I can be the queen of mean. Poor Tabitha had better watch out."

"You mean I actually might wind up feeling sorry for her if she pushes you too far?" Cass laughed at the possibility. "That's hard to imagine." She pushed herself out of her chair.

"Are you leaving?"

"I thought I'd take a walk." Cass plucked at her shorts.

"Would you like some company?"

Cass shook her head. "I think I'd like to be by myself, if you don't mind."

Yawning, Mom snuggled into a corner of the swing and stretched her legs along the length of the cushion. "I don't mind a bit. I'm quite happy where I am. If I can keep my eyes open long enough, I'm going to read to the end of the chapter." She reached behind her for her book, propping it up in her lap. "Then I believe I'll join Steve in a nap. I'm feeling downright lazy at the moment."

Cass paused in the doorway leading into the kitchen. "After my walk, I might go over to the pool for a little while if that's okay."

"That would be fine." Mom erupted in another jaw-breaking yawn. "If I'm asleep when you get back, leave me a note telling me what time you left for the pool."

"Okay."

Five minutes later, Cass quietly let herself out the back door and crossed the lawn to the beach. The tide was going out so she could walk on the sand instead of having to scramble over rocks. Stopping frequently to peer into tidal pools, Cass slowly made her way up the beach.

The sun beat down on her, but Cass realized she was beginning to find Kwajalein's climate more bearable. Maybe Steve was right after all, and she'd eventually

djust to the heat and humidity. Plus, there were some
ood things to be said for island life. She paused for a few
ninutes, staring out at the clear ocean and cloudless sky.
But it's just not Tennessee, she thought, suddenly feeling
old inside.

At the pool, Cass found an empty table tucked away in
he corner and claimed it for herself. As she tugged off her
T-shirt, she glanced around to see if she knew anyone. To
ner surprise she recognized a couple of people her age from
church. When Cass realized they were curiously eyeing her,
he quickly averted her gaze.

Maybe I should go over and tell them about the youth group,
he thought. She glanced at the group again. *Then again,
maybe I'll just wait and see if they come talk to me first.*

Pulling her hair back into a ponytail, Cass made her way
o the shallow end of the pool and eased into the frigid
water. Although she and the two girls snuck peeks at one
another, nobody seemed eager to make the first move. Cass
gathered her courage and dove under the water, swimming
n the general direction of the girls. When she came up for
breath, however, she saw that they'd moved to the other
side of the pool and were chatting with a third girl.

Well, I guess they'll find out about the group soon enough,
Cass thought, somewhat relieved. At the same time, though,
she realized she felt slightly guilty. How could she criticize
Tabitha for her lack of enthusiasm for the youth group when
she wasn't willing to promote it either?

Cass climbed out of the pool to lie in the sun, not wanting to dwell on the possibility that Tabitha wasn't the only
hypocrite in the family.

CHAPTER 19

"Who's Mom talking to?" Cass asked Steve, coming into the kitchen the following morning. She opened a cupboard and scanned the row of cereals to see if a brand she liked had miraculously appeared overnight.

"Your grandparents," replied Steve. "She called to ask them to scour the Christian bookstores for materials to use with youth groups. She's really gung-ho about getting this thing started."

Cass whirled around, her expression alight with excitement. "Papaw is on the phone?" she asked, joy flooding through her. "Can I talk to him?" She hadn't spoken with her grandfather in the two weeks since she'd left home.

Steve smiled. "I don't see why not. Before you talk, though, you need to realize that with long-distance calls, there's a couple second delay between the time you say something, and when the person on the other end hears it. You have to pause after you speak to give the person time to hear and respond. Otherwise, things can get pretty confusing and it's next to impossible to carry on a conversation. It's strange at first, but you'll get used to it."

Along with everything else around this place, Cass thought sourly. *The heat, the isolation, this itsy-bitsy house.* A chirping

154

near the sink drew her attention and she looked over in time to see a small green lizard skitter along the counter, leap onto the wall, and disappear behind the refrigerator. *And geckos*, she added with a shiver of distaste. Although Steve assured her geckos helped to keep down the population of even less welcome guests, Cass still wasn't used to the idea of sharing a house with lizards.

Waving to Mom she whispered urgently, "Don't hang up, okay? Let me talk."

Mom nodded. She listened several more seconds then said, "Dad, there's someone here who's dying to talk to you. Do you have a couple of minutes to spare for a very homesick granddaughter?" After a brief pause, she laughed and passed the receiver to Cass. "He says he's up to his ears in work, but he'll do his best to squeeze you into his busy schedule."

Cass could barely contain herself as she grabbed the phone. "Hey, Papaw!" she bubbled. "How are you? I miss you and Mamaw and Uncle Larry and everybody so much that most days I can hardly stand it."

"Hello there, Sassafras," Papaw's greeting boomed across the line a few seconds later. He sounded so very far away. "Mamaw and I are fine, thanks. Our only problem is missing you and your mom. I swear, your leaving has left a bigger hole in our hearts than Mamaw and I anticipated."

Tears pooled in Cass' eyes and she hastily turned her back so no one could see them. "I'm glad to hear you haven't forgotten me," she tried to joke.

"Never!" Papaw declared stoutly. "Who could forget a sassy one like you? Why, I still expect you to come bouncing through the door any minute. I haven't even begun to get used to your being gone."

"Good. I don't want you to get used to it." Squinting, Cass looked up at the sunshine streaming through the windows on the porch and asked wistfully, "What's the weather like there, Papaw? It's sunny all the time here and I'm sick of it."

Papaw's laugh cackled over the wire a few moments later. "Well, it's been raining four days straight so consider yourself lucky. We've almost forgotten what the sun looks like around these parts. Your mamaw's worried her vegetable garden's going to float away if this keeps up much longer."

Cass barely laughed at her grandfather's humor. Her mind had already skipped ahead to another, more important, subject. As soon as he stopped talking, she inquired, "Papaw, have you seen any of my friends?"

"Funny you should mention it," replied Papaw. "As a matter of fact, we ran into Janette today. Mamaw and I went out for a bite of lunch after church and Janette was at the restaurant with her family. The minute she saw us, she came right over and chatted with us a bit, asked if we'd heard from you and how you were doing. She had a friend with her. I think she said the girl's name was Laurie. Anyway, the friend had stayed overnight at Janette's house and the two of them were going to spend the afternoon baby-sitting the friend's little brothers," reported Papaw.

Cass' heart twisted with jealousy. "That was Lauren," she stiffly informed her grandfather. "She's Janette's second best friend after me."

Or at least I hope that's the way it still is, she added silently. She had a sinking feeling in the pit of her stomach that more had changed over the past two weeks than just her address.

The conversation ended a short time later because Cass couldn't keep her mind off Janette and Lauren long enough to concentrate on anything Papaw said. Without asking to speak to her grandmother, Cass returned the phone to Mom and shuffled to the living room where she sank into the recliner with a gusty sigh.

Steve turned around from the table where he was eating breakfast to study her. "Something the matter?"

Throwing her hands up, Cass gave an airy laugh. "What could possibly be the matter?" she retorted bitterly. "Except for the fact that my best friend has already dumped me for somebody else, everything's peachy. The way I see it, my life couldn't be more wonderful."

"Do you want to—" Steve began.

Cass glared at him. "Please don't ask me anything. I don't feel like talking right now."

"Okay," Steve agreed. "I understand. But when you are ready to talk, I hope you won't hesitate to come to me." He winked. "After all, that's what—"

"Dads are for," Cass completed the sentence in unison with him. She leaned back in the recliner and rolled her eyes at the ceiling. "I know, I know."

The day didn't get any better for Cass. After Steve left for work, Mom headed out to Pastor Thompson's office to talk with him. She returned an hour and a half later, bubbling with excitement. He was impressed with her plan to start a youth group and offered to call a church board meeting the next night to obtain their approval. Meanwhile he and Mom had set this coming Sunday night as the date for the first meeting. Cass was amazed at how quickly things were moving and realized she wasn't sure she was ready to jump into another youth group so soon.

While Cass was pondering her predicament, Tabitha left to spend a couple of hours with her friends. With Tabitha gone, Cass thought about mentioning her concerns about the group to Mom. Mom was so busy chattering away about possible activities, however, that Cass couldn't get a word in edgewise. In the end, she left Mom happily planning and retreated to her room to lie on the bed and stare moodily out the window.

When Tabitha returned for lunch, she reported that her friends were willing to give the group a try. Mom whooped with delight, but all Cass could manage was a wan smile as she set down the sandwich she suddenly had no appetite for. In between the commotion, she'd just heard Steve announce on the radio that there wouldn't be any mail coming in on the afternoon flight from Honolulu. That meant there was no chance of hearing from Janette for at least another day. It was enough to make Cass want to crawl back into bed and pull the covers over her head.

Although Logan invited Cass to the pool on Tuesday, she opted to stay home and brood about Janette. Mom had taken Steve up on his offer to go to lunch and left on her bike at eleven-thirty. Clad in her swimsuit and a towel knotted sarong-style around her waist, Tabitha emerged from her room a short while later. Her eyebrows shot up when she discovered Cass sitting cross-legged on the couch, staring at nothing.

"What's your problem?" she asked in passing on her way to the kitchen. Without waiting for a response, she yanked open the refrigerator door and studied the contents.

"What do you care?" retorted Cass.

Tabitha grabbed a handful of grapes and bumped the door shut with her hip. "I don't. I'm just making conversation. It makes our parents happy to think we're getting along."

Cass made a show of looking around the room then cleared her throat. "In case you haven't noticed, they aren't here. You're not the most observant person, are you?"

Tabitha perched on an arm of the recliner and popped a grape into her mouth. "Maybe not. But I'm observant enough to notice you're still sulking about your best friend tossing you aside for somebody else." She shook her head in feigned sympathy. "Tough break. I don't know what I'd do if I didn't have Kira."

Straightening her legs, Cass planted her feet flat on the floor and leaned forward to glare at Tabitha. "Who told you about Janette?"

"Hmm, I'm not sure." Tabitha pretended to think as she bit down on another grape. "Wait a minute"—she snapped her fingers—"I believe I ... uh ... accidentally overheard Mom and Dad discussing it." She lowered her voice to confide, "They feel really sorry for you."

Cass couldn't believe it. "They feel sorry for me? I don't want anyone feeling sorry for me."

"Oh, really?" Tabitha selected a grape and delicately nibbled at it as she gazed at Cass. "Then why have you been going around for the past twenty-four hours looking like you lost your best friend?" Covering her mouth, she giggled. "Oops, I forgot. You did."

"What's the matter with you?" Cass glared at Tabitha. "Do you get some kind of sick pleasure out of torturing me about this?"

Tabitha waved away Cass' anger as if brushing at a pesky fly. "Calm down. Believe it or not, I'm only trying to help you."

"Yeah, right. By mocking me?"

"I prefer to call it shock treatment." Tabitha held out her hand to offer Cass a grape, but Cass ignored the gesture. Tabitha shrugged. "Suit yourself. Anyway, back to my shock treatment theory. You've been moping around like you honestly thought you and Janette could remain best buddies, in spite of the eight thousand miles separating you. What are you, nuts? She was bound to find somebody else to fill your shoes, just like you'll eventually start palling around with people here. That's the way it goes."

"How can you be so callous?" demanded Cass. "It's like your heart is made of stone. Don't relationships mean anything to you?"

Tabitha's expression hardened. "I learned early on that relationships come and go," she replied cryptically. "It's better not to put too much stock in them. Otherwise you can wind up hurt."

Cass just stared at her. "What are you talking about? Who have you ever lost?" Belatedly, she remembered her mother telling her about Tabitha's mother walking out on her and Steve when Tabitha was a toddler, and she blushed. "Uh—" she stammered.

Tabitha shot her a crooked smile. " 'Uh' is right. I know what I'm talking about. My advice to you is to pick yourself up, dust yourself off, and start looking for a new best friend of your own. Janette certainly didn't waste any time replacing you."

Cass, who, for just a moment, had found herself almost liking Tabitha, bristled. "Thanks so much for reminding me."

Tabitha lazily stood up and sashayed to the door. "Well, in case anyone wants to know, I'll be at the pool for a couple of hours." After opening the door, she glanced back over her shoulder. "Think about what I said. Your friendship with Janette is history. It's time to move on."

Unable to think of a reply, Cass settled for a frustrated scream as the door closed behind Tabitha. She threw herself down on the couch and lay with her fists clenched at her sides.

"I wish you were history," she muttered. "I wish this island were history. I wish they'd blown it to smithereens when they fought over it during World War II. Then it wouldn't be here and neither would I. I'd be back home where I belong, having a wonderful summer with Janette and everybody." She brushed a hand across her eyes and added fiercely, "And, for your information, my friendship with Janette is not over. It'll survive my being stuck here two years. Just you wait and see."

CHAPTER 20

By Wednesday some of Cass' enthusiasm for the youth group had returned, mostly because it was the major topic of conversation at the dinner table every night and she wanted to be in on the planning. It annoyed her to be left out while Mom and Tabitha worked side by side on things, especially when she remembered how negative her stepsister had been about the project in the beginning.

"So...uh...Mom," Cass asked after she and Tabitha had done the dinner dishes, "we're having the first meeting here Sunday night?"

Mom leaned back to stretch and run her fingers through her hair. "Yup, from six to eight. While the kids are here, Pastor and Mrs. Thompson will be meeting at their home with the parents to explain the program and enlist their support. He's had quite an encouraging response from the people he's contacted."

Tabitha smiled. "I told Kira about some of the activities we're planning," she gushed to Mom. "She can't wait to come to the meeting Sunday."

Cass snorted. "You know, it's hard to believe that just a few days ago you didn't think anyone would be interested in a youth group. Now it's like it was your idea in the first place. Why the big change?"

Tabitha arched her eyebrows at Cass. "Not to be mean or anything, but the way you explained it, the group sounded like a drag." She smiled and rested her hand on Mom's shoulder. "Mom makes it sound exiting. Everyone I've talked to is really looking forward to Sunday night."

Mom grinned. "The way things stand now, we're expecting between twenty and thirty teens to show up, and that's just the senior highs. Heaven only knows how many we'd be looking at if we had opted to include the junior high group."

"You're kidding." Cass blinked in surprise. "Between twenty and thirty? I had no idea there were that many people my age on the island. Where have they all been hiding?"

"You're the one who's been hiding," Tabitha retorted. "You never go anywhere unless you're tagging along with my friends and me. How can you expect to know who lives here when you never get out and meet people? You've been holed up in the house practically every day since you got here."

"Honestly!" Cass exploded. "I ask a simple question and suddenly I'm getting lectured about my social life. I don't have to put up with this. I'll be in my room if anybody cares." She shoved back her chair and stood up, breathing hard in an effort to keep her temper in check.

"Cassandra—"

"I said I'll be in my room," Cass interrupted her mother. At the moment, she couldn't care less that she was risking Mom's wrath. "You and Tabitha have fun organizing the group. Like I need to tell you that," she added bitterly, "since you've gotten along just fine without me so far."

With her head held high and her back ramrod straight, Cass stalked down the hall to her bedroom.

Fifteen minutes later, Mom knocked on the door. After Cass grudgingly gave her permission to enter, Mom let herself into the room and joined Cass on the bed.

They sat without speaking for almost a minute then Mom asked softly, "So, kiddo, what's going on?"

"Tabitha," Cass spat out the name. "As usual. I swear, Mom, sometimes she makes me so mad I think, if I don't get away from her, I'll go crazy. I know it's a sin to hate people and I'm trying as hard as I can not to hate Tabitha. But she's not making it any easier with the things she says and the way she acts. It's like she goes out of her way to bug me."

Mom gently rubbed Cass' back, kneading the tense muscles. "It might help if you keep in mind you're still adjusting to each other. After all, you've only been living together a few weeks. You're bound to have conflicts. You're still learning about each other's quirks, as well as your likes and dislikes."

"I already know all I need to know about Tabitha's likes and dislikes," grumbled Cass. "She likes you and Steve, and she despises me. End of discussion."

"Tabitha doesn't despise you." Mom slipped an arm around Cass' shoulders and pulled her close. After resisting a few seconds, Cass gave in and leaned against her. "In her own way, Tabitha's having as difficult a time as you are, getting used to the changes in her life."

Cass snorted. "Puh-leeze! What changes? She's not the one who's had her life turned upside down. She still lives where she's always lived. She still has the same friends, the same neighbors, the same church. Compared to me, she's got it pretty good."

"Yes, but now she has to share everything with you," Mom reminded Cass. "No doubt it's hard for you to see at the moment, but we've all had to make adjustments since the wedding. Everyone's life is different in some way now that Steve and I are married."

"Maybe, but I'm the only one who seems to be having problems adjusting to the changes," muttered Cass. "As far as I can tell, the rest of you are doing fine." A lump formed in

Cass' throat as she rested her head on Mom's shoulder. "I miss Papaw and Janette and the rest of my friends so much. Sometimes I honestly think I can't stand it one more second."

"I know," Mom said softly. "That's one of the reasons why I'm hoping the youth group is a success. It'll give you a chance to meet people outside of Tabitha's circle. You need to strike out on your own a bit more than you've been doing."

"I'm trying," Cass said, close to tears. "It's not that easy."

"I wasn't criticizing you," Mom assured her. "Considering the recent upheavals in your life, you're doing great. Much better than I'd be doing if I were in your shoes." She nudged Cass' chin up so she could look into her eyes as she continued, "I want you to be as comfortable as possible with the group. That's why I'd like you to help plan activities so we'll be sure to do things you like to do."

"Really?" Cass felt a flash of happiness, but it left quickly. Pulling away from Mom, she slumped against the wall and sighed. "It's not like there's anything to do on Kwaj. We can make all the plans we want, but all we're going to wind up doing is swimming and picnicking. That's fun for awhile, but it's going to get old really fast."

Mom's smile was mischievous. "Well, maybe you ought to come back to the dining room and hear some of the things we've cooked up."

"Like what?" Cass demanded with a scowl. She was curious, but she wasn't about to admit it to Mom.

"Let's see," Mom said slowly and calmly, "what was your favorite activity with the youth group back home?"

Cass stared, open-mouthed, at her mother. "You're planning a progressive dinner? Honest?" When Mom nodded, Cass whooped with delight. "That's great! Okay, you talked me into it. I'll help you and Tabitha come up with some more ideas."

"Good." Mom gave her an encouraging hug and teased, "I've always said three heads are better than two."

"Why stop there?" Cass slid off the bed to follow Mom to the door. "Let's get Steve to help us. Four heads are better than three, you know."

The meeting on Sunday turned out to be a rousing success. Promptly at six, seventeen young people, including Cass and Tabitha, converged at the Spencer house for prayer, pizza, and Bible study. Even though she didn't know most of their names, Cass was pleased to discover she recognized about half of those who came, having seen them around the island.

Settling into a spot on the floor between Logan and Tabitha, Cass thought, *That's one good thing about living someplace this small. It doesn't take long to get to know people. Not,* she added hastily as a reminder to herself, *that it makes me feel any better about being here.*

Mom opened the meeting with prayer and then they began an icebreaker to get to know each other. Mom had each person stand and state their name, as well as one little-known fact about themselves. Once everyone had been introduced, Mom went around the circle, calling on different people to identify somebody else and tell their little-known fact.

When it was Cass' turn, Mom pointed to a girl seated across the room. "Okay, who's this?"

Drawing a blank, Cass wracked her brain for several seconds then announced triumphantly, "Marcy." She frowned. "But I don't remember her last name."

"Marcy's good enough," Mom said as the girl nodded her agreement. "You're not off the hook until you give us her little-known fact, though."

"She has a forty-two inch chest," Cass blurted then immediately clapped a hand over her mouth when she realized what she'd said.

The group erupted in laughter. Cass tried to explain that she'd mixed Marcy up with the burly boy sitting beside her, but she couldn't make herself heard above the din.

"Way to go, Marcy!" hooted one boy.

"Forty-two inches?" drawled a girl. "In your dreams, Marcy."

"No, in mine!" yelled another boy.

Cass met Marcy's eyes across the circle and she shrugged an apology. Marcy's grin and airy wave told Cass one wasn't necessary.

As soon as the group broke up to head over to the dining room table to make the pizzas for supper, Marcy made her way to Cass.

"Hey, thanks for the compliment." She elbowed Cass in the side.

"I'm sorry if I embarrassed you." Cass smiled ruefully. "It just popped out. I was thinking of the guy next to you."

"You have good taste. That's Andy, Kwaj's resident body-builder." Marcy glanced down at her flat chest before looking back up at Cass and chuckling. "As you can see, that was the nicest thing anyone's said about me in a long time."

Cass laughed along with Marcy, admiring the other girl's easygoing attitude. She doubted she'd have been as nice about the whole thing, even if it was unintentional.

"So you're Tabitha's new stepsister." Marcy fell into step with Cass as the girls moved to join the throng around the table. "My mother told me Tabitha's dad had gotten married. I'm glad. I really like Mr. Spencer. He's always been one of the cooler fathers."

Cass didn't know what to say to that, so she just nodded and mumbled, "Uh-huh."

Fortunately, Marcy didn't need any encouragement to keep talking. "So how do you like Kwaj?"

Remembering Tabitha's touchiness about the subject, Cass replied cautiously, "It's ... okay. I'm getting used to it."

Marcy laughed. "Translated, that means you hate it with a passion and you wish you could hop the next plane home. Which is where, by the way?"

"Uh"—Cass was having a hard time keeping up with Marcy's rapid shifts in conversation—"I'm from Jonesborough, a little town in northeast Tennessee."

"No joke?" Marcy's eyes lit up. "I've been there. My mom and I used to drive over to the Jonesborough story-telling festival."

Cass paused to eye the swarm around the table. "I don't think there's any room for us here. Let's go ask my mother if there's something we could be doing to help."

Shrugging agreeably, Marcy trailed Cass to where Mom stood, supervising the pizza-making. Mom smiled gratefully at their offer and immediately set them to filling cups with ice and pouring drinks.

"So where are you from?" Cass asked Marcy as they worked side-by-side at the kitchen counter. "It must be near Tennessee if you were within driving distance of Jonesborough."

"We're from Boone, North Carolina." Marcy took the cup of ice Cass handed her and filled it with Coke. "I was born in Georgia, then we lived in Florida for a few years before we finally moved to Boone."

"Is it just you and your mom?" Cass thought perhaps she'd found someone she had something in common with.

"No, I have two younger sisters. Not that I care to claim them on a regular basis." Marcy made a face. "I mean, I love them—but they can be awful pains in the neck. I keep telling my mother she'd have been better off if she'd stopped with me."

Cass laughed. After a brief hesitation, she ventured to ask, "Where's your ... uh ... father, if I'm not being too nosy?"

"I don't mind your asking. He lives in Boone. And yes"—she gave Cass a teasing look—"my parents are still married. My dad's a long-distance trucker and my mom's a teacher. About three years ago they decided that having

Mom come here to teach would help us out financially. Since Mom's employed by the government, the pay is a lot better than what she was making back home, and they don't take out any taxes because she's working overseas. Besides, it's not like my parents spent a lot of time together. My dad was always off driving his truck so it was just my mom and us most of the time anyway."

Cass glanced curiously at Marcy. "But don't you ever miss your father?"

Ducking her head, Marcy concentrated on pouring the cola. "I guess so," she replied in a muffled voice. "Right after school let out, we went home for six weeks. Dad took off from work for three weeks and we visited relatives and went to Disney World." She sighed wistfully. "It was nice being a family again. I sort of wished we"—she cleared her throat and tried again—"we didn't have to come back."

Cass didn't know what to say. She'd been caught up in her own misery for so long that she'd forgotten other people had problems. "How long is your mom planning to stay here and teach?"

"At least another year. I may or may not finish high school here. But all in all, it's really not that bad I guess." She flashed an upbeat smile that didn't fool Cass for a moment. "We're meeting my dad in Hawaii for Christmas, and I've decided I'm going to attend Appalachian State College in Boone. So even if my mom and sisters stay here, I'll be living in the same town as my dad and I'll be able to see him whenever he's home."

Despite Marcy's cheerful tone, it all sounded very sad to Cass. She was suddenly very grateful that Mom hadn't given in and allowed her to stay behind in Tennessee. She couldn't imagine being separated from her mother for months at a time. She realized she'd even gotten so used to Steve that the thought of not seeing him every day wasn't a happy one.

"I didn't think I could stand leaving my friends and family behind when my mother announced she was marrying Steve and we were moving down here. But"—grinning, she gestured down at herself—"here I am. I haven't died yet, like I thought I would. It sounds cheezy, I know—but I know things wouldn't be fine if God wasn't helping me, giving me strength."

Astonished at herself for talking so openly about her faith, Cass nervously awaited Marcy's reaction. *She probably thinks I'm some kind of religious nut or something.*

Marcy didn't seem to think so, however. She set down the soda bottle and turned to Cass with shining eyes. "Thanks. I'm really glad we talked. I told my mom that one of the reasons I was coming tonight was to find someone to talk to. I mean, I talk to my friends, but I needed somebody who could help me see things from God's point of view."

"And you think I'm that person?" Cass shook her head in amazement. "No way. I'm the last person you should be talking to. Believe me, I've done a rotten job of accepting God's will the past six weeks."

Marcy's expression was confused. "But you sounded like you knew what you were talking about, being strengthened by God."

Cass rolled her eyes at the other girl. "I'm not always great about taking my own advice."

Marcy shrugged and seemed about to say something else, but the first pizzas had been placed in the oven and the kids who'd worked on them were clamoring for something to drink.

As soon as the pizzas were set out on the counter, the teens got in line and loaded their plates with four and five slices apiece, then gathered in small groups around the living room. While they ate, Steve and Mom circulated among them, offering drink refills and more pizza the minute they spotted an empty plate.

After devouring ten pizzas and washing them down with gallons of cola, the group settled in for Bible study. Mom led a discussion, based on the First Commandment, about different things that can get in the way of a person's relationship with God. Although she didn't join in herself, Cass was happy to see that a good number of the other kids jumped into the discussion. *Who says this won't work out?* she thought smugly, glancing at Tabitha to see that even her stepsister was absorbed in the discussion.

Despite protests from the group, Mom wrapped up the discussion after twenty minutes, with promises she'd allow more time at the next meeting.

Once the group finally quieted down, Mom announced, "Now let's look at planning some activities for the remainder of the summer. I've jotted down a few ideas," she held up the list, "But I'm open to suggestions." She read through the ideas she had.

Before anyone could respond, Cass raised her hand. "I say we do the progressive dinner next Sunday."

"I don't want to sound dumb, but what is a progressive dinner?" Jack asked. "I mean, I'm all for it if it involves food." The group laughed and he continued, "But how is it different from a regular dinner?"

Cass looked to Mom to answer him, but Mom nodded at her. "Go ahead. You explain."

Cass nervously cleared her throat before replying, "It's called a progressive dinner because you start at one house for the appetizers, go to another house for salad, then someplace else for the main course, and the last house serves dessert. We did them in my youth group back home and they were a lot of fun."

Tabitha's voice suddenly rang out above the murmurs of interest. "I vote for a picnic at the lagoon. We should save the dinner for a special time, like around Christmas. It doesn't seem right to me to do something that fancy right off the bat."

"A progressive dinner isn't fancy," argued Cass. Not wanting the others to see how much she disliked Tabitha, she struggled to keep her temper in check. "Besides, I think it would be fun to try something new. We can do a picnic at the lagoon any time."

"You're forgetting a youth group is new to us," Tabitha pointed out in a syrupy-sweet voice, but Cass could see the anger in her eyes. "Maybe that's all the newness we care to handle at the moment."

Mom stepped in before the debate evolved into a full-fledged argument. "The best way to settle this is by putting it to a vote."

In the end the majority voted for the picnic. Although she knew it was a lost cause, Cass stubbornly raised her hand for the progressive dinner. She was pleased to see that at least a couple of the others did the same.

Cass was so mad at Tabitha that she refused to speak to her after the group left. The minute the cleaning up was done she stomped off to bed without a word to anyone.

"Tabitha knew how much I wanted to do the dinner. She was there when Mom and I talked about it," Cass whispered angrily to the ceiling as she lay in bed, her arms folded beneath her head. "Lord, is there any reason why You keep letting Tabitha win at these things? I'm beginning to think that maybe You do take sides. It's either that or You're not listening to my prayers."

Since neither possibility appealed to Cass, she rolled over and ordered herself to go to sleep.

CHAPTER 21

As the week wore on Cass grew increasingly more depressed. Nothing in her life was going the way she wanted it to. Tabitha seemed to make a point of talking about the picnic whenever Cass was around. The fact that Mom joined in the discussions didn't help matters any. Cass concluded that God wasn't the only one taking sides.

By Friday Cass had decided to skip the picnic, although she hadn't mustered the courage yet to tell Mom. She knew her mother would do her best to talk her into going and she wasn't up to arguing. Then letters from home arrived and the picnic was the last thing on Cass' mind.

"Guess what I found in our mailbox when I stopped by the post office," Steve teased Saturday afternoon when he arrived home from the radio station.

"Cobwebs?" muttered Cass. She didn't bother to look up from the magazine she was flipping through. It was two months old, but it was the only thing she had to read.

"Nope," Steve replied cheerfully. "Didn't you hear on the radio that a ton-and-a-half of mail came in on last night's flight?" He waved a batch of envelopes under Cass' nose. "These are for you, my dear."

Squealing, Cass grabbed them from Steve and clutched them to her chest. "Thank you!" She jumped up and flung her arms around Steve.

He laughed and hugged her back, seeming to enjoy her enthusiastic reaction.

Realizing what she was doing, Cass abruptly pulled away. "I'm going to my room to read them."

At supper, Mom did her best to draw Cass out about who had written and what they'd said. All Cass would say, was that she'd heard from Janette and three other friends. When Mom persisted in questioning her, Cass grudgingly reported that everyone was having a good summer. In order to avoid further inquiries, Cass concentrated on eating while the others' conversation swirled around her.

After dinner, Cass turned down Mom's and Steve's invitation to go bowling with them and Tabitha. The last thing she wanted was anyone's company.

"You go on," she urged with a bright smile meant to hide the aching in her heart. "I don't feel like bowling tonight. As an extra treat, I'll even do Tabitha's share of the chores. That way you can beat the rush at the alley and get right on a lane." *Plus, I have the added benefit of getting rid of Tab that much sooner,* she added silently.

"How about I stay here while Steve and Tabitha head on to the bowling alley?" Mom offered as soon as the others left the room to get ready for the evening.

Cass, who wanted nothing more than to be left alone so she could cry, shook her head. "I wouldn't dream of letting you ruin your good time just to stay home with me."

Mom placed a loving hand on Cass' shoulder. "Sweetie, it wouldn't ruin anything for me to stay here with you. I'd merely be exchanging one type of fun for another."

Cass smiled crookedly at Mom. "Yeah, like spending time with me is fun." Although she intended it as a joke, her remark sounded more bitter than lighthearted.

Mom sat down in the chair next to Cass. "What does that mean? Have I said or done something to give you the impression I don't enjoy being with you?"

Cass looked away from her. "No. I don't know why I said that. I guess I was just trying to be funny."

"Sweetie"—Mom smoothed Cass' hair and tucked it behind her ears—"what's wrong? Did somebody write something that upset you?"

Shrugging off Mom's touch, Cass stood up and started collecting the dishes from the table. "Nothing's wrong. Honestly, if I'd known it would cause this much trouble, I would've accepted the bowling invitation."

"What's happened to the wonderful relationship we once had?" Mom asked softly. "We used to be able to talk about anything. Now I don't know what's going on in your head half the time."

Cass dumped the dishes on the counter beside the sink and whirled to face Mom. "What's happened to our relationship?" she echoed with a short, bitter laugh. "Steve, Tabitha, and this rotten island, for starters. Has it ever occurred to you that maybe the reason you don't know what I'm thinking anymore is that you don't take the time to find out? I used to be first in your life, Mom. What place do I hold now? Am I even in the top ten?"

Two bedroom doors down the hall opened and Cass, breathing hard, spun around toward the sink. She didn't want Steve and Tabitha to see the distress on her face.

"Cass, let me tell them I'm not going," insisted Mom.

"No," Cass ordered in a low, but firm, voice. "I don't feel like talking about this right now. I'm going to my room as soon as I finish doing the dishes. It would be a waste of time for you to stay home."

Mom didn't respond, so Cass took that as acceptance.

As the three of them left, Mom stopped to kiss Cass on the head. "Do you think you'll feel like talking tomorrow?"

"I have no idea," Cass replied coolly. She waited until Mom left the room then added, "Even if I do, the picnic's tomorrow. You'll be so busy getting ready for it that you won't have time for me." She choked back a sob. "Not that that's anything new."

She knew it wasn't fair, but Cass resented Mom for leaving. True, she'd insisted that Mom go. *But if she truly loved me,* Cass couldn't help thinking, *she'd have stayed home, no matter what.*

"All right, I think it's time we had ourselves a father-daughter chat."

Sweeping the hair out of her eyes, Cass looked up from where she lay on her bed to see Steve standing in the doorway. It was twenty-four hours later and, except for church, she hadn't been out of her room all day. Mom and Tabitha had left thirty minutes ago for the picnic. She'd gotten out of going by pleading a headache. It wasn't exactly a lie. After all the crying she'd done, Cass' head did hurt—although not nearly as much as her heart.

Crossing the floor to the bed, Steve held out the tall glass and the plate of cookies he carried. "Here you go. Food fit for a king or, in your case"—he winked—"a queen. I've brought you one of my super-duper chocolate shakes and some of your mom's chocolate-chip cookies. You haven't had anything to eat since breakfast and I figured you might need something while we talk."

"Why? Are you going to yell at me?" Cass looked at him apprehensively and refused to accept the snack.

Looking injured, Steve set the glass and plate on the nightstand. "Me? Give me a break," he scoffed. "In the short time you've known me, have you ever heard me even so much as raise my voice to anyone?"

"Well, no," Cass admitted. She frowned suspiciously. "But there's always a first time." Sitting up, she leaned against the headboard and reached for the milkshake. "So, what do you want to talk about?"

Steve pulled her desk chair closer to the bed and sat down before answering. "I've got a couple of things on my mind, but first things first. Did somebody write something to upset you in the letters you got yesterday? You haven't been your usual bouncy self ever since I brought you your mail."

"Not exactly." Cass took a long drink of the shake. *Steve thinks I'm a bouncy person?* She was surprised at what a warm feeling that gave her.

"You need to be more specific." Steve said. "What do you mean by 'not exactly'?"

"I don't know how to explain it." Setting down the glass, Cass picked up a cookie and took a small bite. "Hearing from Janette and everybody about the places they've gone and the things they've done made me so homesick I could hardly stand it. I guess I realized for the first time that life back home didn't stop when I left. My friends are out doing the stuff I'd be doing if I were still there with them. It's not that I expected them to sit at home and do nothing except miss me, but it hurts—a lot— to know it's business as usual for them while everything's changed for me." She raised troubled eyes to Steve. "Am I a selfish person for thinking that way?"

Steve reached over and briefly squeezed Cass' arm. "Absolutely not. In fact, you're one of the least selfish people I know. You're having a very normal reaction to what you've experienced. However, it seems to me that when you get an opportunity to go out and spend time with people your own age, you ought to take it."

Cass took another bite of the cookie. "You're talking about the picnic, aren't you?" When Steve nodded, she made a face. "I know everyone thinks I stayed home from the picnic because I was mad I didn't get my way. That's part of it," she conceded and exchanged a smile with Steve. "But mostly, the letters from home made me realize that even if I went to the picnic and did other things with the youth group, I'd still be in Tabitha's territory."

"So?" challenged Steve. "Does that mean you can't enjoy yourself or make new friends?"

"I don't want to step on Tabitha's toes." Cass carefully chose her words so as not to sound like she was criticizing her stepsister. Even though Steve thought well of her, Tabitha was his real daughter. Cass had no doubt he'd take her side in an instant if she came right out and spoke badly of Tabitha. "I figure she wouldn't appreciate it if it looked like I was trying to steal her friends."

Steve waved aside her concern. "Kwaj may be small, but surely it's big enough for the two of you. Don't worry about Tabitha. As long as she has Kira—and Micah," he added with a wink, "she'll be fine."

"You think so?" Cass looked hopeful for a moment, then her expression drooped again. "Even if you're right, that's not the only thing bothering me."

"You're not sure you want to make friends, right?" guessed Steve. "Because, if you do, that will mean you're staying."

Cass stared at Steve in astonishment. "How did you know?" she sputtered.

He laughed. "Don't worry. I'm not a mind reader. I told you I had a couple of things to discuss with you and that was going to be my second question."

"But how did you know that's what I've been thinking?" persisted Cass. "Mom doesn't even know I feel this way." She pursed her lips and thought about it a second. "At least I don't think she does."

"I don't know if she does or not. We haven't talked about it." Steve took a cookie off the plate. "I know

177

because there was a time in my life when I felt exactly the way you're feeling right now."

When he didn't go on, Cass prompted softly, "When?"

Steve shifted uncomfortably on the chair and stared out the window on the opposite wall. When he spoke, his voice had a faraway sound to it. "After Tabitha's mother left us. For a long time—close to a year actually—I didn't take off my wedding ring or move from the house we'd lived in. I didn't even make long-term arrangements for Tabitha's care. Doing those things would have made the situation real. It would have meant my ex-wife wasn't ever coming back and I wasn't ready to face that yet." He looked up at Cass. "Just like I don't think you're willing to face the changes in your life either."

"Only not facing them doesn't make them go away, does it?" Cass smiled crookedly.

He smiled sadly in response and they didn't say anything for a minute. Finally, Cass reached her hand out to Steve. He took it and held it firmly in his.

"You're pretty smart, you know," she said, her voice thick with tears. It hurt her throat to speak.

"I should be. I've had 38 years in which to learn a few things," Steve said, smiling gently.

"I never thought I'd say this," Cass confessed softly, "but I'm glad Mom married you."

"Even though it meant moving halfway around the world to this rock?" Cass could see the happiness in his eyes.

Squeezing his hand, Cass nodded. "Surprise, surprise. Most importantly because you're good for Mom." She released Steve's hand, took a deep breath, and added softly, "You're also good for me."

"You know what I always say." Steve got up and went to sit on the edge of the bed. He lifted Cass' chin so that she was looking straight into his eyes. "That's what dads are for."

CHAPTER 22

"Well, hi, you guys."

Cass couldn't help smiling when she heard Tabitha answer the door early Tuesday morning.

"Uh ... did I forget we had plans? I wasn't expecting you."

Micah's cheerful voice carried through the house. "You're not the only person who lives here, you know. We've come to pick up Cass. Do you know if she's ready or not?"

"Here I am." Cass appeared behind Tabitha, smiling brightly.

"Wow! A girl who's ready on time." Micah shook his head in mock amazement. "Between my sister and Tabitha, I never thought I'd live to see the day."

Tabitha remained stone-faced while Cass grinned then turned to call to Mom who was cleaning up the breakfast dishes in the kitchen. "I'm out of here. I'm guessing I won't be gone more than an hour."

"Unless we just happen to get sidetracked at the lagoon, that is," Micah put in with a laugh. "Then there's no telling when you'll see her again. She might not put in an appearance until suppertime. You do have your swimsuit with you, don't you?" he added teasingly to Cass.

Before Cass could think up a witty comeback, Mom leaned over the counter to wave at the boys. "Stay out as long as you like," she told them. "I never worry about Cass when she's with you two. I sort of think of you boys as guardian angels."

Micah and Logan laughed. Then, puffing out their chests, they began to strut and take turns boasting.

"You've got that right, Mrs, Spencer," crowed Micah. "We're definitely God's gift to the women of this island."

"We're trustworthy and respectful," Logan chimed in. "All the mothers feel safe when their daughters are with us."

"The other guys should take lessons from us on how to treat girls right." Micah elbowed Logan who suggested, "We could charge ten bucks a head and make a fortune teaching the guys around here how to be gentlemen."

"That's enough, you two," Mom ordered with a laugh. "I'd advise you to quit while you're ahead. Otherwise, I might decide you're too conceited to allow either of my daughters to spend time with you."

Cass experienced a familiar knotting in her stomach at hearing Mom include Tabitha as one of her daughters. *You'd think I'd be used to it by now*, she berated herself, *but it still gets me every time*.

Glancing at her stepsister, expecting to see a smirk, Cass discovered instead that she looked upset. She briefly wondered what was bothering her, then decided it wasn't worth worrying about.

With a wave to Mom, Cass turned to head out the door. To her surprise, she was brought up short when Tabitha grabbed a handful of her T-shirt. Snapping her head around, she glared at her stepsister.

"What in the world do you think you're doing?" Cass demanded. She jerked her shirt out of Tabitha's grasp and made a show of smoothing out the wrinkles. "Are you nuts?

180

Why did you grab me like that?"

"Where are you going?" hissed Tabitha. "Nobody said anything to me about doing something this morning. What's going on, and why wasn't I told?"

"I have a news flash for you, Sis. The world doesn't have to let you in on its plans," Cass retorted, taking secret delight in the furious flush staining Tabitha's cheeks. "It's none of your business where I'm going or what I'm doing."

"It is when it involves my friends." Tabitha reached out again to take hold of Cass. She hastily withdrew her hand when Cass glared at her. "You can't just waltz in here and take over."

"What's going on back there?" Logan called from the street. Straddling his bike, he gazed back toward the house. "Are you coming or not, Cass? We're supposed to be there by nine."

"Hold on." Cass shot Tabitha a spiteful look. "As you can see, I have things to do. Catch you later," she said lightly before hurrying to join the boys.

Tabitha slammed the door behind her.

"I'm glad you're doing this devotion with us, Cass," Logan said as they rode their bikes to the church. He and Micah had volunteered at the picnic to lead the devotion at the next week's meeting and had signed Cass up to help them.

Cass met his eyes briefly, then turned her attention back to the road before she fell off her bike. *Which would be easy to do if I look at him too long,* she thought wryly.

They arrived at the church and Pastor Thompson invited them into his office. He had several devotional books stacked on his desk for them to look through to get ideas. With Cass in the middle, Logan and Micah drew their chairs close on either side of her so all three could pore over the books together.

After a few moments Logan looked up, slightly puzzled.

"I'm not saying that these are bad or anything," he said hesitantly, "but I guess I was thinking that we could do something more … I don't know … more about us."

Cass looked at Micah and they both looked at Logan, confused.

"I mean, about stuff we're going through. Does that make sense?" Logan looked so plaintive that Cass laughed.

"Yeah, I think I understand," she said. "You want to talk about something we're dealing with every day, right?"

Logan smiled and Cass thought she would die with happiness. *He has such a great smile.*

"That sounds cool," Micah said, then hesitated. "But what do we want to talk about?"

"Relationships," Logan said after a few minutes. "What to do after high school."

"Not doing everything I think I should be doing," Cass said, thinking out loud. She glanced at Micah and Logan to see if they thought what she said was weird, but they didn't seem to respond.

"Knowing what is the right thing," Micah said, glancing at Cass with a small smile.

Pastor Thompson cleared his throat and Cass jumped. She'd almost forgotten he was in the room. "There's some verses in Romans that might work for you guys to develop something," he said, handing them all Bibles. "Try reading Romans 7—starting at about verse 14."

The room was silent as the three of them flipped through pages and then read the verses Pastor Thompson suggested. *"I do not understand what I do. For what I want to do I do not do, but what I hate I do,"* Cass read silently, then paused, thinking of Tabitha. *Wow—is that ever right.*

She looked up. "Maybe," she started softly, then continued a little more firmly, "maybe we could read these verses, and then first talk about what they mean to us—and then

see if anyone else in the group wants to share something."
She avoided everyone's eyes in case they didn't like the idea.

"Sounds good to me," Logan said quickly.

"Yeah," Micah added. "I can already think of a lot of things to say."

Cass looked at Logan, then quickly looked away. He was smiling at her again. "Let's start working, okay?" she said lightly.

Thursday night as the family lingered over dessert, Cass remarked, "I'm really excited about the devotion we've worked on for Sunday. The guys and I spent a lot of time on it this week, but we finally feel like it's ready to go. I suppose I'll be nervous about it come Sunday night, but right now I'm really looking forward to it." She laughed at herself. "Isn't that weird? Usually I hate getting up and talking in front of a group."

Tabitha arched an eyebrow. "Then you're planning on showing up for the meeting this time, instead of sulking in your room like you did last Sunday because you didn't get your way?" she asked in a voice dripping with sarcasm.

Cass opened her mouth to protest, but Steve beat her to a response. "Cass didn't stay home because she was sulking," he disagreed. "She needed some time to herself to deal with a couple of tough issues and I'm proud to say she did."

Cass smiled her thanks at Steve while Tabitha's expression grew stormy. "I should have known you'd defend her," she scoffed, dropping her fork with a clatter. "You're always taking her side lately."

"Setting the record straight isn't taking sides," Steve replied mildly.

"It is when you go against your own daughter," retorted Tabitha.

"I have two daughters now," Steve said quietly.

Tabitha looked as though she'd been slapped. Color flooded her cheeks and her eyes glittered with tears. Cass quickly looked away.

"There! Are you happy now? Are you done taking what's mine? First you stole my friends. Now you're stealing my dad. It's a good thing I don't have a pet or you'd probably try to take that from me too."

"What are you ranting about?" Cass gave a light laugh intended to rile Tabitha. It worked. The red in Tabitha's cheeks deepened to a painful-looking crimson. "People can't be stolen."

Tabitha just glared at her. "You may have Mom and Dad fooled, but I know what you're up to. You won't be satisfied until you've completely ruined my life. This is one sick game you're playing, Cass Devane."

"Now, girls," Mom said quickly.

Tabitha turned to Mom. "It's true, you know. Cass hates living here. Everybody knows how she feels about Kwaj. Kira and I talk about it all the time. The only thing that'll make her happy is making me miserable."

"Tabitha, that's ridiculous," Steve said, his voice betraying a hint of irritation.

"Yeah," agreed Cass. "I don't hate Kwaj anymore. It's not nearly as bad as I thought it was in the beginning. I'm actually starting to like it here."

"Only because you've taken my friends away from me," snapped Tabitha.

Cass rolled her eyes and drawled, "Oh, great. Here we go again."

"That's enough, both of you," Steve ordered, no longer calm. "Your mother and I would like to enjoy our pie and coffee. If you two can't sit here and be civil to one another then you're going to have to leave the table. I can tolerate disagreements, but I draw the line at rudeness."

The girls moved at the same time, sliding back their chairs and picking up their dishes. They avoided looking at each other as they carried their things to the sink. Cass waited until Tabitha had marched down the hall and slammed the door to her room before addressing her parents.

"It's my turn to do the dishes," she coolly informed them, staring over their heads so as to avoid looking them in the eyes. "I'm going out back to sit on the rocks. Call me when you're finished and I'll come in and do them." She walked out without looking back.

The tension between Cass and Tabitha lingered over the course of the next three days. Cass could hardly stand to be in the same room with Tabitha and she suspected the feeling was mutual. They managed to stay clear of each other except for meals (Mom rejected Cass' suggestion that they eat in shifts), and at the youth group meeting Sunday night, they kept to opposite sides of the room.

The closer it got to the time when Cass, Micah, and Logan would lead the devotion, the more nervous Cass felt. By the time she took her place between Micah and Logan in front of the group, it felt like her hands were practically dripping with sweat. It didn't help that on the way up she happened to glance at Tabitha. Their gazes locked for a few seconds before Tabitha sniffed and pointedly looked away.

I guess it's safe to say she's not rooting for me to do well, thought Cass. *Oh, well, Lord, at least I know You're in my corner. Please help me to relax and give me the words to say.*

Micah began by reading Romans 7:14–25. Even though his voice was steady, Cass could see the faint trembling of his hand as he held the Bible. Closing her eyes, she prayed for him to calm down. *And me too, Lord,* she added, as she felt her stomach start to drop.

Trying to ignore her mounting panic, Cass looked around the group and felt better when she received encouraging smiles and nods in return. The only person who refused to meet her eyes was Tabitha, and Cass felt her fear being replaced with annoyance.

You could at least pretend you care about how I do, she thought resentfully, glaring at her stepsister.

The sudden hush in the room told Cass Micah had stopped reading. She wondered why everyone was staring at her.

Nudging her, Micah whispered, "It's your turn."

Cass paled then flushed a bright red as Tabitha snickered. Despite Kira's attempts to shush her, Tabitha continued to giggle as Cass fumbled to unfold the paper she'd written her thoughts on. Only Logan's steadying hand on her back kept Cass from slinking out of the room in utter humiliation.

Clearing her throat, Cass concentrated on what she'd written. Although Tabitha's laughter still rang in her ears, she took a deep breath and began, "I don't know about you, but I know exactly what Paul is talking about. So many times I've found myself knowing what I'm supposed to do— but I end up doing exactly the opposite."

As she neared the end of what she had written, Cass managed to look up at the group. She breathed a quick sigh of relief when she realized she'd succeeded in capturing the group's attention. "Thank God that Christ does rescue me," she finished up, "and that He gives me the strength to do what is right." She smiled at the group and offered up a silent thank-you to God. She knew it was wrong to gloat, but she noted Tabitha's disgruntled expression with satisfaction. Cass figured if Tabitha was unhappy, she had done her part of the devotion pretty well.

After Logan and Micah contributed their thoughts about the verses in Romans, Mom finished up with prayer. Although the experience had turned out better than she thought it would, Cass was eager to escape the spotlight and hurried to the first available empty space beside Kira.

"Good job." Kira whispered. "You gave me something to think about. I'm impressed."

On Kira's other side, Tabitha let loose with a very loud, unlady-like snort. While Kira turned to glare at her, Cass bit back a nasty remark. She had to remind herself they were in the middle of the youth meeting. Even more important, Mom was watching them, and Cass wanted to make sure she appeared blameless in her mother's eyes.

Let Tab carry on all she wants, Cass thought smugly. *I don't mind looking like an angel for a change. Let her see how she likes Mom lecturing her about her attitude.*

Before the meeting broke up, the group decided to go bowling the following Sunday, and a girl named Ashley volunteered to provide supper at her house since it was closer to the bowling alley than the Spencers' place.

Cass climbed into bed that night with a sense of satisfaction that she and the boys had done well. It also lifted her spirits that she'd left Mom and Tabitha talking in the living room. She didn't know what they were discussing, but she guessed from Tabitha's glum expression that it had something to do with her stepsister's behavior during the meeting.

Life hardly gets much better than this, Cass mused gleefully as she snuggled under the covers. *Mom's finally seeing Tab for the lowlife she is, and I came out of tonight looking great.* She stifled a giggle that threatened to erupt. *If this is the only thing the youth group accomplishes, it will have been worth the work it took to get it started.*

CHAPTER 23

The phone rang bright and early the next morning with an invitation from Logan for Cass and Tabitha to join him at the lagoon to go snorkeling. Not sure what the day's plans were, Cass told Logan she'd get back to him as soon as she talked to Tabitha. When she relayed the message at the breakfast table, Tabitha shook her head with exaggerated regret.

"Oh, gee, I'd love to go, but I can't."

The smile she gave Cass set off an alarm in her head. She didn't know what her stepsister was up to, but she'd bet it wasn't good.

"Mom and I already have plans," Tabitha went on, sending Mom a smile sweet enough to make a person's teeth ache. "As soon as we get ready, we're heading over to the library to look at pattern books so we can get patterns and fabric ordered from Honolulu in time for her to make me new school clothes. Then we'll probably eat at the Yokwe Yuk, although we might come back here and pack a lunch to take over to the lagoon."

Cass stiffened in her chair. "Really?" She glared accusingly at her mother. "How come this is the first I've heard of these plans? Were you hoping I wouldn't find out so you could have Tabitha all to yourself?"

"Oh, Cass, don't be silly," Mom said. "How can you think I'd deliberately leave you out? We only decided last night to check out the patterns. Since you'd already gone to bed, I planned to ask you this morning if you'd like to come too."

"Of course, Mom did say you probably wouldn't be interested," Tabitha said sweetly. She widened her eyes in order to look as innocent as possible as she explained, "She said fashion isn't exactly your cup of tea. She told me she practically has to hold a gun to your head to make you go clothes shopping."

"Yeah, so?" Cass retorted, hurt that her mother had shared this piece of information with Tabitha. She imagined the two of them having a big laugh at her expense and bristled. Scowling at Mom, she drawled, "Aren't you lucky that you finally have a daughter who shares your interests? I guess you realize now what you've been missing out on all these years, huh?"

Steve's fork clattered to his plate and was immediately followed by his crumpled-up napkin. Three pairs of eyes swung toward him. Cass realized too late that once again she'd gone too far.

"Look, girls," Steve growled, "I'm tired of every meal ending in a sparring match between you two. Have you been listening while you're in church and the youth group? It doesn't seem like it if you can't live out your faith and love in your own home."

Cass couldn't say anything and, surprisingly, neither could Tabitha. An uncomfortable silence hung over the table, even after Steve left to get ready for work.

Her face burning, Cass stared at her plate of French toast, no longer hungry. She couldn't believe what Steve had said. No one had ever accused her of being a hypocrite before. The worst part was she had to admit Steve was right. She was as guilty as Tabitha when it came to starting fights and being nasty.

Taking care not to get caught, Cass snuck a peek at her stepsister. Tabitha looked as chastened as she felt. Two fat tears rolled down both cheeks, but Tabitha didn't bother brushing them away.

"Uh … I think I'll call Logan and tell him I can't go snorkeling," Cass informed her mother in a subdued voice.

"You've decided to come to the library with us instead?" Sounding pleased, Mom reached over to pat Cass' hand.

She shook her head. "No, I think I'll stay here. Maybe I'll take a walk on the beach or something, depending on if the tide's out. All I know for sure is I need to be by myself for a while so I can think about some things."

Tabitha gave Cass a curious look. "What are you going to think about? What Dad just said?"

Answering Tabitha was the last thing Cass felt like doing at the moment, but she forced herself to respond. "I suppose." She shrugged. "Along with some other stuff."

"Like what?" persisted Tabitha.

"How should I know? I haven't started thinking about anything yet," Cass snapped. Then feeling bad, she added, "I'll let you know when you and Mom get back from the library and eating out."

"How about I call you when we're done looking at patterns?" suggested Mom. "If you're here, you might feel like joining us for lunch."

Cass glanced at Tabitha, expecting her to be annoyed. Tabitha appeared lost in thought, however, as she swirled an already sodden piece of French toast through a puddle of syrup on her plate. Cass shifted her attention back to Mom.

"Okay," she agreed.

After Mom and Tabitha left for the library, Cass changed out of her pajamas into shorts and a T-shirt and headed to the beach. Even though the tide was coming in, she covered quite a bit of ground before the rocks became too steep to scramble over in her sandals. That and the fact that the sun felt like it was burning a hole in the top of her head gave her two good reasons to turn back toward home.

Long-legged sandpipers and hermit crabs skittered away at Cass' approach. Watching a crab drop out of sight into its hole, she thought how nice it would be to bury herself in the sand until she could sort out the jumbled pieces of her life.

"Steve's right," Cass whispered to a sandpiper perched on a rock a few feet away. Its shiny eyes tracked her progress, making sure she didn't venture too close. "I don't seem to be very good at practicing what I believe."

Cass stopped beside the sandpiper's rock to stare at the crashing waves. She thought about what she had said to the youth group last night. The whole thing with Tabitha was just another case of her knowing what she should do— but not being able to do it. When it came to dealing with Tabitha, being Christlike wasn't nearly as satisfying as giving in to the urge to be mean and nasty. Not that it excused her behavior, but Tabitha truly brought out the worst in her.

"Oh, Lord," Cass murmured plaintively as the bird cocked its head as though trying to understand her, "why does doing Your will have to be so hard?"

Suddenly, she stopped. What was it Paul was saying in Romans? *We're human, which means we're sinful. So of course anything we try to do on our own won't work.* "But if You help me—" She looked up at the sky. "Lord, please help me get along with her."

Murmuring a farewell to the sandpiper, Cass continued toward home. Perspiration beaded on her forehead and trickled down her back. She wanted to think of ways to improve the situation between her and Tabitha, but all she could think about was getting inside the air-conditioned house and pouring herself a tall, cold glass of lemonade.

As Cass came in the back door, she heard someone knocking on the front. With a longing look at the refrigerator, she jogged through the kitchen to the front door. She yanked it open just as Logan was turning away.

"Hey!" Cass greeted him. Flipping her hair back from her sweaty face, she flashed Logan a bright smile.

He appeared dazzled by her welcome and it took him a moment to speak. "Uh ... hi. I was ... uh ... just leaving," he explained, then smiled sheepishly.

"I'm glad I caught you in time. Come on in." Cass moved aside to allow Logan to enter. Although Mom's rule was no boys in the house when she wasn't there, Cass figured she'd make an exception for Logan. "I went for a walk on the beach and I'm parched. I was just about to get myself something to drink."

Logan stepped inside and closed the door on the blazing heat. "You're asking for trouble if you go walking between ten and two. That's the hottest part of the day."

Propping her hands on her hips, Cass pretended to scowl at him. "Who died and left you mother?" she teased then dropped the pose. "I realize now it wasn't the smartest idea I've ever had. I wasn't thinking. I needed some time to myself and that was the first thing I came up with."

She led the way to the kitchen where she retrieved two glasses from the cupboard. "Would you like some lemonade?"

When Logan nodded, Cass filled the glasses almost to the brim then added ice. Handing Logan his, she took a long, satisfying drink from her own. When she glanced at Logan over the rim of her glass, Cass saw he was grinning at her.

"What?" she asked uncertainly, wondering if he was laughing at her.

"You weren't kidding. You really were thirsty." Cass raised her eyebrows questioningly and he continued quickly, "Not that I mind. I've known girls who tried to act like they never got hungry or thirsty and it really bugged me. I'd have liked them better if they'd admitted they were human like the rest of us."

Cass took another gulp of lemonade before setting the glass down on the counter. "You don't ever have to worry about that with me. When I'm hungry or thirsty the whole world knows about it. I don't suffer in silence."

Logan laughed. "Good. I definitely prefer it that way."

"What are you doing here anyway?" Realizing how rude that must have sounded, Cass blushed and stammered, "I ... I mean I'm glad you dropped by, but I thought you were going snorkeling."

"I couldn't get any takers." Logan propped his hip against the counter and grinned at Cass. "Everyone I called already had other plans. Are you guys trying to tell me something?"

Playing along, Cass pretended to seriously consider his question. "I don't think so. I can only speak for myself, of course, but I really did go for a walk."

"No kidding." Logan touched a finger to Cass' still sweaty cheek and held it up for her inspection. "At least I know you were telling the truth." Wiping his finger on his shirt, he continued, "Actually, I decided to stop by because I thought you sounded kind of down when we talked. Is everything all right?"

Surprised by his concern, Cass could only stare at him for several seconds. She debated with herself about whether to confide in him, then decided to chance it.

"Well, since you asked"—staring out the window over Logan's shoulder, Cass nervously licked her lips—"I'll be honest with you. Things aren't okay. No matter how hard I try, I still can't seem to get along with Tabitha." She gave a short bark of laughter. "Not that I try all that hard. That's one of the things I thought about during my walk, how easy it is to be mean to her."

Logan's expression was skeptical. "I can't picture you being mean to anyone, especially your own stepsister."

Cass laughed. "Then you don't know me very well. I can be a real—well, not very nice when I set my mind to it. Unfortunately, I set my mind to it a lot whenever I'm around Tabitha."

"So you two don't get along all that well." Logan shrugged. "It's bound to happen when you have more than one kid in a family."

Cass smiled. "I appreciate your trying to let me off the hook, but I've really been rotten. I know"—she swallowed hard and tried again—"I know I haven't been acting the way God would have me act. I did a bunch of confessing about that on my walk."

"Don't be so hard on yourself," protested Logan. "You're still getting used to your mom's marriage and having to move down here. Forget about getting a stepsister in the bargain. Do you think you're Superwoman or something? You think you shouldn't be having problems dealing with it all?"

Warmed by his defense of her, Cass allowed herself a real smile. "You're a good guy, Logan. I may not be happy about moving to Kwaj, but I'm glad I met you."

Logan ducked his head. "I'm glad we met too," he said softly. He looked up and smiled. "And look, don't be too hard on yourself about this thing with Tabitha, okay? I don't like it when you put yourself down."

"How can you call it 'putting myself down' when all I'm doing is telling the truth?"

"I don't know." Logan shrugged. "It doesn't have to make sense, does it? All I know is I don't like anyone ragging on you." He winked. "Not even you."

I think he likes me, Cass thought suddenly, warmed by his smile.

"Thank you." Picking up her glass of lemonade, Cass

saluted Logan with it. "It's nice to know you're willing to protect me from myself."

"It's a rotten job, but somebody has to do it," he said seriously, then laughed.

Cass pretended to scowl at him over the rim of the glass as she raised it to her lips for a drink. "Why do guys always have to ruin it when they say or do something sweet?" she complained.

"Beats me." Logan's shrug was unconcerned. "Because we're guys, I guess. Aren't you girls always saying we don't have a clue?"

Cass pressed a hand to her chest in a gesture of innocence. "When have you ever heard me say that?"

"Maybe you're never said it, at least not to me," Logan conceded, laughing. "But don't tell me you've never thought it."

He was right, but Cass refused to give him the satisfaction of admitting it. Instead she asked sweetly, "Isn't there someplace you have to be?"

Logan took his time draining his glass of lemonade before giving Cass a wicked grin. "You don't have to hit me over the head. I know a hint when I hear one." With a flourish, he gestured for her to precede him. "Ladies first."

Cass didn't budge. "Ladies first to where?"

"Aren't you going to walk me out?" Logan flashed her his most winsome expression. "I thought you southerners prided yourselves on your hospitality."

Knowing she was beaten, Cass tried to look stern, but gave up with a laugh. "You're impossible," she said good-naturedly. "Do you always get your own way?"

"Not always." Looking pleased with himself, Logan hitched his thumbs in the waistband of his shorts. "But I get it often enough to know I prefer it to not getting my way."

"That's it." Cass grabbed his sleeve and dragged him

toward the front door. "You're out of here. I refuse to spend one more minute in the company of such a spoiled brat."

"Hey!" Logan protested, playing along. "I resemble that remark."

Trading insults, he and Cass exited the house then spent another fifteen minutes talking outside. As Logan finally rode off, waving, Marcy came pedaling down the road on her way to the pool.

Another half-hour passed as Cass and Marcy sat in the shade of a pine tree on the side of the house and talked, beginning with the youth group and ending with the school year that would be starting in a few weeks. Glancing at her watch, Marcy suddenly leaped to her feet.

"Oops, sorry. I've got to run." She retrieved her bike from where she'd propped it against the house. "I was supposed to meet a couple of friends at the pool twenty minutes ago. They're not going to be happy."

Cass watched her leave before letting herself back into the house. The air-conditioned rooms were a welcome relief from the heat and she wiped the perspiration from her forehead as she headed to the kitchen.

Checking the time, she saw it was twelve-fifteen and frowned. Why hadn't her mother called? Surely she'd have heard the phone ring since she was right outside. Cass waited another ten minutes in case Mom called, then gave up and fixed herself a grilled cheese sandwich.

As she set her plate and cup on the table, Cass looked out the window at the ocean. The water looked as restless as she felt.

CHAPTER 24

The next morning, Cass was awakened by an unfamiliar sound. As she lay in bed trying to identify the soft, steady pattering, it dawned on her that her room wasn't awash in the usual blinding sunlight. Her eyes flew open and she bolted upright, flinging off the covers. For the first time since she'd arrived on Kwaj, it was raining. Cass burst into tears, taking herself completely by surprise.

Oh, man, I must really be losing it if a little rain makes me cry, she thought in disgust. *What'll I do if it thunders or lightnings? Pass out?*

Eager to savor the unexpected rainfall—the dry season wasn't due to end for another six weeks—Cass crept out of bed and down the hall to let herself out through the porch onto the lanai. It was still early and she was the only one up, which suited her just fine. If Mom and Steve were awake they'd probably order her back inside. Even worse, if Tabitha arrived home from spending the night at Kira's and saw her standing out here getting drenched, Cass figured she'd never hear the end of it. The thought of her stepsister made her suddenly cold, so she abruptly turned and made her way back to her room.

There's nobody like Tab to put a damper on things, she thought darkly. *The amazing thing is she doesn't even have to be here to ruin something for me.*

Climbing back into bed, Cass snuggled under the covers, folded her arms beneath her head, and stared at the ceiling. She winced as the memories of yesterday's disastrous encounter with Tabitha came flooding back. Despite her best intentions, she'd been at her worst with her stepsister and she still wasn't sure how it happened.

After finishing her sandwich, Cass had gotten up from the table, resolved to be a kinder and more loving person to Tabitha no matter how much her stepsister provoked her. As she puttered around the house, washing her lunch dishes and straightening up the living room, Cass found herself actually looking forward to Tabitha's return. She couldn't wait to start being her new, improved self, and she planned several nice things she could say to Tabitha to help smooth over their past difficulties.

Things started going wrong the moment Mom and Tabitha walked through the door.

"Sorry we're late," Mom chirped, juggling packages on her way to the kitchen. She glanced over her shoulder at Cass who was curled up on the couch reading and gave her an apologetic smile. "Looking at patterns took longer than we expected. There were so many pretty ones to choose from. Then we called Steve on the spur of the moment to see if he'd like to have lunch with us at the Yuk."

Remembering her resolution not to be so touchy, Cass worked hard at not looking as hurt as she felt. "You called Steve?" she asked in a small voice. "But you didn't check to see if I was available? You said you'd call."

Setting the packages down on the counter, Mom turned to Cass with a stricken expression. "I did call, Cass. Twice, as a matter of fact. When there was no answer, I decided you were still out walking."

"In this heat?" Cass retorted, her temper burning hotter with each passing second. "Nobody in their right mind takes a two hour walk when it's ninety degrees outside. I was back home before eleven. What time did you call?"

"Mom doesn't have to answer to you," Tabitha coolly informed her. She crossed the floor to stand beside Mom, as if to defend her from attack by Cass.

"You stay out of it," Cass hissed. "This is between *my* mother and me." Shifting her attention back to Mom, she asked again, "When did you call?"

"Although I resent your implication that I'm not being truthful," Mom began, "I'll answer you. The first call was around eleven-thirty and the second one about fifteen minutes later. The question is, where were you?"

Cass gave a guilty blink and looked away from Mom. "I was here," she muttered. "I just wasn't inside. I was out front talking to a couple of people. I'm positive I'd have heard the phone ring."

"So you are saying you don't believe I called?" Mom's voice was ominously soft.

Cass darted an uneasy glance at her. Mom didn't lose her temper often. When she did, it was best not to be within fifty miles of her. "Not exactly. I ..."

"I was right there both times when she called." Tabitha draped a supportive arm across Mom's shoulders. "I can testify she isn't lying."

"I never said she was lying." Glad to have someone to vent her anger on, Cass rounded on Tabitha. "All I'm saying is I waited for Mom to call like she said she would. When she didn't, I ended up eating by myself."

"And that's Mom's fault?" Hands on hips, Tabitha faced off against Cass. "You were outside talking to friends and didn't hear the phone ring, and Mom's supposed to feel guilty because you didn't meet us for lunch?" Her eyes suddenly narrowed. "Who were you talking to anyway?"

"None of your business." It wasn't the snappiest retort, but it was the best Cass could come up with under the circumstances.

A malicious smile briefly curved Tabitha's lips. It was there and gone so quickly that Cass couldn't be certain she'd actually seen it.

"You know," Tabitha purred, "Mom may not have made a real effort to get a hold of you. I mean, she didn't leave a message on the machine. Maybe, deep down, she didn't want you to join us."

Mom's reproachful, "Now, Tabitha," was drowned out by Cass' shriek as she came off the sofa to stand within inches of her stepsister, "Shut up! You don't know what you're talking about!"

Breathing heavily in her agitation, Cass glared at Tabitha.

"Oh, don't I?" To show her indifference to Cass' outburst, Tabitha ignored her as she held up a hand at arm's length and pretended to inspect her fingernail polish. "I know enough to realize I'm never the one left out of family outings. Think about the past several activities. Mom and Dad always made sure I was along."

"That's because you don't have a life," jeered Cass, wanting more than anything to hurt Tabitha the way she'd been hurt. "You never go anywhere now that your friends have switched over to me, so you're stuck hanging out with them."

Blowing on her nails, Tabitha polished them on her shirt. "My, my, my. In spite of all your big talk, it's obvious you didn't spend much time while Mom and I were gone thinking about what Dad said." She heaved a sigh of mock regret. "What a waste of a morning."

"It was a waste all right," Cass growled. She stared into Tabitha's eyes and wished she had superhuman powers to eliminate her stepsister from the face of the earth. "It was a colossal waste of energy trying to think of ways to be nice to you. You're the vilest person I've ever met."

"Believe me, the feeling is mutual." Tabitha's eyes glittered with malice as she returned Cass' glare without flinching.

Mom moved over to stand between them. "Are you through, ladies?" When neither girl spoke, she continued in a voice that vibrated with anger, "I'll take that as a yes. In that case, I suggest you both find someplace to go because if you're not out of here in five minutes I'm going to explode. I've had all of this fighting I can take for the moment."

Cass took off for her bedroom where she hastily wriggled into her swimsuit and escaped next door to the pool. She hid out there all afternoon, venturing home only after she peeked over the wall and saw Steve's bike parked in the backyard. She wasn't sure if her mother was still angry, but she felt safer knowing Steve was there for protection. Cass was pretty confident that if Mom were in a yelling mood, she'd control herself with Steve around.

Supper was quiet, but tense. Tabitha had gone over to Kira's house. Mom and Steve directed some comments Cass' way, but for the most part they ignored her. That was fine with Cass. She ate quickly and pretended to be invisible. After the meal, she declined Steve's invitation to watch a movie with him and Mom, and hurried off to her room where she remained for the rest of the night.

Now that it was morning, Cass figured enough time had passed that her mother couldn't still be mad at her. One of Mom's most admirable qualities was that she didn't hold a grudge.

Getting up, Cass stripped off her damp nightshirt and donned shorts and a T-shirt. She combed her hair and decided to leave it loose, rather than tying it back in her usual ponytail.

Stepping out into the hall, Cass glanced to the left and saw that Mom and Steve's door was closed. That was to be expected since it wasn't quite six-thirty yet. After sticking out her tongue at Tabitha's empty room, then scolding herself for being so childish, Cass headed for the kitchen. As she'd dressed, it had occurred to her that surprising Mom and Steve with breakfast might earn her some much needed brownie points.

"What's that heavenly smell?"

Ten minutes later, Cass looked up from the sausage she was frying to find her mother leaning against the refrigerator and smiling at her. She returned Mom's smile and felt the knot that had been lodged in her stomach since yesterday afternoon begin to loosen.

"I'm treating you and Steve to waffles and sausage," Cass replied. "I thought you might appreciate a break from cooking. Wake Steve up and tell him breakfast will be ready in five minutes."

"Hmm." Mom cocked her head and studied Cass. "It's not anyone's birthday and we have a long way to go until our anniversary. What could possibly be the reason for this V.I.P. treatment all of a sudden?" Eyes dancing, she tapped her index finger against her chin. "I don't have any reason to be suspicious, do I?"

Cass shrugged and busied herself with pouring batter into the waffle iron. "Of course not. I woke up early and decided to do something nice for y'all. Cross my heart, there are no hidden messages in what I'm doing."

"Uh-huh. I'm sure that's all there is to it." Pushing herself away from the refrigerator, Mom turned and went back to the bedroom to wake Steve.

He was a most appreciative diner. After taking his first bite of waffle, Steve closed his eyes and sighed blissfully. "Cass, this is wonderful! It's good to know we have a backup chef in case your mom ever gets so sick that she can't drag herself into the kitchen. Tabitha still doesn't know how to boil water and I'm not much better."

Cass felt herself blush at his compliment.

Once Steve left for work, covered in a poncho to protect him from the rain, Cass found herself at loose ends. She didn't want to stay home in case Mom planned to lecture her about her behavior yesterday. But the rain prevented her from heading off to any of her usual hang-outs. The stores didn't open until ten, which gave her two hours alone with Mom. As far as Cass was concerned, that was one hour and fifty-nine minutes too long. Undecided about what to do, she stood at the dining room window, watching the rain gusts whip the waves into frothy whitecaps.

"It's nice to see rain again." Mom came up behind Cass and smoothed the hair that cascaded to several inches below her shoulders. "It's funny the things you miss, isn't it? I never really thought about our summer storms back home, but I've noticed their absence since coming here."

Leaning back into her mother's touch, Cass emitted a soft sigh. "I was so happy when I realized it was raining this morning that I stood outside in it for awhile, sort of soaking it up. Now I know what the ground must feel like after a long dry spell."

Mom laughed softly. "That solves a little mystery for me." She lifted strands of Cass' hair and let them flow through her fingers. "I thought your hair felt damp, but I couldn't figure out why since I knew you hadn't had your shower yet."

"You know what else I miss?" Cass said, as though her mother hadn't spoken. "Hearing birds sing. All the sandpipers do is cheep, and they only do that when they get mad at you for riding your bike too close to them." Pressing her forehead against the glass, she raised her hand to trace a raindrop's path as it made its way down the window. "I miss the mountains and the mall and Papaw and my friends, especially Janette."

Mom was quiet for a moment. "Isn't there anything you like about being here?" she finally asked.

"I like Steve and I like the youth group." Cass named the two things that immediately came to mind. "But they're not worth living on Kwaj for. Oh, Mom." She turned and buried her head in her mother's neck. Mom's arms went around her to pull her close in a comforting embrace. "I want to go home. Please, can't I go back to Jonesborough? I can't stay here. I've tried to like it. Honest I have. But it's just not working out. I know you said I couldn't live with Mamaw and Papaw, but what if I promised not to be a bother? I'll be so good they won't even know I'm there, and I promise I'll come visit you every summer. Won't you at least think about it? Please?"

Mom held her for a few minutes while she cried, then took her hand and led her to the sofa. She kept a comforting arm around Cass after they sat down.

"There, did that help? Sometimes there's nothing like a good cry to make you feel better."

Cass gave Mom a wobbly smile and wiped the tears from her cheeks with the back of her hand. "A little. But, let's face it, crying doesn't change anything. I'm still stuck here eight thousand miles away from the place I want to be. I'm not kidding, Mom, there are times when I don't think I can stand it one more second."

"I know," Mom said softly, sliding her hand from Cass' shoulder to gently rub her back. "In the beginning, though, you didn't think you'd be able to stand it here at all. And look how long you've lasted."

Cass gave an irritated twitch. "That's because I didn't have a choice."

Mom turned Cass' face so that Cass would look her in the eyes. "You still don't. You're not going back to Tennessee to live. It's completely out of the question."

Cass' lower lip trembled. "But why not?" she protested in an anguished wail.

"Because you belong with me." Mom cupped Cass' chin and held it so she couldn't pull away. "Don't you remember telling me about Marcy's situation and how awful you think it is?"

"I only think it's awful because she has to live here," Cass muttered. "It'd be fine if she got to live with her father in North Carolina."

"That's not true and you know it." Mom released Cass' chin to take her hand. Tightly clasping it, she continued, "You told me you'd hate being separated from a parent like Marcy is. Since I'm the only parent you have, I have to assume you'd hate being separated from me." When Cass didn't say anything, Mom squeezed her hand and prompted, "Am I right?"

"Okay, yes, I'd hate it!" Cass blurted. "Are you happy now?" Jerking her hand out of Mom's, she jumped up and went back to the window. "But I've thought about it a lot and I'm pretty sure I'd get over missing you once I was back home with my friends and where everything's familiar."

"I guess we'll never know if you're right since I won't be giving you the chance to find out."

Cass swallowed. She slowly turned to face Mom. "Is that absolutely your final word on the subject?"

Mom sketched a cross over her heart. "Abso-bloomin'-lutely."

Cass stumbled back to the couch and collapsed on the cushions. "So I'm stuck here for the next two years, no matter what?"

"If that's the way you choose to look at it then I guess the answer is yes, you're stuck here for the duration." A frown wrinkled Mom's forehead. "I can't help wondering what brought this on. I thought you were starting to like Kwaj. You've been making friends and doing things. What happened?"

Cass shook her head. "I don't know. I could say that the scene yesterday with Tabitha messed everything up, but it wasn't like things were great until then. Nothing's really been right since we got here. The fight with Tabitha made me realize, though, that no matter how hard I try, I'm never going to make her like me." Looking away from Mom, she added quietly, "And I'll be honest. I'm never going to like her, either."

"Never is a long time," Mom pointed out.

"Not when you're talking about how Tabitha and I feel about each other." Cass pulled a pillow onto her lap and began tracing designs on it. "We're too different. I don't want to second-guess God, but what was He thinking bringing us together like this? I can't help wondering if this is His idea of a joke."

Mom gave a small laugh. "I can see how you might think that, but I don't believe God plays games with our lives. There's a reason for everything that happens."

"I used to think that, but I'm not so sure anymore." Hugging the pillow to her chest, Cass folded her arms around it and rested her chin on top to stare broodingly at Mom. "It's not just that Tabitha and I aren't ever going to learn to get along. I also realized yesterday that I'm never going to have a best friend here. Sure, Logan and Micah are my friends, but they're guys. It's not the same as having a girl friend like Tabitha has Kira or I used to have Janette."

"What about Marcy?" Mom wanted to know. "I thought you two hit it off at youth group."

Cass dismissed the suggestion with a snort. "She's too whiny. Every time we talk, she goes over the same old stuff about her folks. I don't mind listening to her if she needs to talk, but I'm not interested in being best friends."

"Isn't there anyone else in the group you'd consider striking up a friendship with?" Mom thought a moment. "What about Chelsea? Or Kelly? Or Amy?"

Cass shook her head at each name until Mom finally gave up. "I'm really not trying to be difficult," Cass said softly with a sad half-smile. "I've tried to find somebody to like, but nothing's worked out."

Reaching over, Mom took the pillow from Cass and set it aside. She drew Cass to her and the two of them leaned back against the cushions, listening to the rain pattering against the windows without speaking.

After almost a minute of silence, Mom finally murmured, "I remember a time in my life when I felt totally alone and like there was no reason to go on. Life became nearly impossible to bear."

Cass blinked in surprise. "Really? When?"

She turned her head so she could study Mom's face. At such close range she had no trouble seeing the pain in her mother's eyes.

"When your father died." She absent-mindedly stroked Cass' arm as she continued, "After he died I worked very hard at doing what I considered to be all the 'right' things. Like mother, like daughter, huh?" She glanced at Cass with a rueful smile. "I prayed. I trusted God to take care of us. I stood on His promises that He'd see us through the hard times and bring us out of the valley into new life. I kept at it for months until one day I collapsed, emotionally and physically."

"What happened?" Cass asked in a hushed voice, disturbed that her mother had ever been weak in any way.

"It was about five months after your father's death." Mom's voice sounded faraway as she relived the memory, and Cass had to strain to hear her. "I'd gotten a job in a grocery store—the only work I could find at the time. Between working and being a single mother, I was worn out. Plus, I was still grieving for your father so I was in rough shape. This particular night you had the sniffles and nothing would comfort you except me rocking you. It was around two in the morning and I'd just put you back in your crib for the fourth time and was ready to crawl into bed myself when you started crying again. That's when I lost it. I fell on my bed and cried until I was sure I couldn't possibly have any tears left. I told God exactly what I thought of Him and His empty promises."

Cass sat up and stared, open-mouthed, at her mother. "You didn't! You actually talked to God like that?"

Mom nodded, smiling slightly. "I most certainly did. God loves us enough to let us struggle with Him, you know. He's also big enough to handle whatever we throw at Him. Anyway, I let God know that I didn't feel taken care of, or provided for, and I sure didn't feel like there was any great new life waiting around the corner for us. I told God I was exhausted, discouraged, and lonely. I said I was sick and tired of being sick and tired and I didn't have it in me to go one step further. I'd had it with trying to straighten out my messed-up life." Smiling, she tugged Cass' hair. "Does any of this sound familiar, kiddo?"

Cass gave her a wry smile. "All of it. Unfortunately." Eager to hear the rest of the story, she leaned toward her mother and urged, "Go on. What happened after you chewed God out? What made you keep going?"

"Somewhere in the midst of my temper tantrum you fell asleep, which was a blessing. It was one less thing for me to deal with at the moment." Mom tucked her legs underneath her as she went on, "And then after a while, I quieted down too. I remembered Philippians 4:13, 'I can do all things through Christ who strengthens me.' It dawned on me that I was worn out because I'd been trying to do everything on my own. Yes, I prayed. But when God didn't act fast enough to suit me, or in the way I expected Him to, I took it upon myself to try to answer my prayers. And whenever something worked out, I was prideful because I believed I was the one who'd caused good things to happen. On the other hand, every time I failed and lost hope or patience—which occurred on a regular basis—I had nowhere to turn. I didn't know I could draw on the Lord's strength to see me through. I thought I had to manufacture my own strength and I eventually ran out of steam."

Mimicking Mom's posture, Cass drew her legs up beneath her, then nodded in understanding. "Like me, yesterday. While you guys were out, I thought about how mean I've been and I made all these great plans about how I was going to be so nice to Tabitha. But when she got back, I couldn't follow through on them. All she had to do was open her mouth and I jumped on her. It's the same thing with trying to make myself get used to living here. I can't do it on my own. I need God to help me do both those things, right?"

"That's right." Mom flashed her an approving grin.

"What's that Scripture verse again?" Cass asked, excited. "I'd like to memorize it."

Mom hesitated. "You know I'm all for memorizing Bible verses. But, remember, they're not meant to be used like magic formulas. You don't recite them, and suddenly everything works out the way you want it to. The power isn't in the verse—it's in what God has done for us. He gave His Son to pay the price for all the times we've ignored Him and tried to muddle through on our own."

"I understand." Cass said quickly, "but I think the words will help. I need all the help I can get. I figure, the sooner I memorize the verse, the sooner I plug into God's power source."

"I applaud your enthusiasm. Just be careful, though," Mom cautioned, "that you don't set yourself up for a nasty fall."

Cass tilted her head and frowned, puzzled by the warning. "What do you mean? I thought you wanted me to feel better about Tabitha and Kwaj."

"I do," Mom assured her. "But I know you and you have a tendency to go overboard. For example, I can tell you exactly what you're thinking at the moment. You're convinced you've finally found the solution to the problem of dealing with Tabitha and you can't wait to try it out. Am I right?"

Cass merely shrugged and nibbled at a broken fingernail.

"Of course I'm right," Mom answered her own question. "After all, the past sixteen years haven't been a total waste. I have learned a few things about you." When Cass didn't smile at her joke, Mom went on, "You think all you'll have to do is repeat Philippians 4:13 to yourself a couple of times and everything will automatically be fine. It's not going to be that easy."

Cass frowned and shifted her posisition. "I know that. I'm not stupid. I don't expect things to change overnight."

"Well, I'm glad to hear that." Mom patted her arm in a gesture of apology. "I guess you're more mature than I've been giving you credit for."

"I should hope so since most of the time you treat me like a baby," Cass retorted, then impishly stuck out her tongue. "Just kidding."

Laughing, Mom unfolded her legs from underneath her and stood up. "As much as I've enjoyed our talk, I hear the breakfast dishes calling. Unless," she added hopefully, "you're in the mood to do something nice for your old mother."

"Nope. Sorry." Cass jumped up and took off down the hall. "I have to get my shower, then I want to write a couple of letters."

CHAPTER 25

Tabitha came in the door as Cass emerged from her room shortly before noon, having written letters to her grandparents and Janette. Seeing her stepsister, Cass took a deep breath, silently recited Philippians 4:13, and pasted a bright smile on her face.

"Hey, how are you doing?"

Tabitha paused in slicking the rain off her arms to suspiciously eye Cass. "What do you care?" she challenged.

Cass counted to ten and repeated the Bible verse before responding, "I was just making conversation. It's what people do when they live together. So," she tried again, "how are you?"

"I'm tired, cold, and wet, but thanks for asking," Tabitha drawled, giving Cass a sardonic look. "And how are you?" she asked with exaggerated politeness.

"Fine, thanks. I'm glad it's raining." Having run out of topics of conversation, Cass wracked her brain for something to say. "Uh ... what are your plans for the rest of the day?"

Great, she berated herself, *I sound like Mom.*

Apparently Tabitha thought so too, because she smirked at Cass. "Gosh, Mother, I don't have any. Do you have any suggestions? Maybe there are a few chores you'd like me to do?"

Cass' cheeks burned at her stepsister's sarcasm and she struggled to hold on to her temper. "I was just asking," she muttered. "You don't have to jump all over me."

Raising an eyebrow, Tabitha pushed the damp hair away from her face. "You call this getting jumped on?" She emitted a tinkly laugh that set Cass' teeth on edge. "Honey, I haven't even gotten warmed up yet."

At that, Cass spun on her heels and walked back into her room. She didn't quite slam the door, but it shut with a definite thud. If she stayed one more second in Tabitha's presence, she'd explode. She refused to give her stepsister the satisfaction of knowing she'd rattled her.

Why isn't Mom ever around to see how rotten Tabitha is to me? Cass wondered bitterly, throwing herself on her bed. *Especially when I worked so hard to be nice to her.*

Cass stayed in her room and moped. The fact that the rain had stopped and the sun was peeking through the clouds didn't do much to brighten her spirits. She'd just decided to head to the pool when there was a knock on her door.

"Cass," Mom called, "the phone's for you."

"I didn't hear it ring." Cass slowly rolled off the bed and started for the door.

Mom opened it before she got there. "Hurry up," she ordered, gesturing urgently. She was grinning from ear to ear. "It's Janette."

"Janette?" Cass froze in mid-step for a moment before letting out a squeal and running for the phone in the kitchen. Grabbing the receiver off the counter where Mom had set it, Cass carried it out to the porch for privacy. "Jan?" she breathed into the phone. "Is it really you?"

"Live and almost as good as in person," came Janette's bubbly response a few seconds later. "My mother was in a generous mood tonight and said I could make a ten-minute call."

"Be sure to give her a great, big hug from me." Cass' mind raced with all the things she wanted to talk about, but she settled for, "So how are you?"

"That's why I bugged my mom to let me call," replied Janette. "I'm fantastic! I'm better than fantastic! I'm on cloud nine! Guess who called this afternoon and asked me out."

Cass didn't need to guess. She knew immediately. "You're going on a date with Aaron Hayes? Life doesn't get any better than that. You've only been in love with him since—what?—sixth grade?"

"I know!" Janette's shriek of delight rattled Cass' eardrum and she winced. "Who said dreams don't come true? I'm living proof they do if you're patient and wait long enough."

"When's your date and where are you going?" Cass asked eagerly.

"Aaron's picking me up at six tomorrow night. We're getting something to eat first—I don't know where yet—then we're going to a movie." Janette sighed wistfully. "I wish you were here so you could help me get ready. I'm absolutely clueless when it comes to what I'm going to wear."

"You know I'd give anything to be there," Cass said, her heart twisting slightly. "But let's try something. Give me a few seconds to think about your wardrobe, then I'll give you some suggestions about what you could wear."

"That sounds like fun. Go ahead and … what?" Jan's voice grew muffled as though she were speaking to someone in the room with her.

"Jan, are you still there?" Cass asked anxiously. She hoped they hadn't been cut off since she doubted her mother would let her call back.

"I'm here." To Cass' relief, Janette returned loud and clear. "Sorry about that. Lauren asked if she could borrow a pair of my shorts for tomorrow night. Aaron and I are going to double date with her and Mark."

Cass stiffened as her stomach lurched. "That's nice," she forced herself to respond. As casually as possible, she asked, "So Lauren's there now?"

"She's spending the night." Janette giggled. "I suppose that's not the best idea since we'll probably stay up all night talking."

Cass made a valiant effort to join in Janette's laughter, but her heart wasn't in it. "Then Lauren can help you decide what to wear."

If Jan noticed how quiet Cass had gotten, she gave no evidence of it. "That's what I'm counting on," she said brightly. "You remember what great fashion sense Lauren has."

"I remember," Cass replied dully. Lauren was another Tabitha, always perfectly put together.

The exact opposite of me in my baggy T-shirts and shorts, Cass thought darkly. *No wonder Janette prefers Lauren's help to mine.*

"She'll make me look so good Aaron will kick himself for not asking me out sooner." An idea suddenly occurred to Janette. "Hey, Cass, how about saying hello to Lauren? She talks all the time about how much she misses you."

Slightly less than enthusiastic, Cass agreed to Jan's suggestion. A few moments later, Lauren's voice pounded against her ear.

"Cass! This is so cool! I can't believe I'm actually talking to someone halfway around the world! How are you? What's it like down there? Have you met any gorgeous guys yet?"

Unsure which question to answer first, Cass decided not to answer any. "Hey, Lauren. How's it going?"

"Terrific!" crowed Lauren. "Isn't it just the best news about Aaron and Jan? You should have seen her face when he called. She lit up like a fireworks display on the Fourth of July."

"You were there when Aaron called?" Cass hoped her voice didn't sound as icy as she felt.

"Yup. Cool, huh?" Lauren laughed. "We stopped by here on our way to the mall so Jan could get some money, and that's when Aaron called. Another two minutes and we'd have been gone."

"Wow." There was a sour taste in Cass' mouth and she swallowed hard to make it go away. "So the four of you are doubling tomorrow night?"

"Yup, and we're going to have a blast," predicted Lauren. "Mark and Aaron are such good buddies, plus Jan and I have gotten really close in the past couple of weeks. I can't wait. It's going to be so much fun." Before Cass could think of something to say, Lauren continued, "Anyway, I guess I should give you back to Jan. After all, she's the one who called you. It was nice talking to you. Write me some time, okay?"

Cass' "okay" was lost as Lauren handed the phone back to Janette.

"I guess I should go," Jan informed Cass when she got back on. "The last thing I need is my mother getting mad and grounding me so I can't go out with Aaron tomorrow night."

"All right." Cass clung to the receiver, hating the thought of losing the connection with Janette. "I'll ... uh ... ask my mom if I can call you over the weekend. I want to hear all the details about your date."

"That'll be great." Janette paused then added softly, "I miss you like crazy, you know."

"Oh, Jan, I miss you too." Cass could barely get the words out around the lump in her throat. "Thanks for calling."

"I'm sorry we didn't talk about what's going on in your life," Janette apologized. "I promise I'll do better next time."

"That's okay. You had big news. My life is boring by comparison." Cass licked her lips, anxious to keep the conversation going as long as she could. "Have fun tomorrow night."

"I will," Janette promised. "Say hi to your mom for me. Bye, Cass."

"Bye, Jan."

Cass would have preferred a few moments to herself after hanging up with Janette, but Tabitha instantly appeared at her shoulder. Although Cass tried to brush past her, Tabitha stood her ground.

"Why do you look so down?" she demanded. "I'd have thought you'd be jumping for joy that your best friend called."

"I don't feel like talking right now." Cass squeezed between Tabitha and the door and headed for her room.

Tabitha followed her. "What's the matter? Did she have bad news or something?"

"Like you care," Cass muttered.

She noticed the concerned expression on Mom's face as she walked by her, but kept going. When she said she didn't feel like talking, she meant to anyone.

"Aw, come on," wheedled Tabitha. "You're not being fair. I care. I really—"

"Tabitha, leave her alone," Mom interrupted in a sharper tone than she normally used. "She said she didn't want to discuss the call. You need to respect her wishes."

Smirking at hearing her stepsister being reprimanded, Cass disappeared into her room. A short while later, she came out clad in her swimsuit and carrying a book. Mom looked up from the coffee table she was dusting as Cass came down the hall.

"Is it okay if I go over to the pool for awhile?"

Mom nodded. "Sure. I'm just doing some straightening up. Nothing major, so you're off the hook."

"Would you like company?" Tabitha called from the kitchen.

Cass met Mom's eyes and they exchanged bewildered looks. "What's up with her?" Cass murmured.

Mom shrugged. "I have no idea."

"Cass, are you still there?" Tabitha leaned over the counter and saw that she was. "Did you hear me?"

"Yes, I was … uh … thinking." The last thing Cass wanted was to be stuck with her stepsister, but she needed to find a nice way of telling her that. Holding up her book, she gave it a shake. "I appreciate your offer, but I plan on doing some reading. Mom bought me this book before we left Tennessee and I'm determined to finish it today."

"Oh … okay."

To Cass' surprise, Tabitha actually looked disappointed. *What in the world is going on with her?* Cass wondered. *Well, whatever game she's playing, I don't want any part of it.*

Announcing, "I'm off," she hastily left before Tabitha got any more bright ideas.

To avoid worrying about Jan and Lauren's blossoming friendship, Cass divided her time at the pool between reading and talking with people she'd met through the youth group. The afternoon passed quickly and Cass had just decided it was time to head home when the gate creaked open and Steve walked in.

"Hi." She waved to get his attention. "Is it that late? Did Mom send you to bring me home for supper?"

Steve ambled over to her. "It's just a little after four. Ed came in early and ordered me to go home. His wife is in Honolulu for the week and he said he'd had enough of rambling around an empty house all by his lonesome."

"Would you miss Mom like that?" Cass stood up and pulled a T-shirt on over her swimsuit.

"I'd be a basket case." Steve laughed. "We haven't been married long, but I sure have gotten used to having your Mom around."

"Yeah, she has a way of growing on you," agreed Cass. "She's kind of like a fungus that way."

Steve's yelp of laughter caused several people's heads to swivel in his direction. He shook a playful finger at Cass. "I'm going to tell her you said that unless you take me up on the offer I'm about to make."

"What offer?" Cass slipped her feet into her sandals and set her sunglasses on her nose.

"How would you like to go to the Yuk for supper? Say yes"—Steve's eyes twinkled with mischief—"and your mom need never know you called her a fungus."

Tilting her head, Cass considered the invitation. "Are you talking about everybody or just the two of us?"

"Just the two of us, of course," Steve replied. "We haven't really had any time by ourselves since we went out for ice cream in Hawaii. I don't know about you, but I could sure use a little one-on-one time."

A spurt of pleasure shot through Cass. *He actually wants to spend time with me,* she marveled before another less pleasant possibility occurred to her.

"Did Mom tell you Janette called and ask you to try to cheer me up?" she demanded.

"You're a suspicious little thing," Steve said with a teasing grin. "Why do you find it so hard to believe I enjoy your company? To answer your questions, though, yes, your Mom told me about Janette's call and that it seemed to upset you. No, she didn't send me over here on a mercy mission. Taking you out to eat was my idea."

Cass gave a satisfied nod. "In that case, I accept your invitation. Give me fifteen minutes to shower and change and I'll be ready to go." She followed Steve toward the gate. "Not that this has anything to do with my decision," she added, laughing, "but Mom said something about making spinach lasagne tonight."

Steve pretended to shudder. "It looks like we chose the right night to eat out. Talk about your narrow escapes."

"Yeah, but what about tomorrow night? There'll probably be leftovers."

"Don't worry," Steve reassured her. "We'll think of something between now and then."

After a quick shower, Cass braided her wet hair, slipped into a yellow sundress that highlighted what could almost pass for a tan and, at the last minute, added small hoop earrings to complete her outfit. Steve whistled and Mom oohed as she came down the hall into the living room. Tabitha sniffed and looked away.

"Don't you look lovely?" Mom said. "It's so nice to see you dressed up for a change."

Cass rolled her eyes at Mom, but smiled sweetly at Steve. "Ready?"

The ride to the restaurant was surprisingly pleasant. Even though the sun hadn't set yet, the temperature had fallen to a comfortable level and the steady breeze fanned Cass' face as she pedaled. She grinned at Steve across the two feet that separated them.

"You know, I've gotten so I actually like riding a bike instead of driving a car," she remarked. "I feel like I'm in better shape now than I've ever been in my life."

"Living on Kwaj will do that to you," agreed Steve. "With all the walking, biking, and swimming, a person can't help being fit."

"I need to take some pictures to send back home." Mentioning home reminded Cass of Janette's call and she felt a stab of pain. Pushing it aside, she continued, "Nobody will believe how tan and skinny I am."

"As soon as we get back to the house, I'll find the camera and personally make sure you get the pictures you want," vowed Steve. "Kwaj doesn't have a processing lab so we have to send the film to Honolulu to be developed. It generally takes two to three weeks to get the pictures back. If you want photos to mail to the people back home, the sooner we send the film off, the sooner you get to show your friends what a beach bunny you've turned into."

"Beach bunny?" she scoffed good-naturedly. "Honestly, Steve, everyone knows that term went out in the sixties."

Steve shrugged. "So I'm an old-fashioned kind of guy," he said flippantly but smiling. "Sue me."

The pair rode the rest of the way to the Yokwe Yuk in comfortable silence. After parking their bikes, they entered the cool, dimly-lit restaurant and were quickly ushered to a table.

"Are you up to being adventurous tonight?" Steve asked once they'd been handed menus.

"How adventurous?" Cass asked cautiously. "You're not talking about me ordering shark, are you?"

Steve laughed. "Actually, shark's quite tasty. Don't worry, though," he hastened to assure Cass at her skeptical look. "I'll let you work up to it. How about starting with grilled mahimahi?"

Cass wrinkled her nose. "I don't know. I'm not real fond of seafood. About the only fish Mom ever cooked was fish-sticks."

"Do you like tuna?"

Cass' expression brightened and she nodded. "Uh-huh. Why? Is that what mahimahi tastes like?"

"They're very similar." Steve set his menu down and folded his hands on top of it. "I'll make you a deal. You try the mahimahi. If you don't like it, you don't have to finish it. Plus, I owe you another dinner out."

"You're big on deals, aren't you?" teased Cass. "Is that how you got Mom to marry you? You offered her a deal?"

"I suppose you could say it was something like that."

Steve said, looking Cass straight in the eye. "I told her, if she did me the honor of marrying me, I'd love her, and you," he added pointedly, "for the rest of my life."

Cass' breath caught in her throat. There was no doubting Steve's sincerity. To cover her emotional reaction, she joked, "It sounds like you made her an offer she couldn't refuse."

"Yes, I did," acknowledged Steeve. "I may not be the smartest guy in the world, but I know how to get what I want. Which leads me back to your dinner choice. Do we have a deal on the mahimahi?"

"Okay." Cass leveled a warning look at Steve. "But this had better be good. I'm starving, so I won't be a happy camper if I can't eat my meal."

Once the waiter brought their meals, Cass nervously eyed the plate he set down in front of her. Although she found herself wishing she'd ordered the steak or chicken, she gamely picked up her fork. Resisting the impulse to hold her nose, she broke off a piece of the mahimahi and brought the fork up to her mouth.

"Hey, that's not bad."

Steve burst into laughter. "Did you honestly think I'd talk you into ordering something you'd hate?"

Cass swallowed and took another bite. "Not exactly. I figured it was one of those parent things. You know, where you tell us to try something for our own good. Translated, that means it tastes disgusting, but that's not supposed to matter because it's good for us."

"Hah! Fooled you," said Steve. Taking a sip of iced tea, he peered at Cass over the rim of the glass. "So do you think of me as a parent?"

Cass suddenly busied herself with pushing the food around on her plate. "Well ... sort of," she hedged. "I mean, you're Tabitha's parent so I lumped you in with all parents."

"One of these days I'm going to find a way to convince you I'm your dad too," Steve said lightly. "I know I've said it before, but, as far as I'm concerned, I have two daughters now." His face lit up with a smile. "Which makes me the happiest man in the world."

"I think being married to Mom also has something to do with your feeling like that, don't you?" Cass said quickly. "At least I hope it does, for her sake."

Laughing, Steve shook his head. "That's one of the reasons I enjoy your company so much. You keep me on my toes. I never know what you're going to say next."

Cass beamed at the compliment before turning her attention back to eating. The next several minutes passed in companionable silence as they continued to eat.

"You know the only thing wrong with my liking the mahimahi?" Cass asked after finishing the last of the fish.

Steve patted his mouth with his napkin. "No. What?"

Cass gave him a teasing look. "It means I don't get to go out with you again any time soon."

Steve's expression was a mixture of surprise and pleasure. "Well, I intend to make a regular habit of taking each of my girls out"—he cocked an eyebrow at her—"including your mom, for one-on-one time. I can't think of a better way to stay on top of what's going on in your lives." He paused. "Speaking of which, do you feel like telling me about your friend's call?"

Unsure whether she did or not, Cass stared down at her hands clasped in her lap. She wanted to talk to somebody about the call, but maybe Mom would be the better choice. *But you know Mom,* she argued with herself, *she'll be her usual reasonable self and try to explain why it's natural that Janette would turn to Lauren in your absence. You don't want reasonable right now. You want to tell someone who'll see things your way and be upset on your behalf.*

Raising her head, she looked directly at Steve. "Actually, I would like to talk about it," she declared and proceeded to relate the conversation as best she remembered it.

To Cass' secret delight, Steve's expression grew more and more thunderous as she told him about the call. His eyebrows drew together in a dark line above his nose and his mouth tightened. By the time she finished, he was sporting a full-fledged scowl.

"I don't want to speak ill of your friend, but I don't understand why she bothered calling," Steve remarked the moment Cass quit talking. "One minute she was telling you she wished you were there, then the next minute she all but told you it didn't matter since she has this other girl to keep her company. What gives?"

"That's exactly what I thought." Cass sat back in her chair, grateful that Steve understood. "I mean, I'm happy for Jan and all, but the phone call was all about her and Lauren. She didn't have a clue about how I felt and she never asked how I was doing. I always thought I'd feel terrific after talking to her. Boy, was I wrong."

Steve leaned his elbow on the table and propped his chin on his hand. "I'm sitting here wondering what kind of advice your mom would give you about the situation. I'm afraid I don't do too well when it comes to girls and their problems with their friends. Ask Tabitha. I used to go next door and ask Charlie what she thought I should do whenever Tabitha and Kira would have one of their spats. When all else failed, I'd call my mother."

Cass laughed. "Don't worry. You're doing great. Mainly I wanted to see if I had a right to be put out with Janette. You made me feel like it's okay for me to be annoyed and I appreciate that."

"I'm glad," Steve replied, then frowned. "Although I think I should say something about you forgiving Janette and not holding a grudge."

"I don't hold grudges." Cass toyed with her napkin and avoided looking at him. "But I'll be honest. I haven't forgiven Janette yet." She glared down at the table. "I guess I figured it would take her longer to find somebody to replace me as her best friend. I've only been gone a month."

"I doubt this new girl has replaced you." Steve reached across the table and gave Cass' hand a comforting squeeze. "My guess is Janette decided to get on with her life and this friend was a convenient substitute for you."

"Replacement, substitute"—Cass shrugged—"what's the difference? It all adds up to the same thing. Lauren's there with Jan and I'm not."

"That's right," Steve surprised Cass by agreeing. "You're here on Kwaj forging a new life for yourself."

"Not voluntarily," Cass muttered.

"No, not voluntarily," Steve conceded with a laugh. "But you're doing it and I admire you for it. Now, I have a suggestion," he went on, sparing Cass from having to respond to his compliment. "Let's skip dessert, go home and change, and head over to the basketball courts. I want to see if you're as good as your mom's been telling me you are."

Cass stared at him in surprise. "You mean it? That'd be fantastic! I haven't played basketball since we left Tennessee."

Standing up, he came around the table and held Cass' chair for her. "Of course I mean it. There might even be some people around interested in playing a pick-up game."

Cass hesitated. "O-oh, I don't know about that. I'm bound to be rusty. I don't mind looking like a fool in front of you, but it's a different story when it comes to other people."

Sliding an arm around her shoulders, Steve pulled Cass close for a quick hug. "Thank you. That's the nicest thing you've ever said to me."

The pair arrived home in high spirits, startling Mom

and Tabitha when they burst through the door singing the Notre Dame fight song. As Cass went to her room to change, she heard Steve explain their plans to Mom and Tabitha.

"But I was going to ask you to go bowling when you got back," Tabitha protested.

"Sorry about that, sugar. Maybe tomorrow. Cass and I have already made our plans."

"I guess bowling's not athletic enough for you." Even down the hall, Cass could hear the sour tone in Tabitha's voice.

Steve didn't sound concerned. "I can like both sports, can't I?"

"You can, but you don't. Be honest. You'd choose basketball over bowling any day, wouldn't you?"

Cass waited breathlessly for Steve's response. "That's a stupid question and I'm not going to answer it. See if you can talk some sense into her, will you, please? I'm going to change."

"Honey, you really shouldn't put your dad on the spot like that," Mom was saying as Cass hurried to get ready. "It's not fair, and—"

"You might as well save your breath," Tabitha broke in. "Nothing you say is going to convince me I'm wrong about this. I've known all along how Dad feels. He's tried to hide it, but he finally let on what he really thinks just now. He wishes I were more like Cass. She's like the son he never had or something. He can do things with her that I wouldn't be caught dead doing."

"How nice for your dad that he gets to enjoy both of you."

"He only enjoys one of us. He merely puts up with me because he doesn't have a choice. Sorry to run out on you, too, but I'm going to my room."

Cass almost ran into Tabitha in the middle of the hall.

The tense stand-off lasted a few seconds before Cass stepped aside and gestured for Tabitha to proceed. Tabitha didn't move.

"What? You're being the gracious winner?" she sneered.

Cass frowned her puzzlement. "What are you talking about?"

"Like you don't know." Tossing her head, Tabitha started past Cass. "You and Daddy-dear have fun at your little basketball game."

"Would you like to come?" Cass offered hesitantly.

"And risk breaking a fingernail?" Tabitha feigned horror. "Heaven forbid! No, I'll stay here and watch television while I lie on the couch and eat brownies." She laughed harshly. "You know, like I usually do."

Wow—with the mood she's in, I'm glad I'm leaving, Cass thought.

"If you think of it," Tabitha flung over her shoulder as she disappeared into her room, "would you remind my father, while the two of you are out enjoying yourselves, that he has a real daughter who'd like to spend a little time with him?"

"I can do all things through Christ," Cass whispered as Tabitha slammed the door, "including be nice to my wicked stepsister. Even if it kills me."

CHAPTER 26

Cass soon lost count of how many times she repeated Philippians 4:13 to herself over the next two weeks. Sometimes it was through clenched teeth, at other times with tears in her eyes.

She used it to remind herself not to blow up at Tabitha when her stepsister announced at the supper table one night an upcoming slumber party at Kira's house, to which Cass wasn't invited. As Tabitha gushed about getting together with all her friends, Cass closed her eyes in a silent appeal for help.

A few days later, Cass found comfort in the verse when a letter arrived from Janette. In it, Jan wrote about her date with Aaron as well as a weekend retreat she'd gone on with the youth group from church. She happily reported that Lauren had also attended the retreat and was thinking about switching churches.

Over and over again, every time she was sure she'd come to the end of her rope, she'd whisper the verse and hang on just a little bit longer. *Christ gives me strength*, she'd think, feeling slightly better each time, *Christ gives me strength*.

About ten days after her talk with Mom, a bright spot unexpectedly appeared in Cass' life. Tabitha and Kira showed up at the house with the girl for whom the slumber party had been thrown. Her name was Rianne Thayer, and the two girls had decided to celebrate the fact that she was back on Kwaj after a six-week visit to the mainland.

Cass found she liked Rianne immediately.

"So you're the one Tabitha talked about all last night," Rianne teased after Kira made the introductions. "We couldn't get her to shut up about you. After everything she said, I couldn't wait to meet you."

"If you only believed half of what she told you, I'll bet you were expecting someone with horns and a pitchfork, weren't you?" Cass retorted good-naturedly.

Out of the corner of her eye, she saw Tabitha squirm and stifled a laugh. *Good,* she gloated. *It's about time she got back some of what she dishes out.*

"Actually, a broomstick and warts would have been more like it," Rianne shot back and they laughed. "She didn't paint a very flattering picture of you."

"Surprise, surprise." Cass flashed a knowing look at Tabitha. "Why am I not shocked?"

Tabitha glanced uneasily at Mom and muttered, "I didn't say anything mean. Honest. I just talked about how hard it's been to get used to having a sister."

"Uh-huh." Mom didn't sound convinced, but she continued, "How would you ladies like some pound cake? It's fresh out of the oven. I have lemonade to go along with it."

While Tabitha and Kira wandered off to Tabitha's room with their snacks, Cass and Rianne went to sit on the porch. Cass learned that Rianne was from California and had lived on Kwaj for three years. She had two brothers, one a year older and one two years younger.

"Coming from California, I guess Kwaj wasn't a huge change for you, huh?" Pushing the swing with one foot, Cass nibbled at a corner of her pound cake. "I mean, you were used to palm trees and hot weather, right?"

Rianne laughed. "That's what most people think of when you mention California, that the whole state looks like Los Angeles. I come from northern California. We lived in the mountains. It got hot, but we also had tons of snow in the winter."

"The part of Tennessee I'm from is mountainous too." Her expression grew wistful. "Don't you miss it? The ocean's okay, but it's not the same as the mountains."

"Yeah." Rianne set down her lemonade and gazed out at the restless Pacific. "I really miss skiing. I was getting pretty good at it when we left. I hope my parents decide to go back for a visit around Christmas. I keep bugging them about it." She smiled. "It's hard to get in any skiing in the middle of July."

Realizing she'd made Rianne sad with her questions about home, Cass decided it was time to switch topics. "Does your older brother look like you?" she asked, thinking that Rianne's combination of wheat-blonde hair, brown eyes, and golden skin would look very nice on a boy.

Besides, she reasoned, *if Tabitha can go after Micah, surely I'm allowed to see if Rianne's brother is available.*

To Cass' surprise, Rianne's face tightened with wariness. "I guess we look alike. I never really thought about it." She took a deep breath then said in a rush, "Here's the deal, since you're going to find out anyway. Randy's disabled. He broke his back in a swimming accident five years ago and his legs are paralyzed. He gets around in a wheelchair."

"Oh." Cass didn't know what to say. She couldn't imagine being seventeen and in a wheelchair. "I'm sorry."

"Yeah." Rianne's eyes were bleak. "It stinks, but Randy makes the best of it. One of the reasons my father took the job here was because Randy would get his medical treatments paid for. The problem is, there isn't much for him to do." She smiled sadly. "Not that he was out and about all that much back home. But he's stuck in the house even more here."

"Well," Cass said suddenly, "I don't know if Tabitha told you, but my mom started a church youth group while you were gone. We meet here at the house Sunday nights at six. Maybe Randy would like to come to a couple of meetings to see if he likes them. You too. They're pretty fun."

Rianne's face lit up. "You think it would be all right? I did hear some of the girls talking about the group last night, but I figured it was only for kids who go to church." She hesitated before confiding, "My family doesn't go very much, usually just at Christmas and Easter. My parents have been pretty bitter since Randy had his accident. It's not that they blame God exactly. I think they're mad at Him for not making Randy better."

"I know what it's like to be angry at God." Cass laughed. "Ask my mother and stepfather. I've been throwing one huge pity party for myself ever since I got here." She dismissed the subject with a wave. "Anyway, anyone can come to the meetings. Tell your brother about the group and see if he's interested."

"I will. I think he'll …" Rianne broke off when she noticed Kira and Tabitha standing in the porch entryway. She nudged Cass. "We have company."

Cass looked up and was taken aback by the malice in Tabitha's narrowed eyes. Kira seemed to realize something was amiss because she glanced over at Tabitha with a puzzled expression.

Ignoring Cass, Tabitha focused her attention on Rianne. "Let's go," she ordered harshly. "We're going back to Kira's house."

"Uh—" Rianne seemed to realize she was caught in the middle of the tension between them. "Are you coming too?" she turned to Cass to ask.

"No, she's not," Tabitha answered before Cass could respond. Her ferocious glare dared anyone to argue with her.

No one did. Kira restlessly shifted her weight from one foot to another, but didn't say anything. Rianne reluctantly stood up.

"What are we going to do at Kira's?" she asked Tabitha.

"I don't know." Tabitha's shrug revealed her impatience. "Anything's better than staying here, though." The pointed look she directed at Cass told everyone why she felt that way.

Cass' stomach churned with fury, but she managed to hold her tongue. She leveled a steady gaze at Tabitha that soon had her stepsister averting her eyes.

"Cass and I were talking about the youth group," explained Rianne. "I want to hear more about it."

"I can answer any questions you might have." Tabitha glanced at Cass then hastily looked away. "I've been in on the group since the beginning too. She doesn't know anything I don't know."

"But—" Rianne began.

"It's all right," Cass broke in to assure her. "I don't mind if you want to go back to Kira's. Tabitha's right." She almost choked on her stepsister's name before continuing, "She can tell you whatever you want to know about the group. Besides, with Kwaj being as small as it is"—she produced a faint smile—"I'm sure we'll have other chances to talk."

Still looking uncertain, Rianne picked up her glass and plate to carry them to the kitchen. "Well, okay." She paused in the doorway to smile at Cass. "I'll see you around."

"See you." Cass pushed her foot harder and harder against the floor, making the swing go faster and faster.

Kira waved, then turned to follow Rianne through the doorway. Tabitha spun on her heels and disappeared into the house without saying a word. The triumphant gleam in her eyes told Cass she felt she'd won this latest game of one-upmanship.

"I can do all things through Christ," Cass muttered as she heard the girls call good-bye to Mom and leave by the front door. "It's just that some thing take longer than others, like learning how to live with Tabitha without going stark raving mad."

Rianne called early the next morning, just as Cass was finishing breakfast. Her face lit up when Mom announced the phone was for her. Tabitha scowled when she heard who it was.

Picking up the receiver from where Mom had set it on the counter, Cass said brightly, "Hey—I take it you're another early riser."

"Not by choice. It's a requirement around here," Rianne complained good-naturedly. "My mother likes to think of herself as a drill sergeant. No one is allowed to stay in bed past eight o'clock."

"She must know my mom." Cass laughed at the raised-eyebrow look Mom shot her. "I don't think the woman knows the meaning of the word *summer*. Sleeping in is practically considered a sin around our house."

"How about we get together and whine about our parents?" suggested Rianne. "After that we could go swimming or maybe see if Macy's has gotten in any new clothes."

"Sounds good to me." Cass felt like dancing. "Your place or mine?"

"I don't care. You call it."

"In that case, I'll come over to your place," replied Cass, thinking about Tabitha. "You'll need to give me directions since I don't know my way around very well yet."

They agreed that Cass would be at Rianne's house by ten, which would give her over an hour to finish eating, shower, and dress.

Tabitha pounced on Cass the moment she sat back down at the table. "So you and Rianne have plans for today?" she demanded.

Cass took a long drink of orange juice before answering. She knew it irritated Tabitha to be kept waiting. "Yes, we have plans."

When Cass didn't say any more, Tabitha raised an eyebrow. "Well, what are they?"

Glancing at Mom, Cass silently appealed to her to put Tabitha in her place. Mom, however, merely shrugged.

"Not that it's any of your business," Cass informed Tabitha frostily, "but I'm going over to Rianne's house for awhile. Then we talked about either going swimming or shopping."

"Really?" Tabitha's expression turned sly. "I'll call Kira and we'll meet you at Rianne's. What time is she expecting you?"

Cass checked Mom out again to see if she was ready to intervene. Since she still sat calmly eating her breakfast, Cass concluded she was on her own.

"I don't recall anyone inviting you." She struggled to keep her voice even.

Although Tabitha's eyes flashed with rage, she laughed lightly. "Oh, Cass, this is Kwaj. Nobody needs an invitation to drop in on someone else. Rianne won't mind if Kira and I show up. In fact, she'll be happy to see us. The three of us have been best friends for years. Rianne's mother used to call us the Three Musketeers because we were always together."

"If you and Rianne are such good friends, why do you think she called me instead of you?" Cass' tone dripped with sweetness. She didn't think it fooled Mom, but it was better than issuing Tabitha an outright challenge.

The color drained from Tabitha's face and she glared at Cass with undisguised hatred. "Maybe she was just trying to be nice to you. I told all the girls at the slumber party the other night how desperate you are for friends. I asked them to do me a favor and give you a call every now and then because I'm tired of hearing you moan and groan about how lonely you are."

Unsure whether Tabitha was telling the truth or being vindictive, Cass broke off eye contact with her and gazed down at her hands clenched in her lap. It made her sick to think that Rianne had called because she felt sorry for her. Tabitha had to be lying. The problem was, Cass couldn't be certain.

Tabitha shoved back her chair and began gathering her dishes. "If I'm going to get to Kira's, then make it to Rianne's by ten, I'd better take my shower. Don't worry," she added sweetly, "I'll leave enough hot water for you."

"Sit down, Tabitha."

Mom's steely-voiced command stopped Tabitha in her tracks and made Cass jump. Keeping a wary eye on Mom, Tabitha set her dishes back down on the table and reclaimed her seat.

"Yes?" Tabitha asked hesitantly. "Is … uh … something wrong?"

"Nope, not as long as you let Cass use the bathroom first." Mom kept her attention trained on her scrambled eggs. "She's the one with the definite plans so she gets first dibs on the shower."

"My plans are definite," protested Tabitha.

"You've got that right." Mom looked up from her plate and fixed Tabitha with an unyielding stare. "You're definitely not going anywhere near Rianne's house."

Tabitha's jaw dropped. "You're forbidding me to go to her house? No way!" She jumped up. "I'm calling Dad."

"Be my guest." Mom's tone was completely neutral. "I'll be interested in hearing how you explain what's going on."

Tabitha slunk back to the table and slumped down in her chair. "You're not being fair," she whined. "Why can't I go see Rianne if I want to? I've known her longer than she"—she shot Cass a venomous glance—"has."

"On the contrary," Mom disagreed. "I'm being quite fair. I haven't made you take Cass along when you've gone out with your friends, have I? Why should I force Cass to let you tag along this time?"

"Because ... well ... I mean," Tabitha sputtered. She waved her hands in her agitation. "You can't call it tagging along when you're talking about my friends. Like I said, Rianne will be glad to see Kira and me."

"Sorry, but I'm siding with Cass on this one." Mom bit into her toast. "If Rianne had wanted to include you in the get-together, she'd have asked to speak to you."

Tabitha's face twisted with bitterness. "What a shock," she spat out. "You're taking Cass' side. I guess what they say is true. When all is said and done, blood really is thicker than water."

Without asking to be excused, she got up and stalked to the kitchen where she dumped her dishes in the sink. Her mouth set in a thin line, she then proceeded to stomp off to her room and slam the door with a resounding bang. Mom and Cass exchanged weary smiles.

"Isn't being the mother of two teen-age girls fun?" murmured Cass. The music blaring from Tabitha's room made it impossible for her stepsister to hear her, but she wasn't taking any chances. "Kind of makes you appreciate how easy you had it with just little ol' me, huh?"

Mom pushed her plate aside and propped her elbows on the table. "Hard as it is to believe, I wouldn't go back to the way we were. I must be a glutton for punishment because I actually like the challenge of raising you two."

Cass shook her head. "You really are strange, Mom." She collected both her own and her mother's dishes. "But I love you."

"Thanks. I love you too." Mom placed her hand over Cass'. "Go on and get your shower. I'll take care of the dishes. I need something to keep me busy or I might end up throwing a few things."

Startled, Cass stared, open-mouthed, at her mother. "You're mad?"

"Furious is more like it," Mom replied tersely.

"Really?" Cass studied Mom, searching for clues as to her state of mind. "You look so calm."

Despite her anger, Mom laughed. "It goes with the territory, sweetie. I'm the mother. That means I can't allow my emotions to rule me, except on very rare occasions. Can you imagine what a mess there'd be if all the moms in the world were as moody as their children? Somebody has to stay in control."

Leaning down, Cass gave Mom a hug. "I don't say it as often as I should, but I'm really glad you're my mother."

Mom patted Cass' back. "That makes two of us. It's nice the way that works out, isn't it?"

By the time Cass returned to the kitchen, Mom was putting away the last of the breakfast dishes. Loud music continued to pulsate from Tabitha's room.

"Well, I'm off." Cass hoped the pleasure she was feeling at being able to say those words wasn't revealing itself in a goofy look on her face. "Do you want me to call when we make up our minds whether we're going swimming or shopping?"

"I'd appreciate that." Mom grinned at Cass. "I'm sure you don't want me to make a big deal out of this, but I'm so pleased Rianne called."

"Me too," conceded Cass and let it go at that. "I'll call you later."

The Thayer house was located on one of the interior streets and turned out to be a two-story duplex. After meeting Rianne's mother and younger brother, Robby, Cass followed Rianne up to her room.

"It's nice to be going up steps again," she remarked. "I don't like living all on one level. Our house back home had three floors if you counted the basement."

"It'd be easier on Randy if we just had one floor," Rianne pointed out. "My parents requested a one-story house when we moved here, but they didn't have any available."

Cass was embarrassed that she hadn't given any thought to Randy. "Why don't they ask to move as soon as one opens up? Steve said people come and go off the island all the time."

Having reached the top of the stairs, Rianne turned right to go to her room. "We're settled in here now." She opened the door to a blue and white bedroom that Cass instantly liked. "Besides, Randy doesn't mind. Some of the men my father works with converted the porch off the kitchen to a bedroom for Randy and added a bathroom. The way he sees it, he's got himself a pretty good set-up."

"It sounds like your brother has a terrific attitude." Following Rianne's example, Cass sat down on the bed and scooted back until she leaned against the wall.

"Randy's the best. I'd be a basket case if I had to put up with all the stuff he has to put up with." Rianne beamed with pride for her brother. "He hardly ever gets down. When he does, it's usually over something that doesn't have anything to do with his disability."

"Doesn't it ever bother him to not be able to come upstairs with the rest of you?" Cass tried to imagine what it would be like to have a member of her family cut off from everybody else, then decided it wouldn't be so bad if it were Tabitha. *Actually, I wouldn't mind shutting her out on the porch and leaving her there.*

Rianne gave Cass an amused look. "Who says Randy doesn't come upstairs? His upper body strength is unbelievable. Wait until you meet him. When he wants to see one of us, he gets out of his chair and hauls himself up the steps. He's amazing to watch. He's gotten so good at it that he can almost go faster than I can walk up."

"Wow." Cass was impressed. "Is he here? I'd love to meet him."

"He just ran out to Surfway to get something for my mom. He should be back in a few minutes." Rianne laughed at Cass' stunned expression. "He has a motorized chair so he can go practically anywhere. He's a real speed demon too. We keep telling him he's going to get ticketed if he doesn't watch out."

"I can't believe Tabitha never mentioned him," marveled Cass. "He sounds like quite a guy."

"Randy doesn't socialize with girls much," Rianne explained. "He's self-conscious about his disability when he's around them. Also," she added with a teasing glint in her eye, "in case you haven't noticed, the only brother your stepsister is interested in is Kira's. I just hope when Micah finally asks her out that Tabitha doesn't die of shock."

"How odd. I hope just the opposite happens," Cass muttered then clapped her hand over her mouth. "I'm sorry. I shouldn't have said that."

"Don't worry." Rianne laughed. "I won't tell Tabitha on you. Besides, she's not exactly shy about letting people know you two don't get along."

"Still"—Cass made a face—"I don't want to talk about her behind her back. My mother would kill me if she ever found out."

From downstairs came the sound of a door opening and closing, then a male voice called, "Mom, I'm home. You'd better come get these chocolate chips before I give in to temptation and start eating them."

Mrs. Thayer's response was too muffled for the girls to understand, but her laughter floated up the stairs. Rianne smiled at Cass.

"Randy's home. Let's go say hello."

As Cass trailed Rianne down the steps, she realized she had butterflies in her stomach. *I've never met anyone my age in a wheelchair,* she worried. *What do I say to him? Do I bend down to talk to him or will he think I'm being insulting?*

Rianne led the way past Robby who was playing a video game in the living room next to the kitchen. The girls found Mrs. Thayer leaning against the counter talking with Randy.

Gosh, he's cute, Cass thought immediately.

As she'd expected, Randy was a masculine version of Rianne. If he'd been able to stand, Cass guessed he'd be well over six feet tall. With a start, she saw that Randy was studying her as closely as she was studying him. She wanted to look away, but she didn't want Randy to think she was bothered by his appearance because the truth was, she wasn't. Fortunately, Rianne came to her rescue.

She laid a hand on her brother's shoulder. "Randy, I'd like you to meet Cass Devane. She just moved here last month from Tennessee. Her mother married Tabitha Spencer's father." She shifted her attention to Cass. "Cass, this is Randy."

Cass inclined her head toward Randy. "Nice to meet you."

"Same here." Randy's eyes crinkled at the corners as he smiled. "So how do you like having Tabitha as a stepsister?"

"I refuse to answer on the grounds it might get me into a heap of trouble," Cass shot back.

Randy laughed. "Good answer," he approved. "You must be planning on going into politics someday."

"No, I just want to live to see my seventeenth birthday." Folding her arms, Cass backed up until she was propped against the refrigerator. "If word ever got back to Tabitha that I was going around badmouthing her, my days would be numbered."

"You're not only pretty, you're smart too." Randy gave Cass a thumbs-up. "That's an unbeatable combination."

Blushing at the compliment, Cass looked at Rianne to say something. Rianne, however, was staring at her brother.

"Uh ... Randy," Rianne said quickly after a slight pause, "I forgot to mention it yesterday, but Cass told me about a

239

youth group her mother has started. What do you say we give it a try this Sunday night?"

Randy's grin immediately faded and he looked down at his lap. "I don't know," he hedged. "You know how I am when it comes to crowds."

Cass spoke up before Rianne could say anything. "I don't know what you consider a crowd, but we usually have about twenty, twenty-five kids who attend. I'd really"—she swallowed hard, astonished at her boldness—"like you to come." She flashed Rianne a smile. "I figure any brother of Rianne's has to be okay."

"Yeah?" Randy's smile gradually reappeared. "All right, then, I'll think about it."

"That's all I ask."

Rianne gave her brother and Cass curious glances before nodding toward the stairs. "How about we go back up to my room, Cass? We still have a lot to talk about."

"I'll fix you two a couple of my world-famous grilled cheese sandwiches for lunch," Randy called after them as they headed for the steps.

Rianne halted and spun around, one hand pressed to her chest. "Excuse me? Did I hear you right? Did you actually offer to fix my lunch?"

Randy smirked at her. "Sort of. I was just going to offer to make lunch for Cass, but I figured you'd be put out. So I included you at the last second."

"Gee, aren't you all heart?" drawled Rianne. "I'll tell you what. I'll get back to you about letting you make me a grilled cheese sandwich. I don't care how world-famous it is, I'm not sure I want one."

Cass waved her hand. "I'm not going to play hard to get. I already know I want you to fix me one. What time will it be done?"

They left the living room on a gust of laughter. The minute they reached Rianne's room, she closed the door and faced Cass with sparkling eyes.

"Who are you?" she asked incredulously. "I've never seen Randy as relaxed with a girl as he was with you."

Pleased, Cass smiled but looked away. "You were right. Randy's great. I'm glad you think he likes me. I hope I have a chance to get to know him better."

"If he has anything to say about it, you will." Rianne walked over to her bed, elbowing Cass in the ribs as she went by. "After all, he's going to be making lunch for you. Believe me, that doesn't happen everyday." Sitting down on the bed, she peered up at Cass. "So you weren't uncomfortable around him?"

Cass sank cross-legged to the floor. "I thought I would be," she admitted, "but it turned out I wasn't. He's just"— she hesitated, searching for the right words to explain how she felt—"a regular guy who happens to be in a wheelchair." A troubling thought crossed her mind and she frowned. "You don't think I was being nice to him just to show what a good person I am, do you?"

Rianne vigorously shook her head. "No way. I can always tell when people are putting on a show. They smile too much and talk in these really cheery voices like they think Randy's a two-year-old. It's so annoying. I think one of the reasons Randy liked you was because you were yourself, and you treated him like he's a normal human being. Which, of course, he is," she added loyally.

Cass almost asked if Tabitha was one of the people who put on an act around Randy, but she caught herself before she said anything. It wouldn't be fair to Rianne to ask her to compare the two of them. *Still*, she though, feeling only slightly guilty, *I'd bet anything Tabitha doesn't like spending time with Randy.*

Cass and Rianne went downstairs at noon so Randy could serve them lunch. Cass found herself talking and joking with Randy as though she'd known him for years, instead of a couple of hours. When it came time to head to the store with Rianne, she was reluctant to leave.

"Are you sure you wouldn't like to come with us?" she asked Randy for the third time.

He laughed. "Yeah, like I want to waste the rest of the afternoon watching the two of you look at clothes," he scoffed. "Girls may consider shopping an indoor sport, but I rank it right up there with having a root canal."

Cass made a face at him. "I take it that's a no," she drawled.

"Not just a no," Randy retorted good-naturedly. "But an uh-uh, no way, Jose."

"I don't think it gets much clearer than that," Rianne solemnly informed Cass before sticking her tongue out at her brother. "Good. I'm glad you're not coming. We really didn't want you to anyway. We were just being polite."

Clutching his chest, Randy acted stricken. "I'm crushed." He dropped the pose and motioned toward the door. "Go on, ladies, have fun. Don't buy out the place." He stopped teasing long enough to smile at Cass. "I'll see you around."

She returned his smile. "See you. Oh, and thanks for the lunch," she added over her shoulder as Rianne hustled her out the door. "It really was a world-class sandwich."

Pedaling home from Macy's two hours later, Cass decided this was the best day she'd had since arriving on Kwaj. She'd gone several hours without thinking about Janette and she didn't feel the least bit guilty.

I'd say I'm making progess, Lord, she thought as she let herself into the house. *Thank You for not giving up on me and for letting me have such a good time with Rianne.*

CHAPTER 27

Tabitha returned from Kira's shortly after Cass got back. Other than glaring at her stepsister as she strode through the living room, Tabitha didn't even acknowledge Cass' presence. That was fine with Cass since she wasn't interested in talking to Tabitha either. In fact, she wondered if it would be possible to live with someone for two years without saying a word to them. *I'm certainly willing to find out,* she thought wryly.

A little after four, Cass lifted her head from the book she was reading while sprawled on her bed and sniffed the air. Nothing.

Rolling off her bed, Cass padded down the hall, through the living room and kitchen, and out onto the porch. Mom sat in the swing, reading.

"What's for dinner?" Cass asked.

Mom looked up from her book. "I don't know what you're having, but I'll probably order the shark."

"We're going out to eat?" Cass' mouth watered at the thought.

"Not we," Mom corrected her. "Steve and I are. He called and I'm meeting him and the Nishiharas at the Yuk at five. It's Ed and Lois' anniversary and they invited us to celebrate it with them."

"What are we supposed to do while you're out?" Cass asked. Her skin crawled at the thought of being alone with Tabitha. Maybe Tabitha would stay in her room the rest of the night and she wouldn't have to deal with her.

Misunderstanding Cass' question, Mom arched an eyebrow and drawled, "You and Tabitha are big girls. I'm sure you can take care of yourselves for a few hours. You can warm up the chili, or there's tuna salad, for whenever you get hungry."

"Where are you going?" Tabitha had wandered out onto the porch.

Mom told her about the date with Lois and Ed.

"In that case, can I go to Kira's for supper?" Tabitha gave Mom her most persuasive smile. "I know her mother won't mind, but I'll call and ask if it would make you feel better."

Her smile didn't work. "Not tonight, sweetie." Mom laid aside her book and stood up. "You've both been gone so much this week, it'll be good for the two of you to spend some time together. You can tell each other what you've been up to."

Looking at Tabitha out of the corner of her eye, Cass thought her stepsister looked as thrilled about the prospect of spending time together as she felt.

The minute Mom left to meet the others at the restaurant, Cass went straight to her bedroom and slammed her door. A second later, she heard Tabitha do the same. Cass threw herself on the bed and picked up her book while Tabitha cranked up her stereo until the walls vibrated.

Resolved to remain holed up in her room until she was sure Tabitha had eaten and returned to hers, Cass lay on her back and propped her head up on pillows. Setting the book on her stomach, she tried to concentrate. After a couple of minutes, however, she realized she'd just read the same sentence over three times and still couldn't remember what it said. The music pounding through the walls was giving her a headache. She was about to yell at Tabitha to turn her stereo down when the music abruptly quit.

What in the world? Cass wondered, leaning up on her elbows and gazing around as though looking for the reason for the sudden silence.

At the same time, Tabitha shouted from her room, "Hey! What's going on? Cass, did you do something?"

Cass cautiously opened her door, then stepped out into the hall. Tabitha already stood there, looking puzzled. The house was strangely quiet without the ever-present hum of the air-conditioners.

Suddenly, Tabitha threw her hands up in disgust. "Oh, great. The power went out," she said. "I hate it when this happens. I hope it doesn't take eight hours to fix like it did the last time. We'll have to drag blankets out onto the beach if we want to get any sleep because the house will be a sauna."

Cass gulped. "It could actually take eight hours to get the electricity back on? What'll we do in the meantime?"

"Sweat," was Tabitha's terse reply. Crossing her arms, she leaned against the wall and glowered at Cass as if she were somehow to blame for the power failure.

"Shouldn't we open the windows so it doesn't get stuffy?" suggested Cass. The air was already starting to feel stale to her.

"We can't. Haven't you ever noticed the windows are sealed shut?" When Cass shook her head, Tabitha explained, "It's supposed to be more energy efficient. Personally, I liked it better when we could open the windows. It was nice to let the fresh air in every once in awhile. But some engineer decided that sealed windows were more cost-effective so here we are."

"You mean there's no way—"

The phone rang, cutting Cass off in mid-question. She and Tabitha looked at one another and rolled their eyes.

"I'll bet you anything it's Mom, checking to make sure

we're all right," guessed Tabitha, heading to the kitchen.

Cass followed her and giggled when, after answering the phone, Tabitha said sweetly, "Hello, Mom. What a surprise." She rolled her eyes at Cass. "Yes, it's out here too. Of course we're fine. It's not any big deal." There was a pause then she replied, "Okay. You and Dad have a good time. Don't worry about us. See you later. Bye."

Tabitha hung up and turned to Cass. "They're going to the Nishiharas' house since the Yuk can't function without electricity. Since we can't reheat the chili, we're to help ourselves to the tuna salad, and collect candles and matches for when it gets dark. Mom said they'll be back around ten unless we need them to come home sooner." She chuckled. "I don't know if you've noticed, but your mother really likes to organize things."

"Tell me about it," grumbled Cass. "I've only lived with the woman for sixteen years. She's happiest when she's telling people what to do. But," she went on, "in this case, she has a point. It'll be getting dark in another hour or so. Since you know where everything is, why don't you find the candles and stuff while I make the sandwiches?"

"Sounds like a plan to me," agreed Tabitha. "I want extra mayo on my sandwich and absolutely no pickles." She pretended to shudder.

"I like pickles," declared Cass. "Put a beet in front of me, though, and I guarantee you'll see me gag."

Laughing, Tabitha left the kitchen. By the time she rounded up a dozen candles and set them on the counter along with a box of matches, Cass was finished with their sandwiches. With the air in the house growing warmer by the minute, they picked up their plates and drinks and carried them out back. The low tide allowed them to sit on the rocks without having to worry about their food getting drenched with salt spray.

They sat in silence for a few minutes and then Tabitha

said gruffly, "Thank you for fixing my sandwich. It's really good. You put the right amount of mayonnaise on it. Mom doesn't ever use enough."

With Tabitha in such a mellow mood, Cass figured it was her turn to be gracious. "Thanks for finding the candles. I didn't like the idea of being stuck in a pitch-black house. It's scary to think there's no electricity at all on the island."

"That scares you?" Tabitha was quiet for a few seconds. "I know I said before that I hate it when the power's out, but that's not true. I actually kind of like it."

Cass turned to Tabitha, surprised by her admission. "Really? Why? It doesn't strike me as anything but a major pain in the neck."

Tabitha shrugged. "Because it's—oh, I don't know—a nice change of pace. Think about it. We spend so much time shut up inside air-conditioned buildings that it's good to be forced to come outside every once in awhile. I mean, look around you. When was the last time you saw this many people on the beach? If the electricity were still on, we'd probably all be tucked away in our houses, instead of out here enjoying the breeze and the ocean."

"You have a point," Cass said. She studied Tabitha who continued to stare out at the sea. "You truly love it here, don't you?"

"It's my home," Tabitha said simply, as if that explained everything.

For Cass, who still loved Jonesborough with all her heart, it did. Feeling more at ease with her stepsister than she ever had, Cass decided to risk raising a touchy subject. "You love Kwaj, but you really hate me, huh?"

Jerking her head around, Tabitha gave her a startled look. "Why in the world do you think I hate you?"

Before Cass could respond, the girls heard the faint ringing of the telephone in the house. They glanced uncertainly at each other.

"Do you think we should answer it?" asked Tabitha.

"It's probably Mom and she'll be worried if we don't. No, stay," Cass ordered when Tabitha moved to stand up. "I'll get it." Leaping to her feet, she jogged across the lawn to the house. She picked the phone up on the fifth ring and discovered it wasn't Mom calling, but Kira.

"Tabitha's out back eating a sandwich," Cass informed her. "Hold on a sec. I'll go tell her it's you."

"Cass, wait," Kira said before she set the receiver down. "I'll call her back later. Meanwhile, I wanted to tell you I talked to Rianne a little while ago. She raved about how nice you were to Randy. I'm glad you hit it off with him. I think the world of Randy. I just wish he'd get out more."

"I invited him to the youth group," Cass said.

"I know. Rianne told me." Kira sounded pleased. "She said she thinks he's seriously considering trying it out. That'd be so great."

"I hope he does. And Rianne too," Cass put in. "You know, at the rate we're going, we could be up to thirty kids by the time school starts."

"Boy, wouldn't your mom be excited about that?" There was a whispered conversation on Kira's end, then she came back on the line. "Logan's here and he just realized I'm talking to you. He wants to say hello. Is that okay?"

Cass' stomach did a slow roll. "Sure, put him on," she replied and hoped she didn't sound as fluttery as she felt. "Bye, Kira."

"Bye. Don't forget to tell Tabitha I called."

A moment later Kira's voice was replaced by Logan's "Hi, Cass. How are you doing?"

"Great," Cass said brightly. "How about you?"

Brilliant, Cassandra, she chastised herself. *Way to hold his interest.*

"I'm great too." There was an awkward pause then Logan continued, "I was wondering if you'd like to play handball tomorrow. We could go early, maybe around eight-thirty or nine, before it gets too hot."

"I've never played handball, but I'm willing to give it a try." *Wow, am I willing,* Cass added silently. "Will I need any special equipment?"

Logan's laugh rumbled across the wire. "Uh, Cass, it's called *hand*ball," he teased. "If you've got hands, you have all the equipment you need."

"Very funny," Cass said, grinning at the empty room. "Okay, I guess I asked for that one. Should I meet you at the courts tomorrow or what?"

"I'll come by and get you at eight-fifteen or so. Then we can ride over together." After another awkward pause he added, "I'll see you tomorrow morning."

"I'm looking forward to it," Cass assured him. "Just promise me you won't laugh when I make a mistake." When he did, she added, "Bye, Logan."

Tabitha was eating the last of her potato chips when Cass rejoined her on the rocks. Removing the napkin from Cass' plate, Tabitha handed it to her.

"Here you go. I kept the flies from getting it."

Cass accepted the plate with a grateful smile. "Thanks."

"You and Mom had quite a chat," Tabitha commented as Cass bit into her sandwich. "Was she worried about us?"

Shaking her head, Cass wiped her mouth with the napkin. "It wasn't Mom. It was Kira, then Logan got on and we talked for a couple of minutes."

"Kira?" echoed Tabitha. "Why didn't you holler at me to come in and talk to her?" Her face hardened suddenly. "She wasn't calling for me, was she?"

Heaven help me if she wasn't. Cass warily eyed Tabitha's menacing expression.

Aloud, she replied, "Of course she was. But she said she'd call back later so I guess it wasn't important." Cass set down her sandwich and brushed the crumbs from her hands. "That gets us back to what we were discussing before the phone rang." Tilting her head, she gazed at Tabitha in the gathering dusk. "Why do you hate me so much?"

"If you'll recall, I asked you why you think I hate you," countered Tabitha.

Snorting, Cass drawled, "Oh, gee, let me think." She dropped the sarcasm as she continued, "Come on, isn't it obvious? You never talk to me unless we're fighting. You hate it whenever I have anything to do with your friends. You should have seen your face when you thought Kira had called me. I don't know who you wanted to kill first, her or me."

"Don't be ridiculous," sniffed Tabitha. "I wasn't mad. I was surprised. And as far as not talking to you except when we're fighting, that's not true. We've had lots of conversations about the youth group and stuff."

"Whatever." Cass dismissed her arguments with a wave. "Admit it. You wish I'd go back to Tennessee and never set foot on Kwaj again."

"Well, of course I wish you'd leave and never come back," Tabitha said without the slightest hesitation. "Only it's not because I hate you. Okay, I'll admit that sometimes I can't stand you. But it's because you're so perfect you drive me up the wall with jealousy. I used to think I was something until you came along. You score off the charts on the perfection meter."

Cass dropped her sandwich onto the plate and jabbed a finger to her own chest. "Me?" she squeaked in astonishment. "You're saying you think I'm perfect? What are you talking about?"

"Oh, please. Like you don't know," scoffed Tabitha. "Ever since he met you, all my dad does is rave about how wonderful you are. You're smart. You're funny. You're a super athlete. You've been such a good sport about leaving everything behind and moving here. For three months it's been nothing but Cass this and Cass that. It's practically all

250

I ever hear anymore. It's like I've fallen off the face of the earth as far as my Dad's concerned. You're the only person who matters to him. You and Mom," she added bitterly.

"But—" Cass stammered.

"As if that weren't bad enough," Tabitha went on, ignoring her feeble protest, "you've completely taken over the island in the five weeks since you moved here. You got the youth group started." She held up a hand when Cass opened her mouth to disagree. "Don't say that was Mom's doing. She wouldn't have gone to Pastor Thompson if it weren't for you. Plus, Kira and Micah think you're terrific. Logan worships the ground you walk on. And Rianne"— she shook her head in exasperation—"all she had to do was meet you, and suddenly you're like best friends. Everyone you meet likes you."

"I'm sorry." Cass didn't know what else to say, and she leaned toward Tabitha, her hands clasped in her lap. "I didn't mean—"

Tabitha cut her off in mid-apology. "It's not your fault. You're just … nice. I mean, this right here is a great example. You're apologizing for people liking you. Only a perfect person would do something like that. I can't even make you mad anymore and believe me, I've tried. The problem is I wind up looking like the bad guy because you don't react."

"I'm not perfect," Cass insisted. She frowned in her frustration at not being able to convince Tabitha. "And you do make me mad. Inside, I'm so eaten up with anger that sometimes I think, if I don't get away from you, I'm going to smash something."

"Well, you could have fooled me." Tabitha took a potato chip from Cass' plate. "You drive me crazy when you stand there calm, cool, and collected while I'm ranting and raving. I had no idea I was getting to you."

Cass couldn't help smiling. "Are you happy now that you know how furious you make me sometimes?"

"Honestly? Yes," Tabitha shot back. "I hated thinking I couldn't bug you anymore. I'm glad to know I haven't lost my touch."

"What a weird relationship we have," mused Cass. "I wonder if all sisters are like this."

"Who knows?" Tabitha popped another chip into her mouth. "This is the first time I've ever had to deal with a sibling. Obviously I'm not very good at it," she concluded with an unconcerned shrug.

"That makes two of us." Cass broke off a piece of sandwich to nibble on. "You know," she observed, "you talk about the way your father feels about me. What about you and my mother? It's like you're the daughter she's been waiting for all her life. I hate it when I come into the room and the two of you are talking about clothes or cooking or taking quilting lessons. I feel totally left out. I want to wave my arms and shout at Mom, 'Hey, remember me?' "

"Well, excuse me," Tabitha said stiffly, tossing her hair over her shoulder. "I've never had a mother before. Am I supposed to apologize because I enjoy having one?"

"I've never had a father," Cass retorted, "but you don't see me going around trying to steal yours away from you, do you?"

"That's because you don't have to. He goes willingly. All you have to do is snap your fingers."

The girls glowered at each other until Cass felt her mouth suddenly begin to twitch. After a few moments, she saw Tabitha's do the same. Despite their best efforts to remain angry, the girls soon found themselves grinning from ear-to-ear.

"This is one stupid conversation, isn't it?" Cass asked wryly.

"It does seem silly," agreed Tabitha. "How about we make a deal? I won't be mad at you anymore about Dad liking you if you won't be angry because Mom likes me." She stuck out her hand. "Let's shake on it."

Cass took her hand, but didn't shake it. "That still leaves you mad at me on account of your friends," she pointed out.

"Let me see if I can explain this so it makes sense." Removing her hand from Cass', Tabitha stared out at the ocean. "A lot of why I'm put out about my friends is because it doesn't seem to matter to them that you hate Kwaj. I can't help thinking they should be more loyal and not fall all over themselves trying to get someone who doesn't even appreciate living here to like them." She smiled crookedly at Cass. "So I guess you could say I've been just as mad at them as I have been at you. I know it sounds dumb, but I think I wouldn't feel as bad about you winning my friends over if you at least liked it here."

Since Tabitha was being so honest, Cass realized it was time for her to be honest too. "I don't hate Kwaj as much as I act like I do," she admitted. Unable to look her stepsister in the eyes, she talked to a palm tree over Tabitha's left shoulder. "I've kind of gotten used to being a beach bum. I like being free to come and go as I please because the island's so small and safe. Things were a lot more restricted back home. I had to report in to Mom every hour on the hour or she'd get crazed, thinking I'd been in an accident or something." Cass hesitated before adding, "I also like your friends. Kira and Micah are fun, and Rianne seems really nice. I'm looking forward to getting to know her better."

"What about Logan?" Tabitha prompted with a mischievous expression.

"Logan is ... intetesting," Cass replied carefully. "Very, very interesting."

"Ooh, I'm telling Kira," Tabitha said, laughing. "Right from the start, she said the two of you would hit it off."

"Logan and I haven't exactly hit it off," Cass reminded her. "At least not yet."

"Yet!" echoed Tabitha, clasping her hands to her heart. "I just love a good romance." She leaned closer to add confidentially, "If things keep going the way they have been between you two, I'm pretty sure Logan will invite you to the first school dance. There's a fall formal the first weekend in October."

"In that case, I'm going on record as predicting Micah asks you," Cass replied quickly.

Tabitha raised folded hands to the darkening sky as though in fervent prayer. "I'd be one deliriously happy girl if Micah would only give me a second look."

After a burst of laughter, they launched into a discussion about the upcoming school year, due to start in two weeks. The sun sank abruptly below the horizon, and a full moon rose to send its light shimmering across the water.

Cass was so deep into their conversation about planning what classes they'd take and debating what to wear on the first day that she didn't hear Steve and Mom coming up behind them until Steve spoke.

"Well, Donna, it's finally happened," he said, and Cass saw Tabitha jump as high as she did. He switched off the flashlight in his hand.

"What's that, dear?"

"Hell has frozen over," Steve declared. "Either that or I've died and gone to heaven. Personally, I hope it's the latter."

"Very funny." Tabitha stood up and stretched. "You missed your calling, Dad. You ought to quit your job at the radio station and go into stand-up comedy."

"Yeah," agreed Cass. She rose to stand next to Steve. "You're a laugh a minute"—she hesitated then finished softly—"Dad."

There was a long pause while Steve blinked several times and cleared his throat. "Well, that settles it," he murmured. "I have died and gone to heaven."

Briefly leaning her head on his shoulder, Cass gave him an impish smile. "Don't get all emotional on me. I was just trying it out."

Steve dropped a kiss on the top of her head as she moved away. "I hope, after you try it out a couple of times, you decide to permanently assign me the name."

"We'll see." Cass winked at Tabitha, who grinned.

Sounding a bit breathless, Mom said, "Before I forget, girls, guess what your dad has agreed to do? We talked about it coming home and he said he'll co-lead the youth group with me."

Tabitha stared at Steve in the moonlight. "You're going to help with the group? Mr. I-Don't-Want-To-Get-Involved? I don't believe it."

"Believe it, honey." Steve draped an arm across Mom's shoulders and pulled her close. "This is one very persuasive woman. She convinced me I should be a guiding force in my daughters' lives, not just an interested bystander. Besides, like I always say"—he ignored the girls' loud groans—"that's what dads are for. So, starting this Sunday, the team of Spencer and Spencer will be leading the youth group."

"And the team of Spencer and Devane will be the group's most faithful members," Tabitha vowed, linking arms with Cass. "Isn't that right?"

Cass smiled at her. "You got it, Sis."